FINDING HOME

Dominic
Sheehan

FINDING HOME

Dominic Sheehan

Secker & Warburg

For Albert

First published 1996 by Secker and Warburg, a division of
Reed Publishing (NZ) Ltd, 39 Rawene Road, Birkenhead,
Auckland 10. Associated companies, branches and
representatives throughout the world.

ISBN 0 7900 0462 3

Editorial services by Michael Gifkins & Associates,
Auckland

Printed in New Zealand

I'm sitting on the floor of our kitchen. I have my undershirt pushed right up over my stomach. Charley the cat brushes against me, flicking his tail across my tummy with every pass. I reach out to grab him but he is too quick and escapes me easily. Mum stands at the sink bench and laughs at us, her jet-black hair waving as her head bobs. Outside is summer. It is my happiest memory.

∾

Chapter Zero

Rachel used to kiss her Donny Osmond poster twice a day, straight after she woke up and just before she went to sleep. Twice daily was not a hard and fast rule, mind you. Sometimes she would kiss it more, or less, depending on how tired she was or where Donny's latest hit was on the Top Twenty. Bernadette used to go one better. Whenever Bobby Sherman came on the radio she would let out a high-pitched scream and immediately slip into a trance, like she was possessed, chanting 'oh Bobby, oh Bobby' over and over and over until the song was finished. Then she would give a satisfied sigh, sink back into her chair and smile.

Eddie and I, not being so appreciative of Mr Osmond or Mr Sherman's musical talents, used to tease our older sisters about these things. I especially could imitate Bernadette's excited scream with uncanny accuracy. She retaliated by playing the stereo so loud it made the chandelier in the hallway shake. Ed and I took the battle one stage further when we rolled all her records down the front steps and watched them wobble drunkenly along our red gravel driveway. When Dad, arriving home from work, drove into the front gate, there was no avoiding the swarm of LPs and 45s coming at him and none of Bernadette's records survived the incident intact.

Dad was relieved to find out they were only records because he thought he'd hit the cat which was impossible since Charley, our old cat, had died a month earlier after slipping head first into the downstairs toilet. Poor Charley must have been exploring or drinking from the toilet bowl and got stuck with his face under the water. No one heard any splashing and we only suspected something was wrong when he didn't turn up for his tea-time feed. It was too late when we found him, very dead, his back legs hanging limply over the edge of the seat and the shiny wet fur on his front slicked hard against his skin. Ed and I dressed in our Sunday best to give him a fitting send-off, complete with a cardboard box coffin and a round of 'How Great Thou Art' from Mum's hymnal. We buried him, along with his food bowl, in a far corner of the garden.

All this happened a long time ago, when we lived in a two-storied house in a town called Lumley. We moved to that house from a far less impressive Lumley abode soon after I was born and because of that I regarded it as *my* house and was especially proud of all its special places. Like the den with the fold-out bed; the windows shaped like portholes on the west side of the ground floor; the coal chute that I used to wriggle through until I eventually grew too big; the leadlight arched window in Andrew's room; the stairs that you could roll marbles down or slide on the railing; the linen closet that was so large you could squeeze all us kids into it at once, the perfect place to escape to during a game of Sardines or for a ghost story. Such stories only occurred during the holidays when the older kids were home from boarding school and only when Kate and Andrew were in a particularly bone-chilling mood. They would gather up me and Eddie and sit us cross-legged on the closet floor. Then Kate, armed with a torch, would sit down beside us as Andrew shut the door just like he was closing the doorway of a crypt.

If I close my eyes and imagine hard I can picture us in that closet and I can hear Kate and Andrew and Ed's voices, the young voices they had then. It's a memory from a time in my life I always go back to, when I was nine. It's not a time that was all happy or all sad, but simply the time that comes to me when I reminisce. Maybe that's because so much happened to me then that my subconscious won't let me forget it. Or maybe I like to think of it as my golden time, even though some of the memories are anything but golden.

Sometimes I wonder if I'm making half of it up, because I don't have a photographic memory and I can't remember exactly how it all happened and how we all sounded. Sometimes I wonder if I don't mix in a bit of who I am today with who I was then. The past blurs with the present and although I try to listen and think as I did then, the 'me' of now, the grown-up me, keeps getting in the way and in the end I become an adult trying to talk with the voice of a child, a man who lives in the present yet who often takes a journey through the past.

Chapter One

'Kevin, I'm scared,' Eddie whined and looked at me with huge, terrified eyes.

'Don't worry,' I reassured him. 'It's only Kate.'

Andrew sneered. 'What's his problem?'

'He's only six,' Kate said, as if it was an explanation. She had been holding the lit torch underneath her chin which made her face look like a monster mask, but because Eddie was so frightened she directed the light towards the floor instead. 'How's that?'

Through the half-darkness I could see Eddie nod.

'Welcome to ghost story time,' Kate began with a booming voice. 'Tonight I'm going to tell you about the story of the Hairy Toe. Once there was an old hermit who lived on a mountain.'

'You forgot something,' Eddie said.

'What?'

'The date bit,' I pitched in.

'Okay . . .' Kate wasn't big on formality but this time she relented. 'Welcome to ghost story time, taking place this Saturday night, January the twenty-fourth, in the year of our Lord nineteen hundred and seventy-six. Once upon a time there was an old hermit. He lived on a mountainside all alone. One day the hermit was visited by a hiker who had come from far across the seas to climb this mountain. There was a terrible storm that night and the hiker was cold and tired and needed shelter. But the hermit didn't give him any. He was a mean evil man —'

'I don't like this story,' Eddie said suddenly.

'I've hardly started.'

'I don't like it.' He was snuggled up against Kate, his head nesting in the crook of her arm.

'Let's tell them about Mrs Hill,' Andrew suggested.

'If he's scared about the Hairy Toe he won't want to hear about her again.'

'No, go on. Let's do it.'

Kate finally nodded and Andrew began. It was a story we had been told a hundred times, yet it never lost any of its creepiness.

'You know Mr Hill over the road? I know you've both seen him, driving around in his rusty old van or digging in that stupid garden of his or pacing up and down the street in a filthy mood when we play on the front lawn and make too much noise. You've never seen anyone else over there, have you? But there is someone else. There's a Mrs Hill.

'Mr Hill keeps her locked in a dungeon underneath his place. The dungeon is slimy and full of mould and rats.

'He used to keep her behind bars but she got so skinny that she could slip through and now he has her chained to the floor with manacles, except they're too tight and her hands and feet have gangrene.'

'What's gan-gerine?' Ed asked. Nobody answered him.

'No one has ever seen her. The Hills didn't move in during the day like ordinary people. They came at night. Mrs Hill was brought inside a crate. It had to be padlocked or else she might have broken out and then no one could have ever stopped her. She would have run amok across the countryside. No one would have been safe. Especially not little children.

'Mrs Hill likes to eat little children. Little boys are her favourite. Mr Hill sometimes snatches one as a treat. Who knows? Perhaps he's somewhere near right now . . .'

With that Andrew tickled the back of my neck and I let out a blood-curdling scream, absolutely positive that Mr Hill was in the shelves behind me. Eddie also let burst except that, unlike me, he

11

didn't stop with one scream. Within seconds Kate and Andrew were concentrating not on scaring us, but on shutting him up.

'It's just a story,' said Kate. 'Hell, Andy, what did you do that for?'

'It was Kevin's fault. Grab some towels, we'll see if we can smother the noise.'

I heard the soft plop of towels hitting the ground.

'You'll suffocate him! Bloody hell, Ed! It's just a story!'

'Or so she says,' Andrew added evilly. He was looking at me.

'Andy!' Kate said sharply just as the closet door opened. Bernadette was standing in the blinding light from the hallway with a grim expression on her face. She pulled Ed off the floor and hugged him close.

'What do you think you're doing?' she shouted over his screaming. 'We can hear him all the way downstairs.'

Kate stood up. She was only fourteen to Bernadette's eighteen but was already as tall as the older girl. 'We were having some fun.'

'We were just telling ghost stories,' Andrew let slip and received a black look from Kate in return.

'I would have thought you two were a little more grown up than that.'

'Sorry to disappoint you,' Kate threw back. 'We can't all be contestants for the Miss Maturity Contest.' And she stamped off to her bedroom. Quick as a flash Bernadette dumped the still screaming Ed on Andrew and chased after her.

'Don't you speak to me like that!'

Andrew held Ed for a moment then dumped him onto me.

'This is too good to miss.' He threw the closet door back at us and sprinted off to Rachel's room to listen through the wall. The door shut, plunging Eddie and me into blackness again. As if by magic Ed stopped screaming.

'It's dark,' he said.

'You okay?'

'Yes.' His answer was more than a little doubtful. 'Do you think Mr Hill will come for us?'

'It's Saturday night. He'd shoot straight to Hell if he touched us so near to Sunday. And it was Christmas just a month ago. He gave Mrs Hill some other little boys as a present, I bet. That should keep her going till winter at least. We're safe for now.'

Eddie didn't reply and we sat in a murky silence. Through the walls I could hear Kate and Bernadette arguing. The noise was comforting, somehow.

The topic of Mr Hill was not raised again until later the next day. Before that, we performed one of the miracles of the Garrick household, squeezing all eight family members into our green Holden station-wagon, going to and from nine o'clock Mass. St Peter's Catholic Church was actually within walking distance and if Andrew and I sneaked off to early morning Mass we would go on foot. But the car was essential when the family went together because by the time we had all got through using the bathroom we were invariably running late.

While the ride there was usually an exciting mad dash, the ride home was always the more interesting.

'Did you see that dress she was wearing?' Bernadette was referring to some girl who had been sitting a few pews in front. 'No way should she be wearing minis. She looked like an overripe pear with legs. And did you see Daphne Doron with those platforms? Hideous.'

'What time did you tell the photographer to be there?' Mum asked Dad.

'In about quarter of an hour, dear. Plenty of time for you to make yourself beautiful.' He grinned.

Andrew elbowed me sharply. 'Move over.'

'I can't,' I replied. I was pressed hard against one of the doors with the window winder poking painfully into my ribs. In return he shoved me harder against the door and smiled his appreciation.

Kate half-sang, half-hummed 'SOS' and Rachel joined her for the chorus, really hamming it up like they were Abba performing it live on stage.

'Oh don't sing that.' Mum turned around. 'What about that new one . . . "Feelings"?'

Rachel and Kate stared back at Mum in a way that said 'Feelings' was the last song they wanted to sing, then they looked at each other and began loudly in unison.

'Feel-ings . . . whoa whoa whoa, feel-ings . . .'

At home the three girls scrambled inside to fix themselves up for the photograph. Ed tagged along with them while Mum went off to the kitchen to make a cup of tea. Dad and us other boys hung around the car. When the photographer arrived, Dad and Andrew busied themselves tidying the front porch. I sat on the warm bonnet of the Holden watching them. The photographer set himself up with a precise routine and when he gave the word, Dad hurried the others down with a shout. Rachel, Kate and Eddie appeared pretty quickly with Mum right behind. Bernadette was some way back.

'I can't find my brush,' she complained when she appeared. She had changed into her dress with the yellow flowers on it and was teetering on a pair of wedge-soled sandals. 'One of the other girls must have it.'

'What would I want with your cacky brush?' Kate replied. 'Like I really want your nits.'

'Well someone has it. Rachel?'

'It wasn't me.'

'Mum?'

'Your hair looks fine. You don't need a brush.'

'I would still like to know where it is. It's the third one I've lost this summer.'

Kate couldn't resist. 'Are you talking about hairbrushes or boyfriends?'

Bernadette tossed her head back like she was above the

conversation and pulled out a lipstick from her handbag. Her mood crashed again as soon as she unrolled the barrel.

'There are teeth marks in my strawberry lip gloss!'

Kate peered at the gloss closely. 'That's more than just teeth marks. Someone's clean bitten off the end!'

'Which of you boys did it?'

Andrew threw up his hands. 'Don't look at me. That's more like Kevin.'

Bernadette glared at me but I shook my head. She turned her gaze onto Ed, who was looking exceptionally guilty. He started chewing furiously.

'You filthy little brat! That's what you were doing hanging around my room!' She gripped his jaw and tried to prise his mouth open. 'Spit it up!' Ed wriggled valiantly.

The rest of us kids formed a circle around them.

'Swallow it!'

'He'll make himself sick.'

'Go, Ed!'

'Leave him alone, you're hurting him.'

The drama died in a stalemate. Bernadette gave up, leaving Ed to spit out the waxy mess, applied the jagged stick to her lips and posed for the photographer who had been watching the scene with some interest. He took charge, placing the four older kids at the rear, Mum and Dad on chairs in centre middle, holding hands, and Eddie and me on either side at the front. The photographer looked through his camera then ordered Andrew to move in slightly, Kate to stop slouching and me to stop squinting. He took a step back then looked through the camera again.

'The boy in front, by you, Bob, he's still squinting.'

'It's his lazy eye,' my mother explained. 'The sun must be bothering it.'

'The sun is bothering all of us,' Kate added.

Bernadette agreed. 'It wouldn't be so bad if it wasn't right in our faces.'

'Think its gonna show up your zits, huh?' That from Andrew.

'He's still squinting,' the photographer said impatiently.

'Don't worry about his eye,' Dad replied. 'Try to keep it open, Kevin,' he told me sympathetically.

With an uncomfortable struggle I forced my eye open. Immediately my vision went watery and I felt my head shaking from the effort. I knew that in the photo it would probably look as if I was bulging out my eyes like a fish, which is actually what I was doing, just to keep my one bad eye open.

'Say cheese,' Kate said when the photographer peered through his camera again and shouted, 'Ready.'

'Say hairbrush,' Andrew added quietly.

'Hairbrush,' I said to myself and my lazy eye snapped shut of its own accord just as the photographer snapped his first picture.

Sunday morning breakfast was a weekly ritual in the Garrick household. Dad would change into some casual work clothes while Mum made a pile of toast and set the table. Making toast was no mean feat since our toaster was a smoking, prehistoric monster, dating back to Dad's bachelor days, and regularly delivered up nothing but burnt offerings. However, on that particular Sunday there was no smell of toast when I reached the kitchen. Instead Mum and Bernadette were seated in facing chairs, both of them looking deadly serious.

'It's not fair, Mum. Why should I have to suffer just because I'm the oldest?'

'This has nothing to do with your age, you know that. We're just a bit behind the eight ball at the moment.'

'It's all Dad's fault.'

'That's the last time I want to hear that!' Mum snapped. 'It's no one's fault, certainly not your father's.'

'It's not fair,' Bernadette said again, sounding like an annoyingly scratched record. She pushed her chair away from the table and the chair made a loud scrape on the lino. 'I'm asking him myself,' she promised and headed upstairs.

Bernadette saved her re-entrance until the kitchen was full and the mountain of toast that had finally been made was severely dented. Everyone except Dad and Eddie looked up as she arrived and took her seat. Bernadette, on the other hand, didn't catch anyone's eye, especially avoiding Mum's gaze, but wasted no time getting to the point.

'Dad, I've just been speaking to Michelle. She and Angela have found a place. There's a free bedroom.'

The roundabout remark hung solidly in the air, hovering like a mini-helicopter above the table.

'The Palmers are good people,' Dad said without looking up and with just five words blasted the helicopter from the sky.

'I never said they weren't. But that doesn't mean I want to live with them.'

Mum interjected, 'I don't think this is the time or the place —'

'You have my answer on this, Bernadette.'

'Your order, you mean.'

'The Palmers are our friends.'

'But they're not my friends.'

'Your friends haven't offered you free accommodation.'

'I've told you, I'll get a job. And I have my student allowance. It's my first year at university, I want to flat with my friends.'

'That's all I'm going to say about it.'

Turning to catch Bernadette's reply, I half expected a huge screaming match to begin, World War III with Marmite. But she pursed her lips tightly and with mechanical accuracy took a piece of toast from the pile. She buttered it, spread a light veneer of Mum's plum jam and began to eat, all without looking up from her plate.

'I want to sort out your clothes this morning,' Mum said to Rachel and Kate. 'You too, Andrew. There's only a week before you go, I don't want a last-minute rush.'

Dad pushed off from the table, causing the same sort of startling scrape on the floor as Bernadette had earlier.

'I have to finish some paperwork. I'll be back for dinner.'

After breakfast Eddie and I went upstairs to watch Andrew pack for boarding school. Mum left Rachel and Kate to set out their gear while she moved like a hurricane through Andrew's room, pulling clothes out of his drawers and laying them in careful piles on the bed; underwear, socks, t-shirts, shorts and togs.

'What about my uniform?' Andrew said, tugging at the spongy Hallensteins parcel that had been kicking around his room. He had already attacked the packet more than once and the new-smelling drill shorts and navy jersey were poking out of the gaps.

'I want to fix up your mufti today,' Mum replied. 'How about your sneakers? Where are they?'

Clearly nothing more exciting was going down here than Andrew searching the cupboard for his smelly old sneakers and so I wandered into Kate's room. It was empty, as was Rachel's. The door to Bernadette's room was shut and there were quiet voices coming from inside. The door remained closed till lunch time when the three girls emerged, surrounded by a deathly quiet. Then Andrew suggested that we play tennis-racket cricket at which Rachel and Kate perked up considerably. Mum said the packing could wait till later and we left as a group, stranding her with Bernadette, the big sister from hell.

'Don't say that about her,' Rachel lectured Andrew as she set up the orange-crate stumps. 'You don't understand.'

She handed him the tennis racket and Kate the ball, and appointed Eddie wicket-keeper while she and I fielded. Fielding was hard work, since there were only two of us to cover the whole lawn, but tennis-racket cricket was my favourite game.

'Come on!' Andrew challenged Kate as she turned to face him. He waved the racket in the air. 'I'm going to split this one in half!'

I squinted through the sunlight as Kate bowled the first ball. It hit the back of the crate with a hollow clunk. Everyone except Andrew made quacking noises. Kate laughed.

'Oh yeah, Andy, that's some split!'

I got to bat three times before I hit the big one. I knew it was too hard as soon as I struck it. One of the rules in tennis-racket cricket was that you weren't allowed to hit it for six. But this one was not only a six, it was an eight, or a twelve even.

'Shoot, Kevin!' Andrew complained and the search began. We all poked around the grassy ditch on our side of the road, and in the hedge right at the road's end. I tried to ignore the steady stream of abuse Andrew hurled at me. We searched for a full ten minutes before Kate glanced upwards and spotted the ball firmly wedged high in a piece of weather-worn trellis on the front of the Hill house. My heart sank as soon as I saw it.

Rachel was philosophical. 'It's not like its the first ball we lost on the Hill place.'

'We could get it,' I said hopefully. 'It's not very high. And Mr Hill's van isn't there.'

'And who's gonna go?' Andrew asked me.

'Not me,' Kate replied. 'Mrs Hill's probably inside sharpening up her Wiltshire knife right now.'

'There is no Mrs Hill.' Rachel caught Kate's eye and flicked her head towards Eddie, who was looking absolutely petrified just being this close to the Hill place. 'I've had enough, anyway.' She led Eddie back down the street with Kate snatching up his other hand.

'It's all for the best,' Andrew remarked. 'Mrs Hill can chew on that ball to hone her teeth before she comes to kill you!'

He tried to scare me like the night before but I didn't even blink this time. Seeing my disinterest he spat out a disapproving breath then also headed home. I took one more look at the ball, positive that I could retrieve it. From where I was standing I reasoned I could climb up to the window-sill next to the trellis and scramble up high enough to grab the ball. The trellis looked like it would bear my weight. The only problem was that to get the ball I had to go onto the Hill property.

'Kevin?' Rachel called from our driveway. 'Leave the ball, okay?'

I knew she was right. Realistically, there was no way I could get the tennis ball, yet I was so annoyed at losing it that I kept staring up at that old trellis with its flaky blue paint and rotting wood. I turned the possibility over in my mind, mentally mapping out my movements, but deep down I knew I was only going through the motions. There was no way I was setting even one foot on Hill ground.

Out of the corner of my eye I saw the curtains in the window next to the trellis shudder slightly. At first I thought it had been an illusion, the sun glancing off the window glass, or my lazy eye playing up, perhaps. But as I looked more closely the curtains flickered again, almost like a shiver of fear. Then they moved once more and this time a tiny gap formed between them, a space far too narrow to see through, from the outside at least. The curtains went still but the gap remained. I looked back for the others but even as I did, I knew they were long gone. I wanted to shout to them but suddenly my tongue was like a lead weight in my mouth. My body froze on the spot while a billion things flashed through my head. What if Kate and Andrew were right? What if there was a Mrs Hill? What if Mr Hill did capture little children? Would they kill me straight away or would they take me down to their dungeon and torture me first? Was the dungeon soundproofed or if I screamed loud enough would my family hear me? But most importantly, what would happen to the tennis ball?

By this time I didn't know why I was still there, standing in front of the Hill house, looking into that window, staring back at whoever or whatever was watching me. And even while I was thinking that, totally without warning, the curtains flew open. Flew! It was like some brutal wind had torn them apart! I could hardly breathe for a second, it was such a fright. My common sense said run, but I stayed where I was. The curtains waved wildly back and forth a couple of times and when they calmed down I looked clear into the room. But there was nothing there. The room was empty. Dead empty. The curtains continued to swing with the barest movement. I felt hypnotised by them, drawn in by the gentle to and fro. But then I realised that whoever or whatever had been in the room could now be anywhere. They could even be behind me. With a mammoth effort I pulled myself away from those bewitched curtains, turned tail and sprinted home, checking behind me each couple of steps and not stopping until I was safely inside our house.

By dinner time I had managed to stop thinking about the curtains, or at least I had convinced myself that it was the wind that ripped them apart. In the kitchen Rachel was putting out a bowl of steaming green peas, Kate was asking Eddie what he would like as she piled some fresh salad onto her own plate and Andrew was already chewing on a boiled new potato. Mum brought over a plate of sliced cold meat, the remnants of last night's roast, and found a place for it on the crowded table.

'Did you call Bernadette, Kevin? Go call her again. Andrew, you do it this time . . . just do it. I'm planning to see Aunt Erin some time this week. Do either of you girls want to come?'

'I suppose so. By the way, when are we going to do our school shopping?' Kate asked.

'Tomorrow.'

'Can we go to the city?' Rachel said hopefully.

'That's a good idea,' Kate agreed. 'There's nothing in the stores here.'

'Maybe,' Mum replied, her original question about Aunt Erin lost in a brilliant Rachel-Kate blindside.

'Where's Dad?' Rachel added for good measure.

'He'll be along soon. Ed, wait for grace please. And don't use your fingers.'

Andrew slipped back into his seat and started spooning peas onto his plate.

'Did you call Bernadette?' Mum asked.

'She's coming. But you're not going to like it.'

'What do you mean by that?'

There was a step on the stairs and moments later Bernadette appeared in the doorway, holding a full suitcase in each hand. You could tell the suitcases were full because they were bulging slightly at the sides. She had her best coat tucked under her arm and her white vinyl handbag, the one with the frayed strap, hanging over her shoulder.

'I've called a taxi,' she said quietly, her head dipping as she spoke. 'It'll be here any moment. I'm booked on the late bus to Auckland.' She glanced up at Mum then set a course for the front door.

'Bernadette!' Mum called with a quaver in her voice and walked briskly after her.

'I didn't think Bern'd do it,' Rachel said as soon as Mum was gone.

'What do you think Mum will say?' Kate replied.

'I don't know. Bern was pretty set on going. I'd better see what's happening.' And she followed Bernadette and Mum.

'She can go, for all I care,' Andrew said with a full mouth of bread.

Kate ignored him.

We heard a car's tyres on the driveway, doors opening and closing, a boot being slammed shut, the car pulling away. I kept staring at the door. I wanted to catch Mum's eye when she came in, and give her the same sort of brave smile that she gave me whenever I faced a difficult situation. But when she returned she was looking somewhere into the distance, like she was in a dream. Rachel was right behind. She and Kate gave each other looks, secret code. Kate mouthed something. Rachel nodded. Kate looked confused, then she too nodded. Andrew tried to kick me under the table. He missed, although I could feel the rush of air as his leg swung out towards mine. Eddie was playing with his food like nothing was going on, trekking his fork across the landscape of peas and potatoes on his plate. I peeked back at Mum. I couldn't tell if she was angry or sad. Perhaps she was a bit of both.

Minutes later we all heard the familiar sound of Dad's car cruising into the garage. When he walked through the back door I wondered if he had passed Bernadette's taxi on the road but he gave no clues as he washed his hands under the sink tap then took his seat at the head of the table. Mum sprang into life, her eyes refocused and she picked up her knife and fork. Dad's plate was waiting for him and he piled it up without a word. None of us were speaking. The only sound in the room was the clatter of cutlery on plates.

Usually dinner time was a verbal free-for-all, with everyone jockeying to be the centre of attention. Tonight no one wanted that responsibility.

'Good day, dear?' Mum asked. The slight quaver was still lodged in her throat.

'So-so.'

'Did you get much done?'

'Barely made a dent in the accounts.'

'How does it look?'

'As rosy as ever,' Dad said sarcastically.

'Anything else?'

'Should there be?' Dad glanced around the table and for the first time noticed someone was missing. 'Where's Bernadette?' he asked, putting his fork clean through one of his potatoes.

'She's not here. She's gone to Auckland.'

Mum was studying Dad's reaction. He paused slightly; it was so slight that if you hadn't been watching closely you would have missed it.

'She wanted to get there early, to take that flat with her friends. I couldn't talk her out of it.' Mum was trying to smile as she talked, trying to make her voice sound carefree and in-the-ordinary. 'She said she'd find a part-time job, maybe in a restaurant, as a waitress. I said she'd do well, considering how it is here with so many of us.'

Dad didn't reply. And except for that tiny pause he didn't stop eating. By this time we were all waiting for his reaction. Even Ed sat up and paid attention. I held my breath and looked to Mum. She was watching Dad. I could hear a noise like thunder rolling in over the room only I couldn't tell where it was coming from. My lips felt dry. The lines etched on Mum's face stood out against her set expression. I could make out every strand in the tablecloth. Dad put down his fork. The thunder clapped deafeningly in my ears. My cheeks were fit to burst. Dad looked right around the table then his eyes rested on Mum.

'Pass the bread,' he said. 'And the butter. Please.'

Chapter Two

The haze of discomfort left by Bernadette's departure rested over us
kids for a full day, and then routine returned to the house. Sheer
force of will shook us free from that dark cloud in the end. It was
the last week of the summer holidays and none of us were going to
let our eldest sister ruin it. Kate spent a good part of her time
complaining that Bernadette had stolen her favourite nightie from
the line. Rachel said that didn't make sense but Kate couldn't be
convinced otherwise. She was sure Bernadette had nicked it in
return for the hairbrush, which Kate still claimed she'd never
taken. Mum busied herself with getting all of us ready for school.
There were several shopping trips to buy new clothes for Rachel,
Kate and Andrew, and for me and Ed when we kicked up enough
of a stink. But we never got to the city. It was a full hour's drive
from Lumley and Mum only had time for one day trip that week;
Aunt Erin at the Good Samaritan.

Usually we would make a trip like that as a family but this time
only Mum, Rachel and I went. Dad was at work and Mum decided
not to take Eddie so Kate had to stay at home to mind him. Andrew
didn't go because he was a brat to me all through breakfast and
Mum didn't want us fighting the whole trip. Andrew had planned
it that way, of course, so that instead of spending the day with Mum
in the car he would be left to his own devices.

If I'd been as crafty as Andrew I would have probably done the
same thing. Going to see Aunt Erin was not one of my favourite

outings. Yet the car trip down to Good Samaritan that clear January day was like a little slice of joy. The Holden zoomed through the brilliant morning and the sun patterned the back seat in chinks of pure gold. Mum and Rachel sang along to a Glen Campbell song and we had to laugh when Mum kept getting the words hopelessly wrong though she insisted that she wasn't, just that she was singing her version of the song. Rachel and I played I-Spy and I had her absolutely stumped with A is for air particle. We also played find-the-alphabet on signs and number-plates. All the tough letters, like J and K and Q, came easily for a change, but F and H gave us some grief.

The Good Samaritan was three hours' drive from Lumley. Andrew referred to it as the Nut House. When Mum corrected him she called it a psychiatric institution. Aunt Erin had been there as long as I could remember. She wasn't really our aunt, though, she was some sort of second cousin on Mum's side of the family. Mum and Dad didn't discuss it much, mostly referring to her without saying her name, but you knew what they were talking about because their voices went a certain kind of quiet. Neither of them had ever told me how she got put into the Good Samaritan but I'd heard bits and pieces from the older kids and managed to construct what I guessed to be the story.

Aunt Erin used to be a pretty girl from Lumley who married her childhood boyfriend and went to live in the city where they had a daughter and a son. Mr Aunt Erin had a good job and they owned a big house and had lots of money. But his job took him all over the North Island and Aunt Erin was often left by herself in the house for long periods with just the two young children. This went on for a couple of years until the daughter was old enough to walk. One day, when it was raining and stormy, she wandered onto the road and was accidentally hit by Mr Aunt Erin coming home from one of his trips.

Aunt Erin cried for a full month. She kept talking to her daughter like she was still there and even bought new clothes for her and gave her a birthday party. Then she started doing even stranger things. One day she went to the fountain in the middle of the city shopping centre, took off all her clothes and had a swim. After that she got put into hospital and never came out. Mr Aunt Erin and the son hung around for a while then disappeared overseas in 1972 and hadn't been heard from since.

The Good Samaritan hospital was a criss-cross of different-sized buildings located in the middle of the countryside. Some of the buildings were red brick rectangles but most of them looked like cottages with shingle roofs and small windows. Just outside the Samaritan's gates was a dairy and as we pulled in Mum promised she'd buy us something when we left. There was a big mound of black dirt, clearly visible right from the entrance, looming conspicuously behind the buildings, but never coming into full view. Nothing ever grew on this hill and it looked the same every time we visited.

Inside the main building Rachel and I were directed to a waiting room while Mum followed a woman wearing a white uniform with a scarlet cardigan. We were used to the routine and the room was familiar to us. There were a couple of old armchairs, a formica-topped table with metal legs and some well-read books in a small bookcase standing next to the window.

'Look,' Rachel said as she searched the bookcase. 'They have a Fuzzy Felts.' She pulled out the box. 'Fuzzy Felts farm.'

We sat down at the table and carefully laid out the felt pieces, sorted them into shapes and colours then set them on the prickly back-board. For the first couple of times we did some freehand scenes, but then we tried to copy one of the example pictures on the back of the box.

'Are you excited about school?' Rachel asked me as we worked.

'I guess so.'

'I am. I'm doing UE this year. Do you know what that is?'

'No.'

'University Entrance. It's this hard test you have to sit in the Sixth Form.' She checked out the back of the box, then placed a hat on one of the farm figures. 'I want to get good marks so I can go to medical school. What I get this year matters. And Seventh Form, if I go to Seventh Form. How do you think you'd like it if you had to call me Doctor Garrick, instead of plain old Rachel?'

'Some of the people here are doctors. Are you going to come and work with them?'

'I doubt it. But you never know.'

Mum returned just as we were pulling apart one of our felt creations.

'Can we see her?' Rachel asked.

Mum nodded. 'I think she's well enough to have more visitors.'

Rachel and I were quite excited at this. Most of the time we never got to actually see Aunt Erin and when we did she was always in a deep sleep. We tidied up the Fuzzy Felts in a hurry then followed Mum into the long, shiny-floored corridor.

Aunt Erin's room was dark, shielded from the sun outside with thick cream-coloured drapes. It was an empty room, with only a bed, a wooden chair and an old-type heater, like a big metal accordion, attached to the wall with brackets. Aunt Erin was lying on the bed. Mum went straight over to her.

'Erin,' she said softly. 'I've brought Rachel and Kevin to see you.'

Aunt Erin didn't move. I thought she must have fallen asleep but then I noticed that both her eyes were wide open, staring vacantly towards the ceiling. Her face was twitching slightly and I could hear her breathing in short gasps. She looked the way that our cat Charley sometimes used to look when he slept, eyes open but rolled part-way back in his head so you could see the milky underneath of his eyeballs. You could wave your hand in front of his face and not get any response. It was if he was completely focused on something that you couldn't see.

I took an uneasy step back from the bed.

'Erin,' Mum repeated. 'Rachel and Kevin have come to say hello.'

Rachel leaned over to Mum and whispered, 'What's the matter with her?'

'I don't know. She was fine just a moment ago. Kevin, come over here, she's not going to bite.'

I obeyed, slowly.

'She's gone, I think. She was like this when I arrived then she came out of it and she talked to me clear as day. We won't wait too long.'

Rachel leaned over again. 'What did you talk about?'

'Lots of little things. The weather. This hospital.'

'So she knows where she is?'

'Yes. She's a little confused about the time that has passed. She imagines this is my first visit.'

'Do you think she can hear what we're saying?'

'Maybe.'

'I wish she would wake up so we could talk to her,' I said loudly, hoping it might bring her back from wherever she was. 'She's always like this when we come. Why doesn't she want to wake up?'

'No one is sure. That's why she's been in hospital so long.'

'Maybe she does want to wake up but something's stopping her,' Rachel said.

We stood watching for a moment. Something about Aunt Erin just lying there, unable or unwilling to come into the real world, made me feel tremendously sad.

'I don't know how long she is going to be like this now. Do you kids want to stay?' Mum asked us both.

Rachel looked to me for an answer. I shrugged.

'Shall we go now?' Rachel suggested.

Mum nodded and walked to the door. Rachel stepped over to the bed and touched Aunt Erin's arm lightly, waiting for some response, but Aunt Erin didn't move.

Mum and Rachel talked about medical school in the car going

home. Mum was pretty chuffed that was what Rachel wanted to do. As far as she was aware, Rachel would be the first doctor in the entire history of the Garrick family. Rachel was worried because there were no women doctors in Lumley, but Mum kept saying that if medical school was what Rachel wanted to do then she should go for it. As she had promised, we made a stop for provisions at the dairy. I got a choc-dipped ice-cream and a raspberry K-bar. The ice-cream melted quickly underneath the chocolate shell and ran all over my fingers. I licked them clean then dozed in the afternoon sunshine with the warm chewy satisfaction of the K-bar between my teeth.

Just before we reached Lumley, Mum said she wanted to pop by the timber yard on our way home. Garrick and Son was the very last building before you reached the town limits. Dad's father had started the business when he came over from Britain as a young man and it had once been so large it provided wood to people all around New Zealand. Its glory days were a memory and the yard was far smaller than it had once been, but it was still an impressive sight with two rusty metal towers standing guard over the shoebox-shaped main building, painted brown, red and green, and piles upon piles of fresh-smelling timber neatly stacked on every side.

Mum took Rachel inside with her and I waited for them in the car. I didn't mind because there was a lot to see and hear in the yard. There were men working everywhere, busy filling midweek orders, and behind the main building I could hear the buzz of wood being cut and taste the gritty sawdust in the air.

A couple of the men were on top of one of the metal towers, the rest were on the ground. Some had clipboards and were supervising the loading of timber into huge rigs, like larger-than-life Tonka toys. There were several trucks on the go at once and a couple left the yard even while I was there. The drivers parped their horns as they departed and the men with clipboards waved or shouted goodbye.

In part of the yard two men hauled a tarpaulin over a pile of wood. They fitted the canvas over the timber then tied it down with some rope. On another pile some more men were restacking by hand. The crack of wood against wood echoed all around, bouncing off the boundary fence that circled the whole yard. Most of the men were dressed the same way, in check shirts with the sleeves rolled up to their elbows, shorts and strong work shoes or gumboots. The men who were stacking had thick gloves on as well. It was such a hot day that some of them had taken off their shirts and tied them around their waists.

Rachel came back to the car by herself. A couple of the men gave her a second glance as she crossed the parking lot. I saw them nudge each other and smile when she got into the car.

'Those men are looking at you,' I told her.

'I know. Most of them aren't anything to write home about, but a couple of the younger ones are cute.' She stared out the front window in the direction of the shirtless men. After a while one of the men stopped working and stared back at Rachel at which she pretended she hadn't been looking at all and poked around intensely in the glove compartment like she was really trying to find something. The man went back to work and Rachel looked up again, this time attempting to make it seem like she wasn't looking, but it was obvious to me exactly where her attention was fixed.

'Where's Mum?' I asked her when I got bored watching her watch the man.

'She's coming. She got stuck outside Dad's office talking to some guy. Mr Street. They're talking about you and some kid who's in your class.'

'Richard Street?'

'That's the one. Is he your friend?'

Hardly, I thought. Richard Street had never been the biggest boy in our year, or the strongest, but he had always been the meanest. He was also pretty bright, topping the class in almost every subject, and he rarely misbehaved in class so that the teachers always thought he was this nice guy when in actual fact he was plain nasty.

'He's not my mate.'

'Well Mum's chatting to his dad. I don't think she wanted to, though. You know, when you're stuck talking to someone you don't want to talk to but they won't let you get away so you can't leave even though all you want to do is run like the dickens? Look, she's coming now.'

Mum walked briskly to the car. She waved to a couple of the men in the yard and sighed as she slipped behind the wheel.

'Have fun?' said Rachel knowingly.

'That Street man wouldn't let me go. That's the one with the horrible boy in your class, isn't it, Kevin?'

'Richard.'

'I thought so. He kept talking and talking. When I told him we'd just been down south he wanted to discuss how he took his family to Wellington last year and what the motel they stayed in was like.' Mum shook her head. 'Strange. Anyway, let's go home.'

Rachel put on her seatbelt. 'What does he do?'

Mum started the car. 'Oh, he's just a stock supervisor. His son is a beast, isn't he, Kevin? He's the one who used to bully you last year, until Andrew put a stop to it. I don't understand why some people insist on bombarding you with all this detail about their lives. It's not that I mind talking to him, but he wouldn't stop. I hardly got a word in.'

'Maybe he was trying to get on the good side of the boss's wife.'

'Who knows? He's wasting his time if he is. Listen to me, I only have bad things to say about him.'

The other kids were sitting in a pow-wow circle on the front lawn when we came into our driveway. Before the car had even come to a complete stop I pulled off the Roman sandals Mum had made me wear on the trip and sprinted over to them.

'We have to get them somehow,' Andrew was saying.

'Water fight?' Kate suggested.

'Perhaps. I still think the lemon idea is the best one.'

I waited for someone to volunteer to fill me in.

'So it's lemons?' Andrew proposed.

'Lemons,' Kate agreed. 'Just make sure we get the little creepy one with the rabbit teeth. See if you can hit him in the dick, presuming he's got one.'

'What's a dick?' Eddie asked.

'You are,' Andrew told him.

'Ask Mum,' Kate added.

'What's happening?' I asked at last, annoyed that I could miss an event exciting enough to warrant a war conference.

'Mrs Aston-Peach's grandkids are over from England. We think they've been there for a couple of days now. Bloody Poms. Kate was hanging out the washing when —'

'I can tell it! I'm not Helen Keller, you know. I was out by the line. I didn't notice anything at first but then I heard giggling and they popped up from over the top of the fence. They were saying all this rude stuff and doing this dumb song. I threatened to go over and beat them up but they said they'd enjoy it.'

'They'll enjoy it when I'm finished with them,' Andrew promised.

How old are they?'

Andrew dug at the ground with a stick. 'Dunno. About my age. The younger one's real skinny, but they're both quite tall. Their father is here too. He looks just like a grown-up version of the kids. Haven't seen their mother. Maybe she's dead.'

'I wouldn't be surprised with two brats like that. They probably killed her.'

'Poor Mrs Aston-Peach, trapped alone with them.'

'This is war,' said Andrew. 'I've been studying them all afternoon. I figure we climb up a tree and lure them out in the open then pelt them with lemons, the hard little ones and some of the rotten ones. Mrs Aston-Peach will be out at golf tomorrow afternoon like usual. That's the best time to get them.'

It was only then that I noticed Andrew was juggling a tennis ball from hand to hand like a hot potato. Kate realised I had seen it.

'That's the ball you hit onto the Hill house. We got it back this morning.'

Andrew puffed out his chest. 'Yeah, I climbed up and picked it out of the trellis.' He tossed the ball into the air and Kate swiped it off him.

'Don't listen to him! Mr Hill brought it over. He pounded on the back door and when I answered it he waved the ball in my face and raved about how we could have broken a window and how he's not going up a ladder for us again. Then he thrust the ball into my hand. Yuck, he actually touched me.'

'It's all your fault, Kevin,' Andrew said. 'He'll probably set Mrs Hill onto us now.'

Kate was far kinder. 'Just as well Mum wasn't here.'

'If Mrs Hill comes looking for her ball, we'll know who's to blame.'

'Give it a rest, Andy, you'll scare Ed.' Kate chucked the ball at him but missed by a mile.

'Good shot,' Andrew said sarcastically. 'You better not come up the tree with the lemons.'

Straight after breakfast the next day all four of us stripped the lemon tree of its unripe fruit. Eddie hunted around right under the back of the tree and pulled out some of the rotten ones, managing to find a few with a furry pale-green coating of mould on them. While we picked, Andrew reviewed his plan for the umpteenth time, going over the drill with each of us in turn till Kate got so sick of him she said she might not do it if he didn't shut his face.

The scheme was for Kate and Eddie to position themselves on the back lawn with the box of plastic animals. They would innocently set them up and look like they were playing some involved game. I would wander over to them a couple of times and chat casually. This would hopefully draw out the Poms.

Kate and Eddie would ignore anything the Poms said, lulling them into a false sense of security. In the meantime I would join Andrew at the fir tree halfway down the side fence. We would sneak up the tree, armed with the box of lemons, and hurl them down on the unsuspecting Poms. They would probably run away, but we'd pelt them with a few good ones before then. The real beauty of the strategy was that they had to run right under us to escape. For those couple of seconds they'd be pure target practice. Andrew's plan was so cunning and tactically honed that those two Poms were like dumb sheep being led to the slaughter.

Everything went how Andrew had intended, even better since the Poms turned up straight away, before I could make either of my scheduled visits. I squirrelled silently up the fir and waited beside Andrew. From this angle I could see how skinny and untanned both of the boys were. Their legs were like long uncooked pork sausages, except even more colourless, and both of them were wearing shoes and socks, strictly winter clothing in our family.

'Look at their legs,' I whispered.

'That's the ugliest thing I ever saw.'

We each readied several lemons in our hands and watched vigilantly.

'Hey, sexy tits!' the taller of the two Poms shouted as they both leered across the fence. 'Hey, you!' His voice sounded plummy and correct. There had been a Pom in school the year before and that was the way he sounded too. La-di-da.

'Look at those sexy tits,' the other shouted. His two front teeth poked out below his upper lip. He was obviously the one Kate had described as having the rabbit teeth and in my head I nicknamed him Bugs Bunny.

'Now?' I whispered to Andrew.

'No, let them get cocky. I'll say when.'

'How about coming over here and showing us those sexy tits?'

'How about her sister? The blonde one.' They meant Rachel.

'Now that's what I call knockers.'

'Tits out to here.' Bugs cupped his hands over his chest.

'No, out to here!' The older one began a clumsy mime, hitting his behind and his chest, twice, then strumming low down. 'Bum, tit-tit, bum, tit-tit, play the woolly banjo.'

Bugs joined in.

'Bum, tit-tit, bum, tit-tit, play the woolly banjo . . . bum, tit-tit, bum, tit-tit, play the woolly banjo . . .'

Andrew nodded and we opened fire in unison. My first shot was wide but his caught the younger Pom square on his lard-white leg. Even from the tree you could see the violent red mark that hard little lemon left.

'Cor, what was that!' he shouted painfully.

We didn't give him a chance to figure it out and sent down a hail of similar hard lemons, catching both of them standing stock-still.

The Poms threw up their arms against the rain of fruit then let out some dirty words and ran, as Andrew had planned, right under the fir tree, which is when we switched to the squishy lemons. As Bugs ran past I landed a really mouldy one on the side of his face. A dusty pale-green cloud, like a puff of magic smoke, appeared as it hit him and he stopped in his tracks, shrieking and rubbing his eyes. I'd say between us, Andrew and I landed four or five mouldy lemons on him alone before he finally ran inside, screaming like a girl. The older Pom escaped with only one or two hits before he disappeared, slamming the back door hard behind him.

Kate and Eddie looked up at us with huge grins.

'Ahhhhhoooooooo!' Andrew howled. 'The victors by a unanimous verdict, the Garrick family!' He rocked the branch dangerously. 'Talk about a massacre!'

Kate and Eddie laughed. Me too. It was an evil, infectious laugh. I savoured the moment giddily. Andrew slapped me on the back and smiled.

'I'll swing down,' he said. 'Chuck me the box.'

Before I could reply, Mrs Aston-Peach's back door burst open and a man who looked just like a grown version of the Poms stormed out. The two boys followed, Bugs Bunny holding his face and bawling.

'Christ, it's their father,' Andrew gasped. 'Jump down!' He hurled the box before him and swung off the branch into the bushy undergrowth below.

'Where are you little boggers?' I heard from the ground on Mrs Aston-Peach's side of the fence. The man stormed straight past the tree.

'Kevin!' Andrew said in a loud whisper. 'Jump!'

The Poms stuck close to the back of the house while their father strode up and down the inside of the fence.

'I know you're out there!' He looked up towards the tree and without thinking I skidded ungracefully off the branch. I landed more on my bum than on my feet, hitting the ground so hard it winded me and I lay there, wheezing like a wounded seal.

'Shush!' said Andrew.

Sure, I thought, why don't we swap places and you can lie here and die in silence?

'Come out and face me! Come on!' The father was getting nearer.

'Kevin, shut up!' Andrew clamped his hand over my mouth.

The voice was right beside us now. 'Bloody cowards. Not so brave now are we, you little boggers?' We could hear him pushing through the bushes on their side of the fence. Andrew dragged me behind the fir and tightened his grip on my mouth.

'I'd give you bloody marks on your legs if I had you!' The searching sounds stopped. 'Bloody little Kiwi cowards. You make me bloody sick.' The voice was moving away. 'Bloody little bloody boggers!'

Andrew listened for a moment or two and then let his hand go. I gulped in a huge lungful of fresh air as Kate and Eddie picked

37

carefully through the undergrowth and joined us. Kate and Andrew looked at each other seriously.

'Do you think he'll tell Mum and Dad?'

'Who cares?' Andrew said. 'If they do, we'll just repeat what the Pom kids said to you. Jesus, did you hear their father? He's insane. I thought he was going to smash through the fence for a minute there. Those limey Poms! They didn't even try to fight back. They had to get their dad to fight for them. Deserved everything we gave them. They won't be saying anything about tits now.'

'You okay, Kevin?' Kate asked me.

'I think so,' I said in laboured whoops and breaths.

Andrew pulled me off the ground and hugged me around the neck. 'He'll survive. Damn good shot too. Landed some stunning blows. You should have seen him hit the skinny one in the face. Right on the cheek it was. Hell that was good!'

Kate said that she later spied one of the Poms peeping over the fence at her but he vanished as soon as he knew she had spotted him. Andrew crowed about the victory at every available opportunity, getting progressively more intolerable as the week went on. I supposed it was because he was starting his first year at boarding school and that made him the big man around the house. He certainly acted like it at Mass on Sunday, ushering the rest of the family into our pew like we couldn't find our own way. He sang the hymns louder than anyone else and insisted on handing over the collection envelope with a grand flourish.

After Mass he tried to engage Father O'Brien in conversation, faking this posh accent so badly that Dad eventually dragged him away to stop him making a bigger fool of himself, if that was possible. Andrew didn't notice at all though. He was too excited about school. He and Dad were going to start the five-hour journey to Wellington later that morning; the girls would go up to their boarding school in Auckland on the evening bus. Mum had tried to get Dad to stay the night down south but he insisted that he do a round trip.

'I can't take any more time off work. It's bad enough that I have to miss today.'

He loaded up the car and hurried Andrew through breakfast, then we watched the Holden vanish out the front gate. Andrew was so absorbed that he didn't even look back in the car to say goodbye.

Late that afternoon we took the girls to Lumley bus station in Mum's Mini. The girls gave us hugs and kisses then Mum, Eddie and I stood on the platform, waving as the bus pulled away.

I always used to complain about Andrew and the other kids. Because they were older, they tended to give us two younger boys a hard time. Andrew's nature especially seemed bent towards making life a misery. And until that Sunday it was always Andrew, me and Eddie in our house. A threesome, no matter how you rearranged the names. Now, for the first time, it was just me and Eddie. Eddie and I. I had thought that the house would be peaceful without Andrew, without all of them. But sitting around the large dining room table that evening with just Mum and my little brother, for the first time that I could remember in my whole life, the house felt big. And silent. And empty.

Chapter Three

Lumley was the sort of town that was not so small that everyone knew everybody else, but small enough that most people knew a little bit of everything that happened. Like how Miss Avalon bred cats for international shows. And how the Johnsons without the 't' attended the 'alternative' church out Remihana way. And Mr Ogilvie worked in the city and came back to Lumley for weekends. And James Tower's parents slept in different bedrooms. And old Mrs Rocher from the corner dairy didn't know how to read or write but never forgot a name, a face, or the amount owed on your tab. Lumley was a town large enough for two primary schools as well as the high school. It had ten pages in the district phone book, a New World supermarket, two roundabouts, a railway overbridge and a gardening shop with its own mini-greenhouse in the rear and a real full-sized wheelbarrow stuck on the façade. It had its own public library, located at the end of a long dark corridor that was cold and echoey and lined with pictures of the city fathers. The library also contained Lumley's only elevator.

It was a town big enough for a municipal swimming pool. And a picture theatre with a winding staircase and red velvet curtains that hung so thick and heavy you wondered how they managed to stay on the rails. In George Mayle Park there was a band rotunda which at Christmas time would be decorated around the edges with dozens of coloured lights. The park was named after a lieutenant-colonel from Lumley killed at Gallipoli. A stone memorial arch at the park's entrance commemorated his sacrifice.

In the centre of town was a square-faced clock, which kept perfect time. It was part of the local post office, the largest building in Lumley, which was sided with shiny aluminium and had a flagpole directly outside, placed in the middle of the footpath. No one knew why the builders put a flagpole in everyone's way, but it was such a part of the town that no one seemed to care, and anyway, once you knew it was there you just walked around it.

Lumley was tucked under the shadow of the mountain. No matter where you went in the town, if you looked up, the mountain was there, watching over your shoulder. Around the base of the mountain was a circle of native bush and even in summer the mountain's peak was capped with a dusting of snow which thickened and spread as winter came. It also had a habit of being shy and more often than not it would play peek-a-boo behind a screen of mist and clouds. Being around the mountain all the time, you tended to forget it was there. But you could always sense its looming presence.

That was the town that came out to greet us as we walked through its wide streets on the first morning of school. The people and the places and the mountain. Mum stood on the front porch and waved goodbye to me and Ed. Unlike Andrew the day before, we waved back. Ed and I had been up for hours. We had both woken early, when it was still dark, then lain excitedly in bed, talking about the new things we would do during the school year ahead.

Although I let Ed tag along with me the whole way to Lumley Primary, I ditched him in the Primers as soon as we arrived, sternly ordering him to meet me by the school gate at the end of the day. Then I hoofed it over to the Standards block. I was in Standard Three and I could hardly wait to see our new classroom and my old friends. On the way I bumped into Julie Dwyer. In actual fact it was more like she was waiting for me. Julie's older brother had been one of Andrew's best friends. David Dwyer was most famous for giving my older brother the same present Andrew had given him the birthday before. Because of that, the friendship was ultimately doomed, but despite their falling out and the fact that she was a class ahead of me, Julie and I had always got on well. You could say we were friends, but it wasn't best friends or even close friends. It was more the sort of go-to-the-movies-once-in-a-while-and-get-invited-over-for-a-swim kind of friends. But more and more her interest in me seemed to be changing.

'Hi, Kevin,' she smiled, her golden Shirley Temple curls nodding dangerously.

'Hello,' I said politely but didn't stop walking.

She matched my stride. 'My family went to Australia for Christmas.'

'That's nice.'

'I saw the Sydney Harbour Bridge.' She paused, waiting for a response. 'And some kangaroos. What did you do?'

'Nothing much.'

'Who do you have this year?'

'Miss A'Court.'

'We have this new teacher called Mr Harris. Raewyn Kelly says she met him in town last week and that he's a real dish.'

'Uh huh.'

'Miss A'Court is nice, though. You're lucky. I liked her last year.'

'Uh huh.' I looked around for an easy escape. There was none.

'Kevin, it's my birthday in a couple of weeks' time.' Julie batted her eyelids expertly. 'Mummy is going to have a party for me. I was wondering, maybe, if you would like to, if you're not busy that day, maybe, you'd like —'

The hard sound of the first bell of the year sliced through the morning air, giving me the perfect escape.

'Didyouhearthat?It'stimeforclass.Ihavetogo.Bye.' And I sprinted away.

42

Miss A'Court's Standard Three was already waiting outside the classroom, divided into two neat groups, girls on one side, boys on the other. I joined the boys and searched the other group for Sheree, who unlike Julie *was* my best friend, but she wasn't there. Kingsley Helms tried to have a conversation with me about his Christmas holiday spent camping in a tent but had about as much success as Julie. I wasn't being rude; everyone ignored Kingsley.

'Hey Kev, did you hear about our teacher?' Steve Armstrong asked when he saw me.

'Miss A'Court, yeah,' Paul Tuck answered before I could. 'Weird, huh?'

'What's happened?' I asked Steve.

'She's gone. Left town last week sudden like. Not a word to anyone. My Dad says she must be up the duff.'

'Bull.'

'Nah, isstrue. We're getting a new woman. Name starts with R.'

Annette Luney must have been listening because she strode across to no-girl's land.

'Are you sure we have a new teacher?'

'Sure am, Looney-bin.'

Annette ignored Steve's remark. 'What's her name then?'

'Dunno. It starts with a R.'

'Maybe it's Rabbit.' Paul grinned.

'Or Wriggle?' Steve suggested.

'That doesn't start with "R", you idiot,' Annette sneered.

'Maybe . . .' I said mischievously, 'it's Rabies.'

'Yeah!' both Paul and Steve shouted together.

'And maybe . . . she really has rabies.'

'Like a dog.'

'Maybe she is a dog.'

'Hi, I'm Miss Rabies,' I said. Egged on by the giggles from the rest of the class I threw myself completely into the role. I put on a high-pitched, lilting voice and strutted inside the circle of kids that had formed around me.

'I'm Miss Rabies. Pleased to meet you.' I woofed a genuine dog bark. The crowd let out a whoop of approval. 'Do you like my collar? I got it from the pet store. For morning tea I'm having dog biscuits then I'll lie down in my kennel in the staff room.' I got down on all fours and howled into the morning air, tossing in a couple of loud growls and snarls. 'If you misbehave I might bite you! And then you'll have rabies. Just like me! 'Cause I'm Miss Rabies.'

The other kids started chanting the name over and over. 'Miss Rabies! Miss Rabies! Miss Rabies!' Then suddenly the laughter and the chanting stopped. The crowd parted and a serious-looking woman in a plain brown dress strode through the gap. She looked down at me and my stomach flip-flopped in a perfect imitation of a see-saw. The woman, who I guessed to be the real Miss Rabies, regarded me with a disdainful glance then turned away without saying a word. That only made me feel worse, because if she had told me off straight away it would have all been over in an instant; I would have known that she'd twigged onto what I had been doing. Instead she left me in an uncomfortable middle ground, wondering whether she had realised it was her I was poking fun at, or whether she had only looked at me strangely because I was acting silly.

The teacher's keys hardly jingled as she unlocked the classroom then hooked the door open. We were all silent as we entered.

'Your names are on your desks,' she said coolly. 'Find your place and sit down.'

There was some pushing and shoving while we fought to find our names which were written on small labels stuck to the tops of our desks. Mine was deep in the heart of the room. Steve had been placed to one side of me. Paul was right in the front row. You could see he didn't appreciate that at all. Sheree was still nowhere to be seen.

The woman waited until we had all settled down and then walked from the back of the class to the blackboard.

'My name is Mrs Riddle,' she announced, writing on the

blackboard as she spoke. 'R-I-D-D-L-E. It's pronounced as if you are saying the word "rid" and then the letter "L". Not riddle, rhyming with middle, like a joke.' She turned and pinned me to the back of my seat with her eyes. My stomach, which had just begun to recover, lurched sickly again. 'I will be your teacher this year.'

'Please, Mrs Riddle,' Annette said from the back of the room. 'What happened to Miss A'Court?'

'Fortunately for this class, Annette Luney, Miss Jennifer A'Court is no longer a teacher at this school. You will hear many stories about what happened to Miss A'Court. Most of them are probably true.'

Some of us kids turned to look at each other, wondering how she knew Annette's name straight off. Steve leaned over to whisper something to me.

'Head forward, Steven Armstrong!' Steve's head snapped forward so fast I thought it was going to fly off his shoulders. By now the entire Standard Three class was thoroughly spooked.

'I have been teaching for fifteen years, the last twelve of those years in Wanganui. I enjoy reading and netball. I hope that I can make your year interesting for you.' She looked over the class with a neutral expression, almost like she was bored, but when her eyes reached me her face hardened visibly. By then my worried stomach was a tangle of knots. Steve stole a glance towards me and crossed his eyes but I didn't dare smile.

Just before morning playtime our class was trooped off to the assembly hall for stationery purchases and we grumbled, watching the children from other rooms running about in the brilliant sunshine. The line was so long and moved so sluggishly that when we got back to our room there was only enough time for Mrs Riddle to hand out copies of the *School Journal* before the bell went for lunch. Steve, Paul and I took up our haunt of previous years by the back boundary fence. The obvious topic of conversation was our new teacher, or Rabies-woman, as Steve had nicknamed her.

45

'I hate her guts,' Steve began.

'I hate the rest of her,' Paul replied.

'She's an alien.'

'A witch.'

'How did she know our names right away?'

'They're on our desks.'

'She couldn't read that little writing all the way from the blackboard. Could she?'

'At least you're not at the front of the room.'

'Did you see Looney-bin greasing up to her?'

'Typical.'

'When she said my name straight off I almost lost it.'

'She *is* an alien.'

I didn't say anything. Secretly I was worried that Mrs Riddle had the area bugged. I wouldn't have put it past her, not after what I'd seen already that morning. I looked beyond the fence to the road and wondered if it was too late to ask Mum if I could go to Lumley Main. There was no Rabies-woman there.

'Kevin?' I heard behind me. 'Kevin!' Steve was calling me. 'What planet were you on?'

'I was thinking.'

'Must have been hard for you.' He laughed.

Paul took a second to get the joke. 'Hard? Oh, haha-hahahahahhhh.'

Steve and Paul weren't my best friends. Steve was okay mostly, a beefy kid with a prickly blond crew cut that was tingly to touch, but Paul, smaller and sporting a crooked pudding bowl hairdo, was not the smartest kid in the world. They both bussed in from the country and could be really crude sometimes. I supposed that had something to do with them both coming from farms. They exploited every situation for its double meaning. Like when Julie Dwyer came over to us that lunch time. Steve and Paul went into overdrive.

'It's your girl-friend, Kevin.'

'He won't be long. He's just picking out a wedding ring, Julie.'

Julie was obviously embarrassed about what was being said but she didn't leave.

'I have something for you,' she told me.

'Ohhh, she has something for you, Kevin. A kiss perhaps?'

'A big sloppy smooch. Mmmwah!'

'Kevin and Julie up a tree . . . K-I-S-S-I-N-G.'

'Is there another line to that?'

Julie rocked uneasily in place. 'Here.' She handed me a pure cream-coloured envelope with pictures of little angels around the edges.

'What is it?' I asked, not wanting to open it in front of Hekyll and Jekyll.

'An invitation to my birthday. It's Saturday in three weeks. I hope you can come.' Then she turned tail and ran back towards the classrooms.

'What's that?' Steve asked.

I pretended not to hear him and folded the envelope roughly into my pocket.

Sheree was missing from class all morning and she didn't appear until after lunch. She tried to sneak in the open door and take the only free seat without Mrs Riddle spotting her. But nothing happened in Mrs Riddle's room without her knowing it.

'What are you doing?' she boomed from the teacher's table at the back of the room. Sheree kept creeping to her desk.

'Little girl . . . Sheree Humphries!'

Sheree slid into her seat, then turned around with a broad grin.

'What do you think you're doing?'

'Going to my desk.'

'Going to my desk, what?' Mrs Riddle prompted, getting up from her seat.

'Going to my desk, here,' Sheree replied cheekily. A tiny ripple of approval swept through the class.

'Were you aware that school began this morning, Sheree Humphries?'

'Yeah, and I'll be here early tomorrow but today I had to help Mum with my brother. He's sick.'

'I expect a note next time,' Mrs Riddle said and slapped a *School Journal* on Sheree's desk. 'You'll have to fix up your stationery later. Right now we're reading silently, page twenty-four.' She returned to her table and Sheree watched her go, catching my eye. She winked at me and I smiled back, glad that someone else had got on Mrs Riddle's bad side, taking some of the heat off me.

At the end of school I collected Eddie from the front gate and we began the walk home. He had done some crayon drawing and he pulled out a picture of a pony which I said was really good even though it looked more like a giraffe than a horse. His teacher, Miss Joyce, was really sweet. She'd been in the Primers forever and had taught all the Garricks, even Bernadette.

'What else did you do?' I asked Ed as he put his drawing back in his satchel.

'Miss Joyce showed us this map of the town.'

I remembered it. 'Did she mark where all you kids live?'

'Yeah. I didn't think much of it at all,' he said with grand disapproval.

'Why not?'

'She knows where I live now.'

'So?'

'What if she comes home in the weekend?'

'Why would she want to do that?'

'To teach me.'

'That's not going to happen.'

'It might.'

'Somehow I doubt it.'

'Well, if she does, I'm not letting her in. She can knock all she wants and I'm not going to answer the door.'

I shook my head in disbelief. Ed could be really eccentric sometimes. He spent half his life in a dream world but even when he came back to reality he was never quite all there. Some people had suggested to Mum and Dad that Ed was retarded but my parents wouldn't hear a word of it. I didn't think Eddie was retarded either. He wasn't dumb, just pretty weird. Oddness followed him around. Not even Saturn Girl from the Legion of Super-Heroes with her mighty telepathic powers could have figured him out.

To begin with, his real name wasn't Eddie, Ed or even Edward, but Jerome. Jerome Hubert Victor Garrick. He was really sick when he was born so they not only christened him in hospital but they confirmed him as well. That's how close he came to dying. Mum was undecided on what to call the new arrival and neither she nor Dad was in any condition to choose so an old priest thought up some names on the spot. Jerome Hubert Victor came to be called Ed because ever since he was a baby he was fascinated by horses. He even had Mum sew him a horse costume for his kindergarten fancy dress party and then refused to wear anything else. Mum finally cut it off him when he tried to rein himself with a duffle bag cord on one of the coathooks in the alcove underneath the stairs. He was as blue as the sky when she found him. Then one day little Jerome saw Mr Ed on TV and became convinced that he and the talking horse were related, like Mr Ed was a person stuck in a horse's body and he was a horse stuck in a person's body. It was Andrew who nicknamed him Eddie and the name stuck.

Arriving home, Ed and I saw a strange car parked in front of our house. Crouched like a huge beetle beside the porch, the shiny black vehicle was hard to miss. Mum must have heard the front door shut because she came out from the living room to greet us.

'Did you have a good first day?' She had a wine glass in her hand and she swung the living room door closed behind her.

'It was okay,' I fibbed.

Eddie nodded. 'Look,' he said, whipping out his drawing.

'It's a horse,' I explained quickly so Mum didn't put her foot in it and say it was a giraffe.

'A very fine horse too.'

'Who's in the living room?'

'Your father. He's with Mr Cleaver. He's a man who's come down from Auckland to help Dad with the timber yard. Are either of you hungry? Mr Cleaver suggested that we go out for dinner.' Mum looked critically at what we were wearing. 'You'll have to change, though.'

She followed us upstairs and pulled out our Sunday Mass clothes. Ed and I had these nice t-shirts with matching pictures on them, the same shirts we wore on the day of the family photo. I asked Mum why Mr Cleaver wanted to go out to dinner and she told me it was for business and because he liked us. Eddie said he was going to show Mr Cleaver his picture. Mum found Julie's birthday card in my shorts pocket and I told her I didn't want to go to the stupid party. She thought it might be fun but I held my ground. Then Mum went to her bedroom to get changed but not before she sent me and Eddie, still clutching his picture, downstairs to say hello to Mr Cleaver.

Behind the living room door was a cloud of swirling, acrid smoke. Both Dad and Mr Cleaver were standing at the back of the room, puffing on cigars. Eddie covered his mouth and nose with the top of his t-shirt. I left the door open behind us.

'It's pure economics, Bob,' said Mr Cleaver as we entered. 'Less staff means less wages, think about it.'

'I suppose that's one way of looking at it.' Dad saw us and beckoned us across. 'Come and meet Mr Cleaver.'

Mr Cleaver shifted his cigar to his left hand and thrust out his right. I shook it, feeling his fat sweaty palm, and held my breath as he expelled a lungful of smoke right beside my face.

'Pleased to make your acquaintance . . . Eddie is it?'

'No, that's Kevin. Eddie is the younger one. Ed, take the shirt away from your face. No, Ed . . . take the t-shirt away.'

Mr Cleaver ruffled Ed's hair playfully. 'Hello, Eddie.'

'First day of school,' said Dad.

Eddie held up his crayon masterpiece. 'I did a picture at school today.'

Neither Dad nor Mr Cleaver heard him. They turned their backs on us and went back to their conversation.

'Do you know what your problem is, Bob? You're too close to the workers. You've got to stop being their friend and start acting like their employer.'

'But they are my friends. I grew up with most of these people.'

'And now they're your employees. Too many human emotions, that's what's wrong here.' Mr Cleaver blew smoke into the air. 'Don't worry, Bob, we'll soon sort that one out.'

Ed and I listened to them for a moment, then I realised we were missing *The Tomorrow People*. We never missed *The Tomorrow People*. I switched on the TV and we had both just settled down to watch when Dad strode over and turned it off with an exaggerated motion.

'We're trying to have a conversation here.'

'But *The Tomorrow People* is on.'

'We're going to dinner soon,' Dad said, like it was the last word on the matter.

'But I want to see *The Tomorrow People*.'

Dad ignored me, chuckling something to Mr Cleaver about the bloody goggle-box. Eddie and I sat staring at the dead screen as if it might magically start up. I could see the adults behind us reflected off the grey glass. Mr Cleaver dwarfed my Dad. Mr Cleaver was big and round and moved his hands a lot.

The first hour at the restaurant was dead boring. Mum, Dad and Mr Cleaver sat in the bar and talked. The men smoked some more as well. Mum was wearing her best blue dress and she looked very beautiful. Eddie and I tried to wait quietly but as the time crawled past we grew more and more restless.

Ed kept saying how ravenous he was. Neither of us stifled our large yawns. Mr Cleaver made a big deal of buying us these drinks called Traffic Lights, which were lemonade with red, orange and green layers. We sucked on them slowly, trying to make them last.

After what seemed like forever we were led through to the restaurant. Mum placed Ed and me on either side of her. Even though the room was dimly lit I could see that the floor wasn't clean. Mum was trying to hide her reaction but I knew she wasn't impressed. The waitress handed us all menus, even Eddie, and said she'd come back for our order.

'What will you be having, Kevin?' Mr Cleaver asked me almost immediately.

Considering I had only got to the words 'Lumley White Horse Hotel and Restaurant — Est 1915', there wasn't much I could tell him.

'Do you like fish?'

'Not really.'

'How about steak?'

'Kevin and Eddie will have a half portion of chicken and chips each,' Mum answered.

'Awww, come on, Meg. This is a growing young man here.' Mr Cleaver ruffled my hair the way he had done to Eddie's earlier. His hand smelt of cigars and soap. 'He needs some meat put on him. It's rugby season soon and I'd say you had a potential winger here. Winger, is that right, Kevin?'

'I don't play rugby.'

Mr Cleaver looked to Dad with surprise.

'Ed's already keen,' Dad answered quickly. 'Kevin's older brother plays. Andrew's a natural. Plays fullback. I've seen him take down boys twice his size.'

'But not you, eh Kevin? Not going to turn out to be one of these limp-wristed pansies are you?'

'No!' I defended hotly.

Mum came to the rescue. 'Kevin's talents lie elsewhere. He's got a lovely singing voice and he likes reading . . . Ed, stop sucking on the menu . . . he's a very bright boy.'

Mr Cleaver nodded and studied his menu. Mum smiled at me and I too looked at my menu, but I couldn't see the words because it was a swirl of black on white with all the letters blurred into each other.

'Kevin.' It was Mr Cleaver. I pretended not to hear. 'Kevin. Kev-in.' He nudged me with his elbow. 'You're not packing a sulk are you?'

'He'll be all right,' Mum said.

'Kev-in.'

'I'm all right,' I said, without looking up.

Mr Cleaver leaned towards me and talked in one my of my ears. 'I apologise for what I said, little guy. I didn't really mean you were a pansy. I was just joking. You can take a joke, I hope?' He made a face at Dad who grinned in agreement. 'Kevin, you're not a pansy, okay? Not like that Dick Emery character, now there's a full-fledged fairy!'

'I heard he was married with a couple of kids,' Dad said and suddenly the conversation turned from me to the merits of Dick Emery. Mum told Eddie to stop sucking on the corner of his menu again. I pretended to be absorbed in my menu, letting it blur in my vision once more.

The waitress returned for our orders.

'I'm paying, of course,' Mr Cleaver said before we could order.

'Adam, you don't have to.'

'Uh-uh, Meg, tonight it's my treat. Have anything you want boys, it's all on me.'

'That's kind, Adam, but I insist that we pay for you.'

'Bob, it's my shout, and that's the last I want to hear about it. Order up, man!' He slapped Dad on the back. Mr Cleaver was a very slappy kind of guy.

Mum and Dad thanked him as the waitress took our orders. Mr Cleaver kept looking around the table and beaming at everyone. He belly-laughed at just about everything either Mum or Dad said and cracked jokes with expert timing. As he laughed, the saggy flap of skin under his chin jiggled hypnotically like a shaking jelly. Both Dad and Ed seemed caught up in the spell of that wobbling flesh. But when I exchanged glances with Mum I sensed she felt that something was wrong. I studied Mr Cleaver's face. He had red, round cheeks and a stub little nose. There were drops of sweat dotting his forehead. His mouth was smiling, but his eyes were like hard, glassy marbles. As I stared at him I felt a strange chill, though I couldn't explain why.

'He's possibly the most generous man I know,' Dad said in the car going home. Eddie was dead asleep against my shoulder and I was barely hanging in there myself. 'He's a nice guy too and a financial genius. You don't get that combination much nowadays. He'll turn the business around, you wait.'

'I'm sure you're right, dear.' Mum's voice was flat but Dad didn't notice.

'He has some big plans, you could see that, couldn't you? Some of them are a bit bold, I'll admit that, but they're exciting, don't you think?'

'Just be careful, dear.'

'I know what I'm doing, Meg.'

'I didn't say you didn't, Bob. But we don't know much about him except that he comes from Auckland. I know that you had to get a partner to save the yard but he owns almost half the business now. I'm worried that you're putting too much faith in him.'

'Christ, Meg!' Dad smacked both hands down on the steering wheel and the car jerked out of control for a second. I bolted upright, my eyes instantly snapping wide open. Ed stirred but didn't wake. 'How about you have some faith in someone for a change?'

'I'm worried, that's all.'

'Let me do the worrying. Look, I didn't want Adam Cleaver coming in any more than you did, but we're stuck with him, right? Let's just try and make the best of it, okay? And don't forget, I still own over half of Garrick and Son, I'm in control.'

Mum didn't reply and the car was silent until we got home. She carried Eddie to bed and I followed them up the stairs while Dad locked up the car. Even from the bedroom I could hear the doors slamming shut with the force of his anger. Mum kissed us both on the forehead and returned downstairs. I lay awake, studying the wall and listening. It wasn't the first time I had heard them argue. But it was the first time I had heard them argue about Dad's business.

Mum and Dad didn't fight the next night, or the next, but they did the night after, and during the weekend, and regularly the following week. They always argued about the same things. The amount of time Dad was spending at the timber yard and the bills for new equipment Mr Cleaver had suggested Dad buy. Mum wanted Dad to slow down. She said he always jumped head first without looking. Dad told her to stay out of it, the timber yard was his business. He said they needed to spend money in order to get out of debt.

Ed, who always fell asleep as soon as he hit the pillow, never woke but I lay there every night, waiting to hear Mum and Dad's angry voices start up. They rarely, if ever, fought in the morning but if there had been a row the evening before, breakfast was a cool, polite affair.

School was no escape. Julie Dwyer tailed me like an assassin, reminding me about the party until I plucked up the courage to tell her I couldn't come. She then proceeded to give me sad, forlorn looks from afar for days afterwards. I noticed that she stayed away from me when I was with Sheree and so I tried to hang around with Sheree as much as possible. It wasn't hard, as we often walked home together; our place was on her way.

Sheree lived in a part of Lumley called The Hollow. Its real name was Halloway Road, but almost no one called it that, not even the people who lived there. The Hollow was a row of tumbly-down houses with messy tangles of weeds for front lawns and rusting roofs. Sheree never seemed to care that her house was run-down and poor-looking but I had never been invited inside. Mostly Ed would tag along with us when we walked but sometimes he had gone ahead with the McGann kids who lived in an adjacent street.

On those days Sheree and I joined in the regular game of bullrush that took place on the back sports field. Although I always got tackled early on, Sheree was usually among the last ones left at the end of a match. No one dared touch her and sometimes it took four or five kids just to bring her down.

'Look!' Sheree said one day on the way home. She had just won three straight games of bullrush and was feeling pretty invincible. 'I'm Mrs Riddle.' She stared at me with both her eyelids inside out. Sheree was able to flip her eyelids over so that you could see the wet, pinkish underside.

'It's Rid - L,' I reminded her.

'Not to me, it's not. It's Riddle. Come here Kevin! Have you done your reading today? Where were you this morning, Sheree Humphries? Face towards the front, Miss Humphries.' We both laughed.

'I hate her,' Sheree said.

'So do I.'

'She's an ugly cow. Not gonna win any beauty contests, that one. Miss A'Court was nice. We should have had her.'

'Miss A'Court wouldn't shout at us.'

'Mrs Fitzpatrick didn't shout at us last year.'

'Only once or twice and we deserved it those times.'

'We should have got Mr Harris. The girls talked about him

56

today. Said he was so nice he holds the door open for them. They think he's a spunk-bubble.' Sheree paused. 'I think he's a spunk too.'

We detoured down by the railway line and searched unsuccessfully for tadpoles in the stream that ran parallel to the tracks. The surface of the water was covered with oil rainbows and I doubted anything could live in it. Then we walked, talking about everything in the universe, until we came to the start of my street. I invited Sheree in but she shook her head.

'I'd better get home. Mum'll be mad if I'm not there soon.' She turned to go then changed her mind. 'Do you like Julie Dwyer?'

'No.'

'She invited you to her birthday party.'

'I told her I couldn't come.'

'But do you like her?'

'No! Why?'

'Nothing,' Sheree answered and without warning punched me so hard on the shoulder it made my whole arm go limp and useless. My eyes began to water but Sheree didn't see. 'Bye!' she called behind her as she sprinted away down the street.

'Yeah, bye!' I shouted back, rubbing my shoulder and trying to pretend that it didn't hurt.

Chapter Four

Right next to our house was a field. It was not only our neighbour on one side but it also ran behind us, falling backwards from Lumley in a wide, green expanse. Diagonally across the field was a swamp and beyond that there was a handful of houses. I always thought of those houses as 'country', with bits of town near them, rather than, as with our place, 'town', with a slice of country next door. You could say our house marked where the town ended and the country began although in reality there was never such a clear distinction as that.

One Saturday afternoon I headed for the swamp, which was one of my favourite places in the world. Eddie wanted to come with me but I managed to give him the slip. He'd been bothering me all morning to play the Adventures of Black Beauty game in which he pretended to be the famous horse and I had to chase him around the lawn trying to round him up. It was such a pointless game that I avoided it at all costs.

The swamp was a sort of basin with trees right around the outside and pools of oozing liquid and dead tree-trunks rotting in the middle. Andrew had dragged across one of the trees to create a bridge over a patch of particularly wet ground. The bridge sagged when you walked on it but the prospect of it collapsing underneath you was one of its main attractions. That afternoon I jumped onto the bridge and pretended I was the Billy Goats Gruff, imagining there was a troll under the tree, trying to entice me below. But it soon got boring doing the voices of all three goats, the troll and the narrator, so instead I pushed sticks into the mud, trying to build a fortress, but even that got boring. While I was playing the Billy Goats game I swore I heard Eddie creeping up behind me, yet although I called out his name several times he didn't appear.

Back in the open field the afternoon sun covered everything with gold leaf and there were so many cicadas chirping that it felt as if the whole sky was throbbing. I flopped down in the dry, scented grass in the shade of our back hedge. There the afternoon was cool enough for comfort. A cricket jumped beside my ear. Bees were buzzing around my head, sounding low and heavy in the air. A fantail swooped and dived curiously above me. I lay there and thought about how I wished Mum and Dad would stop fighting and about why Sheree liked to punch me on the arm and about Bernadette. Her name hadn't been mentioned in the house since she left. I also wondered how Andrew was doing at boarding school. Mum had already fired off three letters and a food parcel which meant he was either loving it and getting a reward, or hating it and getting a bribe to stay. In a lot of ways I was glad he was gone. I liked being the oldest kid still at home. But there were things about Andrew that I missed, all the 'Andrew' stuff he used to do or say. I thought I should write to him and tell him that but I figured he would just keep the letter and tease me with it when he came home for Easter.

Then I must have fallen asleep because the next thing I felt was a kick in the side.

'Eddie,' I said dreamily. 'Go away.'

There was another kick, harder this time.

'Eddie, I don't want to play Black Beauty. Go away.'

The third kick made my ribs ache.

'Eddie!' I repeated and sat up suddenly hoping to scare him. But it wasn't Eddie. Two lard-white pairs of legs stood above me. I tried to scramble to my feet but was thrown back down and pinned securely across the chest and legs.

'Got him, Gil?'

'Yeah. Little bogger!'

The older Pom boy looked down at me with a deadly expression. 'Looks like we bagged ourselves a Garrick at last, even if it's only a baby one.'

'Hey!' The one who had my legs shouted as I threw him off and thrashed out, connecting with a couple of the kicks. The older Pom grabbed me by the neck and slammed my head hard against the ground, three or four times.

'You like that? You bloody well like that?' The older boy sneered. 'You all right, Gil?'

'I think so.'

The older Pom hung onto me, throwing me against the ground again and again. There was a bright searing pain in the back of my head every time my head connected with the dirt. My brain was red jelly sloshing about inside my skull.

'Not too hard, Quentin.'

'He hurt you, didn't he? And we owe him payback for the time with the lemons. Wish his brother was here.'

'I wish his sister was here. The blonde one with the knockers.'

Quentin let my head fall back one last time. 'Okay, Garrick, where is it?'

'He's not saying anything,' Gil answered for me when I didn't reply.

'My grandmother gave me that snorkelling mask for Christmas. Where is it?'

'What snorkelling mask?' I said.

'The one we left on the back step last night. It's gone and it had to be you.'

'I've never seen your stupid mask!'

'Liar!' Quentin smashed my head back against the ground until my whole body seemed to be rocked with the same thumping headache. 'Get up,' he ordered and the weight on my chest and legs lifted. 'Get up!' I was dragged to my feet and forced to start walking. Each of the Poms held one of my arms. I made a break for it, managed to throw Gil off me for a moment too, but Quentin was too big. He caught my shirt and reeled me back effortlessly. I let fly with my best right hook but missed by a mile and instead his elbow slammed into my stomach, knocking all the breath and the rest of the fight out of me.

The two Poms half-dragged, half-shoved me along the back hedge, to Mrs Aston-Peach's little grey corrugated iron shed at the very back of her section, where she kept her gardening gear. The lead-headed nail that usually latched the shed had been removed and the door was open, ready to receive me. While Quentin held me down Gil tightly wrapped my wrists and ankles with an old piece of rope. The shed smelled mouldy and I knew that Mrs Aston-Peach rarely, if ever used it. It was the perfect jail. The Poms pushed me against the wall and I slid down to the rotten floorboards. The rope was prickly against my bare skin. The floorboards were spongy and damp.

'What do we do with him now?' Gil asked his older brother.

Quentin thought for a moment. 'Maybe we'll just leave him here to die.' He said it with such delight that I half-believed him. 'We could just forget about him when we leave tomorrow. Gran never comes out here. Might be years before they find his body.'

'Maybe we could make him eat things like slugs.'

'Or slug repellent.' Quentin grabbed the yellow cardboard box that had caught his attention.

'That's poison.'

'I know.' Quentin glanced at the back of the pack then put it back on the shelf. 'But he's a POW so we can do what we like. Perhaps we'll take him over the road to that crazy man's house. Hill? Is that his name, Garrick? We'll dump him on the front porch for Mrs Hill to find.'

I would have preferred the slug repellent.

'Let's leave him for a while,' Quentin said definitely. 'He can sweat it out until he's ready to tell us where he put the mask.'

61

'Won't he shout for help?' Gil asked as Quentin secured the latch.

'No one can hear him from here. And even if they did they — only think — game —' Their voices were moving away, out of earshot.

I blinked a couple of times and gradually the darkness dissolved to a gloomy haze. I was sitting against the back wall of the tiny shed. The neon strip of light surrounding the door was directly in front of me. It burned into my head as my mind raced with questions. How long would they wait before they came back? Would they really leave me here? Would I die from the cold or starvation or would I get eaten alive by slaters? How had they known about Mr and Mrs Hill? A memory from the past stuck in my head and wouldn't get out, one where Kate had just played a flying monkey in the Lumley Primary production of *The Wizard of Oz*. She, Mum and I were collecting Kate's clothes from the Form One classroom. Kate couldn't remove the thick red greasepaint and she walked around the room searching for her gear with her face and hands still bright crimson. I couldn't tell whether it was something I really remembered or whether my mind was making it up, but it was such a clear picture that I felt it must be real.

I sat on the floorboards and shivered for ages before I heard a noise. At first I thought it was just some other memory playing in my head but after a couple of seconds I realised I was actually hearing the scuffling noise from the back of the shed. An animal? It sounded like a dog sniffing through the shrubs and bushes in Mrs Aston-Peach's garden. The noise floated away for a moment then reappeared right behind me. Suddenly it was at the door. The neon strip winked and I heard the lead nail being removed. The door opened with a brilliant burst.

'Eddie?' I said as the owner of the shape in the light became clear.

'Kevin?' He looked at me with surprised eyes. 'What are you doing?'

'The Poms caught me. They've tied me up.'

Eddie nodded then started to go.

'Eddie?!'

'What?'

'Come here and untie me!'

Ed trod cautiously across the shed and crouched down beside me.

'Where were you going just now?'

'Dunno,' he mumbled, tugging at the rope.

'How did you know where to find me?'

'Dunno.'

I rephrased the question. 'What were you doing over here?'

'Just looking.' He pouted. 'I can't undo the knot.'

'Try and slip it off.' It dawned on me that Eddie had found me not on purpose but during one of his bizarre 'wanderings' when he would take off all by himself. Mum used to stand at the back door calling for him and even if he was close by he would never answer.

'Did you see those Pom kids when you were outside?'

'No.' Ed tried to pull the rope over my wrists but it wouldn't budge.

'Find something to cut it!'

Eddie stood up and started to leave again.

'Eddie!'

'What?'

'Find something here!' I was sure if I let him out the door he'd forget all about me in microseconds.

Eddie tiptoed to inspect the contents of the shed shelf but was far too short to see. I told him to climb on a pile of terracotta flowerpots and that gave him enough height to reach a rusty pair of secateurs. It took a bit of effort but he finally gnawed through one loop of rope, enabling me to slip my hands free.

I used the secateurs to free my feet. Then, instead of climbing over the fence back to our place, we crept around the side of Mrs Aston-Peach's house until we reached the footpath on the street right outside her front door. There was no exact reason why we went this way rather than go the safer route but it seemed far more daring plus I hoped the Poms would see us so I could gloat at having escaped. I told Eddie off as we walked down the hot concrete path.

'What has Mum said about wandering off by yourself? You're not big enough to be doing things like that. What if you walked in front of a truck or got lost? What if the Poms had found you today, instead of me? It'd be you trapped in that shed and you'd still be there 'cause I wouldn't have found you.'

He pouted again but seemed to listen.

Then without warning a door slammed in the afternoon air and the Poms were suddenly barrelling down upon us, doing a ton along the footpath. A strangled gurgle came out of Ed's mouth, sounding like a death rattle. We sprinted to our front gate, Ed's gurgle vibrating the whole way. I shoved him behind the stone gatepost then stood my ground in the middle of the driveway. If I was going to go down, I was going down on my feet, not my knees.

Gil came around first. He got a surprise seeing me just standing there with a wild look in my eyes. I dodged his punch but he caught me on the side of my neck with his girly fingernails. In return, I presented him with the right hook I hadn't managed to plant on Quentin and the rat stumbled back, clutching his nose. Quentin himself was right behind.

'Little Kiwi bogger. Now you're for it.' He didn't even bother to check whether Gil was okay. 'No one hurts an Aston-Peach and gets away with it!'

I took three steps backwards, further down our drive.

'Think I won't come in?' He scoffed and advanced step by step till he was on our property. 'You won't even be able to see out your ugly little face when I'm finished with it! Your eyes will be so swollen they'll have to operate on you. Not even your fat old mother will recognise you.'

My blood boiled. He could see he had touched a sore point.

'Yeah, your mother's fat. She's got the biggest knockers I've ever seen! And old. She looks like she came out of the Bible. And did I mention she's ugly? She's uglier than you, Kiwi-boy, you and your runt of a brother. Must have been all that screwing with your Dad. All that screwy-wewy stuff they did so she could drop babies like —' There was a whoosh of air and a hollow banging sound. Quentin stopped talking. He staggered around in a small circle with the oddest look on his face, like he was surprised and dazed. Ed was behind him, struggling on one end of a dirty metal pipe. It was so heavy he could hardly keep it up in the air. He'd found it behind the gatepost and had sneaked up and donged the Pom with it. Quentin walked around like a drunk man, one hand pressed against his head, and Gil half-crawled along the footpath cupping his bleeding nose.

'They're blooming insane,' one of them said, Gil it sounded like.

I told Ed to drop the pipe and we ran down the driveway to our porch. From there we watched the Poms stumble and crawl out of sight.

'They're blooming insane,' Ed parroted. 'Blooming insane.'

I rehid the pipe straight after Sunday Mass then Ed and I spent the day inside, just in case Gil and Quentin or their crazy father came back for more. But although we kept an ear out and spied down from Andrew's bedroom onto Mrs Aston-Peach's place, we never heard or saw any of them again.

Ed and I kept the whole thing our big secret. I didn't even tell Sheree, or Steve, although I really wanted to and had to stop myself from blurting it out several times. But there were plenty of other things to talk about at school. Annette Luney said she was in love with Mr Harris, so Steve, Paul and I performed a mock wedding ceremony in front of her which made her run off crying. And Julie had her birthday, which from the sound of it was more of an event than a party, complete with a foot-long white-iced cake in the shape of a 'J'. But the big buzz in the air was the school swimming sports day, which was to be held at the end of the week.

Heats had been taking place since school began and the top swimmers for the championship races were posted outside the staff room one lunch time. I pushed and shoved with the other kids to read the typed-up schedule but my name was nowhere on the sheet. Like the other non-champions in my class, my only time in the water would be to take part in the Standard Three freestyle event, a mad sprint across the width of the Lumley pool. As I walked away from the schedule I vowed to win that race.

Mum had asked Eddie and me to meet her at the hairdressers on the way home. Even after school the summer sun was still high and yellow, turning the roads and parts of the footpaths into slabs of hot black fudge, and our bare feet were pitted with tar and gravel long before we reached the salon. Mum was waiting for us outside the salon door.

'We have to buy some eggs on the way home,' she said as we all got into the car. 'How was school? Kevin?'

'I didn't make any of the championship races for the swimming sports.'

'Maybe next year.' Mum patted my shoulder tenderly. 'What about you, Ed?'

'I did a painting of a horse.'

Mum grinned to me. 'Another horse? Anything else?'

'A stable and a tree for the horse to lie under in the sun.'

'That's very thoughtful of you.'

'And some grass for him to eat.'

'Even better.'

'Your hair smells funny, Mum.'

Mum grinned again. 'Should I take that as a compliment, Ed?'

She drove to the farm-store on the outskirts of town where she always bought her eggs. They were fresher here, she reckoned, since the woman had the chooks out the back. You could hear the birds when you were in the store and you could certainly smell them.

Mr Hill's old van was parked outside the store though Ed and I didn't realise it was his until we were walking towards the entrance. We both got a fright when Mr Hill himself came out of the door and walked straight between Mum and us.

'Hello,' Mum said as he passed by.

Mr Hill didn't reply like a normal person but instead held up the bag of eggs he had just bought. 'Supplies,' he grunted.

Mum nodded and went into the store with Ed right on her heels. Mr Hill ambled to his van and I watched him go. We rarely spotted him out of our street and I found it so bizarre seeing him somewhere else that I couldn't help but stare. He was wearing a grey jersey with holes in both elbows and old brown corduroy trousers. On his head was the tatty cloth cap he was rarely seen without. He wore it pulled down in front, with the brim just about resting on the bridge of his nose. The cap cast a heavy shadow over his eyes, like a mask, keeping them dark and hidden.

Eddie stood at the door of the store and called to me to come inside. He was worried that Mr Hill would snatch me there and then, but I knew that our evil neighbour was far more cunning and devious than that. He'd choose his time to grab me, a time when no one else was watching.

'You said hello to Mr Hill!' I said to Mum when I was beside her. 'You sound so surprised.'

'He eats children,' Ed told her.

Mum half-laughed. 'I doubt it. Look, I know he's a bit grumpy and he does keep to himself, but he's got a good heart.'

'Maybe he ripped it out of someone else.'

'Kevin!'

'It's probably true.'

'Well I think you're being way too hard on him.' Mum tinkled the little bell on the counter. 'That poor man. His ears must be burning now, red-hot.'

Eddie and I looked at each other. I couldn't believe that my mother was sticking up for Mr Hill.

'Maybe she doesn't know about Mrs Hill,' I whispered to Ed. 'We'd better not worry her with it.'

Mum tinkled the bell again and the cherubic-faced chicken woman appeared through the back doorway, which was hung with brightly coloured strips of plastic. Mum politely asked for a dozen eggs.

'Certainly, Mrs Garrick,' the woman nodded and carefully counted the eggs into a brown paper bag. 'How are the children?'

'As you can see, they're well.'

'And the ones away?'

'Fine. Andrew is enjoying boarding school. Rachel's just topped her class for a biology test. And Kate's already in training for the hockey season.'

'She's starting early.'

'That's how it is when you love something.'

'Mary Robinet said she saw your eldest at the bus station a month back. All by herself, getting on the bus for Auckland.'

'Yes, that was Bernadette.'

'Strange, that she should be getting on the bus by herself. I thought you usually saw the children off.'

'Bernadette is very independent.'

'Supposedly she got out of a taxi. She didn't even want you to take her to the station?'

Mum paused momentarily and spoke as if she was carefully choosing each word. 'As I said, she wanted to go by herself.'

'Mary said she looked grim.'

'You know teenage girls. Slaves to fashion. The wan look is in this year. It's not the thing to look happy anymore.'

'Hmmmm,' the woman hummed as she pushed the bag across the counter. 'Mary also heard a rumour about the timber yard. Is it true?'

'I suppose that would depend on what the rumour is and

whether you can believe anything Mary Robinet says,' Mum replied tersely.

'Hmmmm,' she hummed again.

Mum paid. The chicken woman handed across the change and Mum crammed it into her purse. 'Thank you,' she said icily and herded us back to the car. 'We won't be coming back here again,' she mumbled and deposited the eggs on my lap, then drove slapdash away from the store. The bag bounced up and down as the car flew onto the road and I could feel the eggs jiggle against one another.

The whole way home Mum gripped the steering wheel so tight it turned her knuckles deathly white. I handed back the bag as soon as she stopped the car. A sliver of gooby egg-white arced between us. Mum felt the slimy patch underneath the bag and sighed angrily.

'Why is it that I can transport two dozen eggs unbroken, all the way from Remihana, by myself, and you can't even manage to hold half that amount across town without smashing them to pieces!?' She slammed her car door behind her and strode into the house.

Eddie ran after her, I took my time. Mum had left the back door wide open but I sneaked inside like a thief. She was in the kitchen, at the sink bench with her back to me. I heard a rustle followed by a tap then a wet smashing sound, like 'splbam!'. I tiptoed halfway across the lino. Rustle. Tap. Splbam! I watched as Mum carefully took the eggs out of the bag one by one, laid them on the metal bench top and pounded down on them with the palm of her hand. Rustle. Tap. Splbam! Rustle. Tap. Splbam! I left before she emptied the bag. Later there was no trace that we had ever bought any eggs. The mess on the bench had been cleaned away and even the paper bag was gone.

Needless to say there were no omelettes in the Garrick house for a while. Dad mentioned Friday morning that he would like scramblers for breakfast but settled for toast and tea after Mum came up empty-handed. He remarked what a hard day he was going to have and Mum agreed. I was honestly only half-listening because it was the day of the swimming sports and winning the width race was all I could think about. I remembered to put on my togs in place of my undies and I'd crammed my rolled-up towel into the bottom of my bag. Mum said she'd meet us at the pool, in the middle of the stands.

'Remember to bring Eddie to me before your race so he's not wandering around the pool by himself. Have you got something warm to wear after your race? I'll bring a jumper for you anyway.'

Swimming sports fever engulfed the entire school. No one was immune. Even Mrs Riddle was less alien-like and cheerily wished everyone luck as the lunch bell rang. We ate outside our classrooms then the teachers led us one class at a time out the gates and down to the Lumley Pool, ten minutes' walk away. A sign across the entrance declared 'Fully Olympic Sized' in bold, weather-beaten letters. The man at the ticket office watched us uninterestedly as we filed past him, not having to pay. I thought how horrible it must be for him, stuck in a tiny, dark room when out by the pool the sun was glinting silvery off the water. I spotted Mum and ran to be with her. Ed was sitting beside her already.

'I thought you were bringing your brother down,' she said curtly, pouring milky tea from a red thermos.

'Everyone had to come with their own classes,' I answered, wondering what was wrong. There was a huge tiredness about her that had not been there at breakfast.

She nodded. 'Your race is up quite soon, third in fact. You'd better change now.'

'I've got my togs on under my shorts.'

'You're well prepared.'

I joined her on the smooth wooden seat, which burned hot on the underside of my bare legs. I could feel the stand vibrate slightly as spectators tramped up and down trying to find the best spots. The teachers were taking their assigned places around the pool. A swarm of girls from several classes, including Julie Dwyer and Annette Luney, buzzed around Mr Harris. He looked fit and healthy dressed in a pair of togs and a singlet. Richard Street walked by with his mother. Mum said hello but Mrs Street walked on without reply. I glanced at Mum as if to say, 'How rude!' but she didn't look at me. An announcement came over for the first race. Even then people were still climbing and descending the stands. There was room on the bench either side of us, and behind, but no one sat down. The second race came up, along with a call for the third.

'You'd better go. I'll watch for you,' Mum promised.

The far side of the pool was in shadow and all of us kids huddled together in a pack. From where I was I could see Mum and Ed sitting in the sun. Ed looked like he was asking one of his bizarre questions and Mum half-smiled and replied. Someone poked me from behind, hard enough to be painful. It was Richard Street, flanked by his cronies John Ramsay and Doug Llewellyn. You didn't cross any one of the three and you didn't mess with them. Stay out of their way and there were no problems. However, when they came looking for you, that was another deal altogether.

'My dad got laid off from the timber yard by your dad this morning,' said Richard with a mean look.

'That's not very nice,' I said, not sure of what else I should say.

'He said your dad promised him that his job was safe but now he's dropped him in it. My mum's hopping mad. She said if I do nothing else I have to beat you in this race. Or maybe we'll just do you over right now.'

I edged away from the Street gang. Sheree, Steve and Paul were in the championship races so I was on my own. I looked across to Mum again. She was still talking to Ed. I waved to her, hoping that if I drew attention to myself the Street gang wouldn't touch me.

Miss Joyce, ready on the other side of the pool, looked at me then turned away. Doug made a menacing movement towards me but Mr Harris, lifesaver that he was, chose that moment to stride across and explain that our race was next. One by one he spaced us out along the edge and gave those who couldn't dive the chance to jump in and cling to the side of the pool. I moved as far away as possible from the three bad guys and tried to concentrate on the water below me.

I looked up towards Mum one last time. Mrs Street was beside her now. They stood facing one another. Mrs Street made big gestures and Mum watched on with her arms folded.

'Ready!'

Richard leaned out of the line. 'You're dead meat, Garrick.'

'Set!'

I shut out Richard's voice. I had survived two murderous Poms; I didn't care about his empty threats.

'Go!'

The water that had looked so good was cold and unwelcoming. I swallowed a mouthful as I hit it and choked for a moment but once I surfaced I took a huge breath and started swimming as hard as I could.

Yet deep down I did care. The Poms were gone for good but I had to face the Street gang every schoolday. It wasn't my fault Richard's stupid father had lost his stupid job. Maybe his father had lied anyway. Dad wouldn't lay off people. I remembered him telling Mr Cleaver that the staff were his friends. Richard Street was a dishonest kid. There was no reason why his father should be any different.

I glanced across the pool and saw that I was in the lead. The other side was ahead of me, looming up fast. I imagined my glory at winning. The proud look on Mum's face, Ed's admiration. I would be given a certificate in front of the whole school. In my mind I heard my name called and I stepped up proudly to shake the principal's hand and hold my award aloft as the audience roared.

In the real world I felt someone grab my leg. They held me back and I came to a dead stop. I heard cheers and shouts from the crowd before I could get moving again. With just a couple more strokes I hit the hard wall and stood up. Richard and Doug were already there and John surfaced from the water behind me.

'Hard luck, Kevin,' he said as he pulled himself out of the pool.

'Yeah, hard luck,' Richard repeated with a smirk.

My face began to burn. I couldn't believe what had happened. Maybe Mr Harris had seen something, or Miss Joyce. But no, she was taking down the names of the three placegetters and didn't even look concerned. Mr Harris was nowhere in sight.

Out of the pool the wind had whipped up and in seconds goosebumps covered my arms and legs. I dashed across to Mum and Ed. Mrs Street was gone. An open towel was waiting for me.

'Did you see that?' I complained. 'Did you see John Ramsay grab my leg? I would have won if he hadn't cheated.' I wrapped the towel around my waist and slipped into my jumper but I was still cold.

Mum was thin-lipped. 'We're going. Grab your bag.'

'Aren't we going to complain?'

'Kevin, that's an order. We're leaving!' She said it loud enough for a couple of people to turn and stare at us. I was instantly embarrassed.

'But we're supposed to stay for the whole sports,' I said as quietly as I could.

'I'm sure they won't miss you,' Mum said loudly again. She slung my school bag over her shoulder, grabbed Ed's hand and strode away. Someone in the stand behind me murmured, 'Good riddance.'

'Mum?'

She didn't stop or turn back. I chased her, past the stand, through the front entrance and out into the parking lot.

'Mum!'

She paused enough for me to catch up. I took her outstretched hand.

'They held me back!' I tried to explain hoping that now she would listen to me. 'I was winning and John Ramsay grabbed my leg.'

'They're an ungrateful lot,' Mum replied. 'They're all smiles and laughter when it's going well but you have to watch your back when things go wrong.' She held my hand so tight that my knuckles were mashed together and I began to lose the feeling in my fingers. 'You'd think the people who lost their jobs would have been grateful for the settlement package. They all got their pound of flesh from your father on this one!'

Pound of flesh? I tried to imagine exactly where on Dad they had taken it from.

'I'm not sitting there as a target for their snide remarks. I tried to be polite today but never again. I've put up with more than enough already. Your father gave them the news first thing today and by ten o'clock I was getting phone calls about it. One of the wives even came to the door and tried to have a go at me. Well the next time someone has a go at me I won't put up with it! Bob Garrick has done more than his fair share for this town. What did Marjorie Street's husband ever do?'

We reached the car and Mum dug in her bag for the keys. 'Your father didn't want to make those layoffs, he was forced into it. I knew we couldn't trust that Adam Cleaver. I knew it the first time I met him. Buying all that new equipment. How are we going to pay for it, I asked. How? Well this is how, laying off staff. And it won't be the last time, mark my words. Meanwhile your father looks like Ebenezer Scrooge and Adam Cleaver comes up smelling like a rose.'

Ed and I listened to her rant while we waited to be let in. Ed looked around the lot. I watched Mum. She was scary like this. I turned to see Ed facing back towards the mesh fence that surrounded the pool. He was waving.

'Who are you waving to?' I asked.

'Dad, stupid,' Ed replied, but when I looked up there was no one there.

Chapter Five

Ed and I gave up lollies that Lent. My little brother didn't understand why he had to make such a sacrifice, but if you turned things into a competition you could make Ed do just about anything, so on Ash Wednesday Mum presented each of us with a screw-top jar and issued a challenge to see who could collect the most lollies by Easter Sunday. I traced pictures of a rabbit and a tortoise from our *Aesop's Fables* storybook, helped Ed colour them in crayon, and sellotaped them onto our jars, the rabbit for him, the tortoise for me.

At first the lolly collecting went great guns. We held a ritual counting every couple of days and our largest disagreement was whether the licorice straw in a packet of sherbet was counted as a separate sweet. Mum judged that it wasn't. But half a jar into Lent, Ed pulled ahead. He claimed that kids at school were giving him sweets and that he had found some Fanta bottles to take to Mrs Rocher's dairy where he bought a whole bag of those sweets that were three for two cents. The level in my jar didn't move, even though I regularly added lollies to it. I suspected that Ed was stealing from me but since I had no proof I had to let it slide.

Lent began with the first proper rain of the year. It hit Lumley one weekend and after it passed we didn't get much really bad weather for another month or two. But that storm was a boomer. To keep me busy while I was stuck inside, Mum suggested I make some papier mâché. I spent Saturday afternoon sticking strips of paper onto a balloon with flour-and-water paste and then dried it in the hot-water cupboard.

'Isn't that wonderful?' Mum beamed when I showed her.

'What do I do with it now?'

'You pop the balloon and pull it out from the small hole that you left in the bottom and then you paint it.'

'And then what?'

'Nothing. It's finished, Kevin. That's it. You can put it on your dresser or hang it on some string. Maybe you could take it to school and show everyone what you did on your rainy weekend.'

Not bleeding likely, I thought and that was the end of my adventures with papier mâché. The useless paper sphere rolled around the back of the living room for weeks until Ed and I finally used it in a game of indoor soccer for which it was perfectly suited.

The weekend wasn't a complete loss. Mum, Ed and I made chocolate chip biscuits and sat down in front of the TV to watch a movie musical on Sunday afternoon. It had a library with a spiral staircase and a marching band in it. The hero won the heart of the librarian. Mum cried.

Halfway through the movie we got interrupted by Mrs Smith who lived across the road, right next door to the Hills. It was a fate I wouldn't have wished on even Richard Street, but someone had to live there. Mr and Mrs Smith didn't seem to mind. Mr Smith worked for the Lumley town council. He strolled to work every morning, summer or winter, in walk shorts and knee-high socks. Mrs Smith worked nights in the ticket booth at the Lumley picture theatre. I considered it a very glamorous and exciting job. She and Mum quite often visited each other for tea and a chat but on that afternoon she popped over to borrow some flour. As Mum got her a cup Mrs Smith joked it was her hobby, starting recipes with only half the ingredients. She told Mum that their letterbox had disappeared during the downpour on Friday night. She felt it was their own fault since Mr Smith had just sat the box on top of their wall and it could have fallen into the road. A passerby had probably wandered by and picked it up. Mum wondered who would want someone else's letterbox.

The wet weather continued into the week, and after several days of being stuck inside at school our class became increasingly stir-crazy. The thought that summer might have deserted our town drove us all wild and Mrs Riddle could hardly keep control. By the middle of the week she'd had enough and we were sent to visit Miss Miles in the dental clinic to, as Mrs Riddle put it, learn what a dental nurse does.

It was supposed to be a rainy-day treat but it had to be the biggest joke of the year. The dental clinic was no mystery and everyone knew exactly what happened when you stepped inside that chamber of unspeakable horrors. You were buckled into the torture chair, Miss Miles stuffed your mouth with cotton wool until your cheeks puffed out like Chip 'n' Dale's and then she drilled you to within an inch of your life. What was there to learn? And sure enough, after being shown the foldy-back chair, the spitting basin, the drawing of Shaggy Dog — the overused toothbrush — and the bumble-bees made out of cotton wool balls I had seen enough. So had Sheree.

'Look what I've got,' she whispered and brought her hands from behind her back to reveal a huge wad of cotton wool. 'Pinched it when she wasn't looking.'

'What are you going to do?'

'Beats me. I don't wanna listen to her any more, that's for sure.'

Miss Miles took the class into her little office at the rear of the clinic and when she disappeared inside we stepped back in unison towards the clinic waiting room. Sheree looked about. Her eyes lit up.

'Ever seen a witch's cauldron?'

'Not yet.'

'Then it's time to whip up a brew.'

We went into the clinic bathroom and locked the door behind

us. Sheree handed me the cotton wool. 'You unwrap this,' she ordered then searched behind the toilet, coming out with a brush. 'This can be our ladle to stir the pot.'

While I struggled with the wrapping she spun the toilet roll bare. Long white snakes of paper ribboned all around us, the toilet bowl and the floor. I tried as hard as I could but I couldn't get the cotton wool open.

'Give it here!' Sheree said impatiently and ripped off the plastic wrapper with one huge tear. 'First we throw in the sheep's brains.' In went half of the cotton wool. 'Then the snake's skin.' A handful of toilet paper. 'Frogs' legs.'

'And a dog's eyeball.' I added some more toilet paper.

'A wart from an old man.' Sheree pitched in the rest of the cotton wool and its wrapper.

'Some smelly socks.'

'One rice bubble.'

'A squashed hedgehog from the road.'

'And finally,' Sheree declared swankily, 'Mrs Riddle's head.' We gathered up the remaining toilet paper and dumped it in. Sheree took the brush and jammed the mess hard down to the bottom of the bowl. 'Then we stir and cook it until it's done.'

'When it's finished we can use it to turn anyone we want into spiders, like Richard Street.'

'Or Julie Dwyer.' Sheree gave me a turn with the brush then grabbed it back. 'Prepare yourself for the final step.'

She pressed down the cistern handle and there was an instant rush of water. We stood on either side of the bowl watching in excited anticipation. The wad of wool and paper jerked violently then stuck. The toilet slurped. It bubbled. It let out a tortured groan. The water started to rise. Sheree and I exchanged a smile. I felt like an inventor who had successfully pulled off a dangerous experiment. Sheree chuckled under her breath. And below us, the water kept rising.

'When does it stop?' I asked.

'Beats me. Should be soon.'

But as the water continued to rise it became obvious that it wasn't going to be soon. The level hit the inside rim of the loo and still kept coming up. Sheree thrust the brush back into the bowl and stabbed at the blockage.

'It's stuck!' She let out a squeal as the water reached the top of the bowl and wet her hands. I pumped at the handle, hoping that would kill the beast. A few drops of water splashed onto the shiny lino floor then became a full-fledged flood. I tried the tap at the side of the cistern but it was stuck tight.

From the other side of the door we heard the sound of a concerned dental nurse. 'What's going on in there?' Miss Miles demanded to know. The door knob rattled. 'Unlock this door, now!'

'Jesus! What are we gonna do, Kev?'

'Sheree's been sick,' I shouted, thinking on my feet. 'It's all over the room.'

'Let me in!'

'I'm sick, Miss Miles. I'm really sick!' Sheree yelled then said in a half-voice, 'I'll put down the seat.' She pushed me out of the way and after throwing the seat down, sat on it. 'Is it stopping?'

'No.' I was standing right against the door, on the only patch of floor the water hadn't reached.

'If you don't open this door now I'll have to call your teacher.'

'What now?' I asked.

Sheree shrugged. We climbed onto the toilet seat for a bird's-eye view as the water glided gently under the door in a smooth curve. Miss Miles let out a shriek.

'Flipping hell!' Sheree gasped.

Mum arrived half an hour after school had finished. The class was both empty and quiet by then with only the noise of Mrs Riddle's pen scraping against paper and the sound of my own breath, shallow and anxious. I sat at my desk and stared straight forward, the way both Sheree and I had been made to sit after Mrs Riddle frogmarched us both back from the clinic. Sheree had been lucky. Mrs Riddle wrote out a note and sent her home with instructions to hand it to her mother. That piece of paper wouldn't have made it out of the school grounds, let alone all the way to The Hollow. Mrs Riddle had phoned our house, though, and Mum said she'd come as soon as she could.

She gave me a frown as she entered then introduced herself to Mrs Riddle. They spoke some hushed sentences before I was ordered outside. The rain had eased and Ed was playing his version of hopscotch on the concrete in front of the classroom. It felt like hours before Mum came out and told us to get into the car. We drove home in silence. You could tell she had something to say, but she was saving it. I, on the other hand, was rendered dumb by my shame. This was the first time either of my parents had been called down to the school because of me. I think Mum was partly in shock.

At home Mum took me into the kitchen and stood watching me, her arms crossed, her mouth a thin, downturned line. I stared at my cloudy reflection in the formica tabletop.

'Why, Kevin?' she said at last. 'Why would you do something that stupid? It's something I would expect from Andrew or Eddie, not you.' I hung my head lower. 'Do you know what your teacher said to me? She told me that I wasn't keeping you in check. That you're her rudest, most difficult to control student. Then she said you've been a problem ever since the first day. You're disruptive in class . . .'

'No I'm not.'

'Pardon? Kevin Garrick, look at me!'

My head was glued down.

'Why did you do it?'

'I don't know.' My voice cracked as I spoke.

'If you did know, what would it be?'

'I just did it.'

'Was it that Humphries girl? Was it her idea?'

I shook my head.

'If she's anything like her mother it wouldn't surprise me if she had led you astray. And growing up without a father can't help.'

'It wasn't her fault.'

'Kevin, why are you acting up at school?' The tone in Mum's voice changed. 'I'm so confused. You're not a rude boy. I just don't understand why you would do something so stupid. It's just like the time you left the lid on the deep freeze open. Remember that? You thought you'd turn the wash-house into the North Pole. Was it for fun? Was that all this was?'

'Yip,' I managed sadly.

Mum sighed. 'I won't tell your dad about this. But if anything similar happens again I'll have to.'

'Can I go?'

'Yes. Go upstairs and look after your brother.'

Ed was playing with his building blocks in our room.

'Make me some houses to knock over,' he asked. 'Please.'

I sat down beside him and built a row of towers, each one standing alone, then he balled up his fist and pretended to be a wrecking ball, smashing them down one at a time.

Most of the kids in class wanted to know what my punishment had been. Sheree and I had become minor heroes of sorts, since we had struck a blow against the dental clinic. Our fame spread even wider than our classroom, all the way to Forms One and Two. My stock story was that it was none of their business, making it sound like I had really caught the wooden spoon. Sheree hooted when I confided I had gotten off lightly. Just like I had thought, her mother never saw the note. Straight out of class Sheree had chewed it up and spat it at Kingsley Helms.

'How did you do it, Kev?' she said, punching my permanently bruised shoulder. 'I thought for sure you were gonna get it!'

We were closer after that. Sheree seemed to develop a deeper regard for me. Maybe I'd made an impression by not dobbing her in to Mum. Or perhaps I'd shown her I wasn't afraid to break the rules, sometimes.

But things only got worse with Mrs Riddle. Whereas earlier she had treated me coolly, now her manner was absolutely sub-zero. I honestly had no idea why she had such a low opinion of me. She had told Mum I was disruptive and difficult to control, but I always tried to be good in class. On occasion, like the time on the first day when I imitated the dog, and at the dental clinic, I was bad. But they were only a couple of times. Mrs Riddle thought that I was her worst student and that I was rude. To me there was almost nothing worse than being thought of as rude. Mum had been right, I wasn't a rude boy. I knew that, but I had to get Mrs Riddle to feel the same. I decided that she and I had got off on the wrong foot on that very first day. She obviously had a warped impression of me. I made up my mind to try and be extra-pleasant to her. I would never play up in class again, or talk out of turn or look bored. I would be a model pupil. She couldn't help but like me then.

It was about this time that Ed and I invented a new game. It all started when he crawled under his bed one afternoon and I threw a blanket over it, pretending I had him trapped in prison. Over time it became a prison boat and then I joined him in the dark and we pretended we were on a modern version of Noah's Ark. The entire world had flooded and he and I were the only survivors.

Fortunately we had managed to build a big boat and push many pairs of animals into it. Although we didn't have a lounge or a bathroom, we did have a kitchen with a large store of food and cooking pans. Each time we cooked something we put the dirty pots aside and brought out some clean ones. We called the game 'A Hundred Pots and Pans', for obvious reasons. Because there was no land left on the planet, all we could do was drift about and cook things for ourselves and the animals.

Most times we played it straight after school and if the voyage that afternoon had been particularly eventful, picked up the game again in the evening when Mum and Dad's angry words and shouts came clear through the floor. Things had gotten worse at the yard. We owed lots of money and couldn't pay it back. Mum blamed Mr Cleaver but Dad stuck up for the fat cigar man. 'Adam will come through, have some faith.'

One night as we played, trying not to listen to them argue, I suggested that we build a real boat. I said that I wanted to sail down the river to the sea, leaving Lumley far behind. Ed quivered with excitement and said he wanted to come as long as we built somewhere for a horse to live.

Dad had a heap of old wood at the back of the garage, though not an impressive pile when you considered he owned a timber yard. On the first day of boat-building we dragged the two longest, thickest pieces to the middle of the front lawn and arranged them in a loose 'V' shape.

'Why is it like that?' Ed asked.

'The bit where the ends are close together is going to be the front of the boat,' I explained. 'We'll lie more wood across the bottom pieces then build a living area on top of that.' I had the entire design worked out in my head. 'We'll have this railing around the side so that we don't fall out. And there'll be round windows just like on a real ship.'

'Where is the part for the horse?'

'On the roof. We'll build him a stall and a trough for hay.'

We pulled out the rest of the wood and some of Dad's old tools; a hammer, a saw and some nails. His good stuff was all locked away so there was no choice in the matter. Ed also insisted we pull out some paint cans and a brush so we could paint as we built.

To begin I made Ed sort the wood into lengths but some of the bits were too heavy for him so I got him to check the pieces for nails instead.

'When are we gonna go, Kevin?' he asked.

83

'When we finish the boat. That'll probably be in a week or two. You should start thinking about what you want to take. We'll need to put in some food and some clothes. And some real pots and pans.'

'And some food for the horse.'

'I want to bring the TV too, so we don't miss any good shows.'

'Are Mum and Dad coming?'

I couldn't believe he asked that. 'Of course not! You haven't said anything to them, have you?'

'No,' he said quietly.

'Ed, we're leaving Lumley. That means we have to leave Mum and Dad behind. If they find out they'll stop us. If anyone asks, just pretend we're building a hut.'

'I don't want to leave Mum and Dad behind.'

'If they come you won't be allowed to take a horse with you 'cause there won't be any room for it.' I let him think that one over and while he picked around the smaller bits of wood, feeling for nails, I dragged the largest ones onto the back of the boat, arranging, rearranging and re-rearranging them in place. By the time that was done the light was beginning to dim around us. The air was also getting nippy. We left the boat at the end of that first day with a sense of real accomplishment.

During the next few days we positioned wood all along the base supports and I got Ed to nail down floorboards but he spent more time yakking about his blooming horse and what would happen if we accidentally went over a waterfall, than he did working. He saw all three of us — him, me and the horse — living in one dark room, with no windows and nothing to sleep on but bare floor. Eventually I shut out his voice completely and concentrated on painting the bottom supports.

I had my own vision of the Kevin-Ed voyage. We would sail right down Lumley river to the sea and from there we would find a desert island. Ed could be my Man Friday, tending to my every need, although I would give him some free time to ride his horse. We could live in the ship, either on the beach or anchored just offshore, like a houseboat. Maybe we would even build a tree-house, like the Swiss Family Robinson had done.

We stayed out every afternoon for as long as the light, and Mum, would allow. The days were shortening and the gradual shift of seasons was becoming apparent all about us. They were subtle changes. The mornings took on a chilliness that hadn't been there before. The afternoon light had a gentle, golden glow to it, in contrast to the hard brilliance of summer afternoons. The warmth from the sun, which earlier seemed to linger even after it had set, now vanished by late afternoon. My nose got drippy while we worked and my hands went blotchy pink and blue and it hurt every time I knocked against something. Ed and I got stuck doing the same things every day. He would hammer another nail into a floorboard. I would paint another coat over the base support. We ended up talking far more than working, complaining about the cool weather or that it was too dark to see what we were doing.

It was neither the lack of light or the cold or even our own slack progress that eventually killed our boat-building, though. One afternoon we trooped out and I took up my usual painting position. Ed, on the other hand, wandered about, lifting up the scattered pieces of wood with a concerned look on his face. When I asked him what he was doing he said he couldn't find the nails.

'You usually leave the tin where you're up to,' I told him. Since he had yet to progress past the third board there wasn't a huge range of possibilities. I helped him hunt but the nails were nowhere to be seen.

The next day I managed to scare up a handful of nails from the garage but this time it was the hammer that was missing.

'You must have put it somewhere,' I complained. 'Did you take it inside?'

Again we searched for as long as the light would allow but the hammer was most definitely gone. The same thing happened the day after, but with the old paintbrush. Then it was a can of paint. And finally Andrew's genuine Little Traveller water-resistant orienteering compass. That was the last straw, not only because it was the coolest compass ever invented but because I had 'borrowed' it from Andrew's room thinking we would be in the middle of the Pacific before he discovered it missing. Ed and I literally turned the boat frame upside down looking for it then we sat down, defeated, on the point of the 'V'.

'Someone's definitely taking our stuff.'

'What are we going to do, Kevin?'

'Figure out who it is. It has to be someone from around here.'

'Maybe it was the Poms.'

'No, they went back to England ages ago.'

'Maybe it's Dad.'

'Why would he take it? And where is he storing it? Not in the garage.'

'Under their bed?'

'Do you think Mum would allow a smelly old paintbrush into their bedroom? It must be some kid from around here, from school.' Richard Street's face shimmered before my eyes. 'We need to set a booby-trap, something to catch a thief.'

The trap I devised was an intricate web of rope, woven around each piece of wood in the boat and threaded through the remaining tools and paint cans in such a way that you couldn't remove any one item without dragging along all the others. I deduced that all of the thefts had occurred during the night, since after the second robbery I had taken to checking the building site as we left for school. That evening I placed Andrew's pen-torch, the companion to the compass, underneath my pillow and readied myself to wake at the sound of wood and paint cans banging together. But it was Mum who woke me as usual the next morning. I was dressed and out by the boat at ultra speed. Because I hadn't heard any sounds I didn't expect anything to be gone. I was wrong. This time the robber had not only taken the remaining tools, but unthreaded the rope and stolen that as well!

Another damp weekend kept us inside the following couple of

days, frustrating any search attempt. I moped around the living room, endlessly pushing back the mesh curtains to stare out at the grey drizzle. Ed was happy enough with his Horse of the Year showjumping game. He could amuse himself for hours, making the plastic animals throw off their riders, stampede the audience into the ground then escape into the wild where he had them hold a Horse Olympics, complete with events like horse-gymnastics and horse-swimming.

Once again, Mum came to the rescue and suggested I might like to help her clean out the attic. When I agreed, she brought Eddie and his game upstairs then she and I climbed through the trapdoor in the ceiling of the linen cupboard.

We didn't have a real attic, just an open space between the ceiling and the roof, but Dad had nailed down some sheets of bison board and rigged up a light in there. Mum used the area to store all our junk, the stuff that probably should have been thrown out or given away, but which she just couldn't bear to part with.

Mum set me to work dusting while she sorted through the cardboard boxes of old clothes and toys, deciding what should stay and what should go to the St Vincent de Paul.

'Look at this,' she said and held up a small navy blue dress with frills on the collar. 'This was Kate's first party dress when she was Ed's age.' She pulled out another lemon-coloured dress in a similar style. 'This was Rachel's. She looked like a china doll. She was so tiny, like porcelain. I was always terrified she would break.' She dug deeper in the box. There were other dresses, pairs of shoes and winter clothes. Mum laid them out carefully, handling them like they were precious treasure.

It struck me out of the blue that some of the stuff had been Bernadette's. I hadn't heard her mentioned in the house since she had left and there had been no word from her. I reasoned that no one knew how she was. I grew instantly worried that she was lying somewhere, sick or even dead.

'We should go and see Bernadette,' I blurted out suddenly.

87

Mum stared at me in surprise.

'We don't know what's happened to her,' I explained.

'Why do you say that?'

'Because we're not allowed to talk about her.'

'But we're talking about her now.'

'What if she's been hurt?'

'She's okay,' Mum reassured me.

My worry was not satisfied. 'But how do you know?'

'She is. I'm positive.'

'But how can you be sure?'

'She's written to me a couple of times. She's . . . well. She said in her last letter that she was enjoying her lectures, but not some of the lecturers. She has a job waitressing in a restaurant. They get some famous people through it. One time she waited on Ray Columbus.' Mum's voice faltered for a second and the attic went quiet, with only the faint sound of the wind outside blowing against the roof directly above us. 'Kevin, your father doesn't know that Bernadette has been writing to me. He doesn't need to know. Do you understand? He's still angry with her for leaving. That's why we don't talk about Bernadette and why I haven't told him that she's writing to me. I need to break it to him at the right time. Until then I don't want you to say anything about the letters, not even to Ed. This can be our little secret, all right?'

I nodded so that she knew I understood. She seemed uncomfortable so I dropped the subject of Bernadette completely. However, I could feel the ghosts I had unsettled flying about the attic like moths spinning in circles. And Mum was in the middle of it, lost among the memories, folding most of the clothes she had unpacked into a 'to keep' pile.

'How are you going over there?' she asked me. We had worked without speaking for several minutes.

'I'm almost finished,' I said cheerily.

'Good. The dust and this hard floor are starting to get to me.' Mum pushed back one box and pulled out another. I heard her gasp. By the time I turned around she was looking straight at me. 'Come and see this,' she said in an odd voice.

I hunched across the bisonboard. Mum pointed to a rag-tag pile of bits and pieces, neatly stashed behind one of the boxes so that you wouldn't have seen it unless you pulled out the whole thing. It was a peculiar assortment of objects. Several hairbrushes. Handkerchiefs. One of my Justice League of America comics that had gone missing from my collection months ago. An assortment of knives, forks and spoons. A couple of pieces of coal from the scullery. A snorkelling mask. A pair of Andrew's socks. Something that looked like it had once been a bread roll. And more.

'This isn't yours, is it?' Mum said, but even as she did I knew she didn't really suspect me.

'No.'

'Eddie.' Mum sighed. 'I don't believe this.'

She sorted through the pile and held up a hairbrush.

'This one is mine.' She put it to one side along with the hankies that I knew had come from Dad's drawer. I fished out the comic for myself.

'I think he's been stealing some of my Lent lollies as well.'

'Kevin, that's the least of my worries right at this second.'

'And some tools have gone missing from the front lawn.'

'Do you see them anywhere?'

I searched carefully but drew a blank.

'Maybe he's hiding them somewhere else. Whose is this?' She held up the snorkelling mask.

'I've never seen it before.'

Mum held it thoughtfully then added it to the 'give away' pile. She crawled across the floor to the trapdoor. Halfway down the hole she turned back with a deadly serious expression.

'Not a word, to anyone.' She shook her head. 'I don't even want to imagine where the Smiths' letterbox is.'

The weather kept us away from the boat for another couple of days and when we finally did get back out there I wasn't surprised to find my building desire had shrivelled up to nothing. By now all that was left was an old can of paint with an unbroken leathery skin on the inside, and the boat frame itself. Ed asked me what we were going to do and I just about popped him one. I told him that we had to find our missing stuff before we could build more of the boat. I thought maybe I could implant a suggestion into his tiny brain and get the stuff back that way. I later searched all the obvious places where Ed might hide the tools but I didn't find even a single nail.

I finally pulled the frame apart, careful to avoid the dozens of slaters and glossy black spiders that scuttled out from its underside. The frame left a perfect yellowed 'V' on the grass. There were similar yellow stripes where the cross-boards had been and the grass around the frame had grown till it was long and straggly.

My dreams of sailing away from Lumley died and the last traces of summer went with them. Mrs Riddle was still stone-faced but I was working on her. I knew that when I finally won her over she would never even think the word 'rude' again. I got perfect scores on all my spelling tests, beating even Annette Luney, and volunteered to empty the bin every day.

Paul got a dose of flu that laid him out for half a month. The class all signed a get-well card for him. The Street gang ambushed Steve one lunch time by the back boundary fence. Steve drove them off and gave Doug Llewellyn a black eye which pleased me no end.

I went to Miss Miles for a dental check-up. She gave me a filling when I was sure I didn't need one. The school had a nits epidemic. We had to go to the staff room four at a time and the nit-woman searched our scalps with a comb and kept the unlucky ones behind. The rest of us were sent away with a leaflet entitled 'Your Child and Nits' to take home. And part of the Hills' front hedge toppled over. Mr Hill was out on the footpath one morning when we left for school, propping up the sunken portion with some boards and twine. He glared down the street at Ed and me and shook his fist at us as if we might have been responsible.

Through it all Mum and Dad kept arguing. Sometimes they would make up in a big way. Dad would apologise, Mum would cook him a favourite meal and I would think that this time they had sorted out their problems. But a couple of nights later Dad would be discussing his day, Mum would make a careless remark and they were off. When they ran out of new things to fight about they dragged up old disagreements and argued them all over again. Timber yard. Money. Bank. The timber yard owed lots of money to the bank. The bank wanted its money but the timber yard didn't have any. Timber yard. Money. Bank. The arguments went round and round, back and forth. Some nights I cried myself to sleep, wishing Mum and Dad would stop. I thought maybe that I should write to Andrew, to tell him how miserable things were, but I realised I'd have to ask Mum for the address and she might get suspicious. I finally found his address, and the address for Rachel and Kate, on the backs of some old envelopes and printed a note to each of them explaining what it was like at home. I felt like an enemy spy as I posted the letters and I was still feeling guilty days later.

Paul returned to school just in time for a show by some travelling puppet people. The whole school turned out in the hall one morning to see it. As we filed inside we saw an old bus with 'Puppet Magic' written on the side parked next to the Dental Clinic. To begin a man in a tatty jacket with tails came out from behind the set and told us a story about a dragon who was in love with a beautiful princess, a story he promised would be acted out later by the puppets. Then the curtains drew apart for the first number with flashing lights and two puppets in flowing outfits jiggling up and down while the Elton John song 'Island Girl' blasted out of the speakers. Sheree made a silly remark about the puppets' heads being wobbly which totally cracked me up. Mr Harris was sitting in the row in front and he smiled at us, making Sheree blush. I'd never seen her embarrassed before.

They never did the story about the dragon because during the intermission one of the kids from Ed's class got round the back of the set and accidentally stood on the head of the beautiful princess, crushing her skull beyond repair. Nevertheless the puppeteers were swamped after the show and later in class several kids mentioned that they wanted to be puppeteers when they grew up. Mrs Riddle replied that those show people were transients and degenerates and believed in free love. It sounded like a put-down but I wasn't sure because no one in the class knew what transients and degenerates were exactly and I reasoned that free love, the definition of which also escaped us, wasn't such a bad thing if having to pay for it was the other option.

I went to sleep with 'Island Girl' stuck on endless repeat in my mind but when I woke up suddenly in the middle of the night the song was gone. I lay in bed wondering why I had woken up so quickly. Sometimes I woke up when Mum and Dad had been arguing but they must have been asleep because I couldn't hear them. Apart from a few squeaks and pops the house was quiet.

I tossed and turned trying to go back to sleep, but the mattress had become uncomfortable, the pillow lumpy. Then I heard a sound from outside. It was a crisp noise like the crunch of footsteps on our driveway.

I leaned out of bed and pushed back the side of the curtain. Outside was inky black with the moon just a scooped-out sliver in the sky, but I could make out someone walking down the driveway. And from where I was it looked like Mum. I thought I could see her curly hair and the lines of her flowing nightdress. She was carrying something in her hand, like a bag. As she walked towards the front gate all I could think was that she was leaving us. She was running away, like Bernadette! We might never see her again! I would have to hide her letters from Dad and would only be able to talk about her in the attic. I had to go after her and persuade her to stay.

Without even bothering to throw any clothes over my pyjamas I crept downstairs. I had to be quiet because I didn't want to wake Dad. The front door had two locks, a modern one and the original lock which you turned with a big old key. Through the square panels of plain glass set into the door I could see Mum reach the end of the driveway. The first lock, the newer one, slipped back smoothly. The older lock refused to shift without a click that echoed like thunder in the house.

I slipped through the door and pulled it almost shut behind me, careful not to close it completely. Mum probably hadn't taken a key, since she didn't intend to return. I would change all that of course and we would need to be able to get back in.

The gravel was cold on my bare feet and I silently wished I had taken the time to pull on some shoes. Ignoring the numbness I jogged to the end of the drive, expecting to catch Mum walking down the street. But she had vanished. It was less dark beyond our place. The odd street lamp threw pools of yellow-white light along our short street and into the crossroads further down. I sprinted to where the streets met but although I looked hard down each one in turn I couldn't see Mum at all. Maybe like Bernadette she had met a taxi. If so, I realised I would have to get Kate's bike and hope I could cycle to the station before the bus left. I dashed back along our street. As I rounded the driveway I narrowly missed colliding with someone going the other way. I got such a scare that I just about lost my dinner out both ends.

'Eddie?' I puffed, catching my breath and swallowing all at the same time. 'What the heck are you doing here?'

'Where are you going?' Ed replied. My brother, in times of stress, always answered a question with one of his own.

'None of your business.' I was instantly annoyed that I had been found out. 'Why are you here?'

'I saw you leave. I wanted to come with you. Are you running away?'

I shook my head then realised he might not be able to see my head shaking in the darkness, so I said no. 'You have to go back.'

He looked down the drive then took a step towards me. 'I don't wanna go back alone. I'm scared, Kevin.' He reached out and slotted his hand into mine.

'Eddie . . . you have to go back.'

'No!' His grip tightened. 'No, no, no!'

'Shhhhhh!' I hushed in a loud whisper. 'You'll wake up the whole flipping neighbourhood!'

Ed tugged at my hand. 'Kevin, come back home with me.'

'I can't. I saw Mu— I saw someone in the driveway. I was following them and they disappeared. I'm looking for them. Do you want to help me?'

'No,' Ed answered in a sorry-sounding voice.

'It'll be fun. Maybe they're wandering around with amnesia and we'll get a reward for finding them. Or perhaps they're just lost and we can help them get home.'

Ed was unmoved. I brought out the big guns.

'I saw a horse too, a bit earlier. I think the person was looking for their horse.'

'Really?'

'Of course,' I lied like a pro. 'Do you want to come now?'

Ed didn't sound sure but he agreed.

Still holding hands we walked across the street. I abandoned my plan to cycle to the bus station. I'd just have to make as good time as I could with my deadweight little brother by my side. On the opposite footpath Ed stopped.

'C'mon,' I said out the corner of my mouth, tugging at him. 'Ed?'

'I saw the person, Kevin, over there.'

I peered down the end of our street. There was no one there.

'C'mon!' I tugged harder. 'We're gonna miss the horse.'

'No, I saw them.' He pointed down the street.

Again I looked. This time I too could make out a figure beside the hedge at the end of the road. The figure dipped down, then vanished. 'Maybe the horse is in the paddock,' he said.

'Yeah . . . maybe.' I led the way down our dark street. I didn't know why Mum had decided to go this way to the bus station. Her actions were making less and less sense.

Ed and I passed the Smith place then detoured onto the road in front of the Hills'. If that house was foreboding during the day, at night it was positively sinister. I tried not to look in its direction but something made me sneak a peek at it. The mere sight of the curtains in the window by the trellis zapped my spine like an electric shock. Ed was being dead quiet too and God only knew what was going on in his grey matter. I quickened our pace. Ed kept step until we reached the hedge. Mum had crawled underneath it, there was enough of a gap to do that at several spots.

'I'll go first,' I said.

'No!' Ed cried. He looked around nervously. At the Hill house mostly. 'I want to go home, Kevin.'

'What about the horse?'

'I don't care any more.'

Secretly I too was feeling far less brave than when I had started out. The shadows around us were spooking me something dreadful. And just having the nightmarish Hill house on my shoulder terrified me down to my frozen toes. But I told myself that Mum was out there somewhere. Maybe she was running away or sleepwalking. Whatever was happening, she needed us.

That gave me strength. I jiggled Ed's hand playfully and pulled him along with me. We passed duck-style under the scratchy hedge then I let my eyes adjust to the black void of the field. On this side there was no light at all and I couldn't see a thing. It was Ed who spotted Mum to our right, picking her way along the hedge, so we too followed the hedge along our boundary. The longer grass in the field was sopping wet and after only a few steps the bottoms of my long pyjamas were flapping uncomfortably about my ankles. Eddie was shaking but I couldn't tell whether it was from fear or the cold. Up ahead, we lost Mum around the back corner of our place. When we got there, she had disappeared again.

'Let's go home,' Ed repeated pathetically.

'We practically are home,' I whispered. 'It's right through the hedge. We're not more than twenty yards from the back door. Just shut your trap for a while longer.'

Right beside us was the hole in the hedge that we used to get to the field. I decided that was the way Mum had gone. Ed and I felt our way through the opening and he followed me through the bush on the other side. The trees threw up branches into my face. In the dark they were like witch's fingers clawing at my eyes.

'Kevin . . .'

'We're almost through,' I said behind me. I shouldn't have looked away for even a second, though. I walked smack into a low branch and the ground rushed up to meet me. I lost Ed's hand on the way down.

'Kevin? Kevin?'

I was disoriented for a moment, not sure of what had happened. I heard Ed's voice grow desperate. 'Kevin?!'

'I'm here.'

'I can't see you.'

'Ed, I'm right beside you!' I struggled to get up but in the darkness I stumbled around, tripping over undergrowth and banging into trees.

'There are things crawling on me.' Ed's voice was moving away.

'You're going the wrong way. I'm right beside you. Eddie? Say something to me!'

His voice had become dispersed with sobs and breathy sucks. 'Ke-vin? Ke-ke-ke-vin?'

I staggered through the bush in a panic, beating back the trees. I protected my eyes with one hand and tried to ignore the heavy dew on the branches as it wet my sleeves and pyjama top. The sound of Ed's cries was coming closer.

'Ed, just stay where you are!' His sobbing was right beside me. I did a full circle and reached out blindly, hoping to find him by pure chance. My hand connected with something. Or someone. The squishy flesh surprised me. I knew straight away it wasn't Ed.

'Mum?' I said, straining to see through the inky bush. 'Is that you, Mum?' I groped into the black and felt flesh again. An arm? A pencil-thin arm? Two hands grabbed my shoulders. Something like hair brushed against my cheek. I smelt stale breath. I realised in a sickening instant that it wasn't Mum. Before I could pull away the hands shoved me backwards and I flew like a limp doll into the bush. The world crashed and spun around me. There was an instant of pure, white light and then the blackness came down again like a wave.

Shaking my head clear I fully expected to feel the hands on me again. Maybe around my throat this time. But instead I heard two sounds. One was Ed screaming like the devil, howling my name over and over at full volume. The other was the sound of someone picking their way through the bush and, as they got clear, running across the back lawn. And then there was just the sound of Eddie's screams.

A light went on in the house. It pierced through the night like the point of a sword. I managed to stand painfully. Across the void came voices. Shouts. Dad. Mum. Ed still screaming. I tried to pick my way along to him. Torchlight sprayed the bush. More shouts. More screams. And beyond it all, way in the distance, so far it was more like an echo than a sound, I could hear laughter. Peals of broad, hyena laughter pitched high into the cool, dark air.

Chapter Six

Mum cleaned us up when we got inside but no amount of soap or hot water could wash away the clammy feeling on my shoulders. She and Dad tried to work out what had happened from my careful story and Ed's jumbled sobs and wails. All they extracted from him was that we got lost in the bush at the back of the house. My version was that we were exploring late at night and I tripped over and Ed started screaming. I knew that if they learned about the mysterious figure they'd freak for sure so I left it out completely.

The gamble paid off and Ed even helped when he babbled about trying to find a horse in the dark. I got the hard word from Dad and was ordered never to go outside at night again. Mum fussed over the impressive scratches on my arms and legs and put Dettol on them which stung so bad it was worse than any punishment Dad could have dished out.

Ed was clingy for several days afterwards and rarely left Mum's side. I, on the other hand, was out in the bush the very next afternoon, searching for some clue as to who the mystery walker was. But I found nothing but some squashed plants and broken twigs.

The memory of the midnight walker was soon overshadowed by preparations for Easter. All the kids were due home for the holiday but one morning at breakfast Mum told us that none of them were coming. I wondered if it was my letters that had kept them away.

Rachel and Kate stayed in Auckland for the break and Andrew spent the long weekend with some new friend from school. So for the first time ever all of them missed the annual Catholic fair.

Stalls were set up on the church grounds on the Saturday before Easter and everyone in the parish pitched in to help towards it. On fair day, Ed and I strolled around the tables, jingled our spending money, and chose our purchases carefully. I bought a pepper shaker in the shape of a sitting black cat for Mum's Christmas present. With such a large family, it was good to get an early start on gift-buying. The cat had a tiny chip out of one of its paws but I thought it was something small and pretty that she would like. I would hide it at the back of my bottom drawer and hope she wouldn't spot it. The man with a missing finger who often did the reading at Mass sold rides on a dappled grey Shetland pony and as soon as Ed hopped on the horse there was no getting him down. He rode until he was out of money, and then some. The man with the missing finger tried to lift him off but Ed threw a fit, gripping those reins like a vice, and stayed on the horse until I lured him down with a promise to buy him a toffee apple and a paper cup full of pink and white coconut ice.

Easter was one of my least favourite holidays. To be sure, we got a couple of days off school and a chocolate egg, but Mum and Dad also took us along to Mass on Easter Friday, Saturday and Sunday and Mum even went on the Monday. They weren't ordinary Masses either, but slow-moving, drawn-out ceremonies with much more standing up and sitting down than usual. Good Friday Mass was particularly painful, being a two-and-a-half-hour afternoon marathon during which the most devout of the congregation shuffled behind Father O'Brien as he sombrely visited each Station of the Cross, hung about the walls of St Peter's, while incense gobbled up all the fresh air in the church. It was a large price to pay for some hollow chocolate and the chance to gorge on the lollies you had been saving all Lent.

Easter brought with it the winter frosts. Mum said we were in for a cold snap because her chilblains started giving her grief and like clockwork, the very next morning a white blanket stretched across all the lawns. Eddie and I got dressed in warm clothes and gumboots and scuffed patterns into the stiff, frozen grass until Mum ordered us inside for porridge with brown sugar and a little bit of milk.

The frosts were like a new toy to us and every day for a week we played on the lawn before breakfast. However, after they began to appear day after day, week after week, they lost their newness and soon they were a pain rather than a present as they made our feet numb on the way to school, made the porch steps and the footpaths dangerously slippery and put the playing fields off limits until they cleared.

At school the class photos arrived. Like in our family portrait, my lazy eye had acted up on the day and in the picture it looked like I was in extreme agony. We took the bags of photographs home and just about everyone in Standard Three bought the class picture as well as some of the individual portraits. My solo one wasn't too disgusting, so Mum ordered the whole lot. She said she'd send them to Nana and some of our lucky relatives.

When Mrs Riddle asked for the photo money I handed her the ordering envelope with the exact money in it. There were a couple of us who had bought everything. Everybody else handed back some of the photos and the envelope, except Sheree. When her turn came she passed back the whole bag. Mrs Riddle did a double-take.

'Sheree, you're not ordering anything?' It was a question but it came out like a put-down.

'No, Mrs Riddle.'

Mrs Riddle examined the bag carefully.

'You wouldn't have slit the bag and taken out some of the pictures, would you?' she said and checked all sides of the bag. 'Why, you haven't even looked at the photos.'

'I can see them through the plastic bag,' Sheree answered. 'Mum doesn't want any. Said she sees me every day, so why does she need a picture of me?'

'I would have thought she wanted a memento of your year in Standard Three. Or doesn't she think this will be a special year for you?'

Sheree shrugged. 'Maybe, maybe not. It's not like I care. I don't want the photo either.'

Mrs Riddle looked around the room. 'Did you hear that? Miss Humphries doesn't want a photo of any of you.'

No one knew what to say. A couple of the girls giggled nervously.

'It's not a very good photo,' Doug Llewellyn offered.

'Only because you look like a girl in it,' Paul said and got a mean look in return.

'You got it wrong,' Sheree said to Mrs Riddle. 'It's not that I don't want a picture of the class, it's that I don't want your picture on my wall. I don't wanna wake up and have to look at your face in the morning.'

Mrs Riddle put her hands on her hips. 'That was a particularly vile remark. I suggest you apologise for that right now.'

'Mum says you never apologise for the truth.'

'Your mother isn't here now and your mother does not run this class, thank goodness. In my class we apologise when we say something mean or unthinking.'

'I didn't say anything I don't believe. I'm not gonna apologise.'

Mrs Riddle turned away as if she had had enough of Sheree. 'You could at least say it correctly,' she said as she walked back to her desk. 'It's "I'm not going to apologise."'

'Me neither.' Sheree was smiling when she said that. There were a couple more nervous giggles in the class then Mrs Riddle lost it. She flew down the aisle with her arm raised. Her open hand hit Sheree on the back of the head with such a slap that Sheree got thrown forward in her desk and her forehead hit the lid with a thud. The sound of the slap cracked into the air like a gunshot, silencing the whole class.

There was one of those moments when you're not sure what to do, whether to say something or get up and shout your lungs off or run over and help or what, so you just sit there and watch, which is what we all did. Sheree picked herself up from her desk top and straightened herself in her seat. Mrs Riddle stood in the aisle, rubbing her palm.

'Now what do you say?' she asked Sheree.

'About what?'

Mrs Riddle readied her hand again. Sheree would have taken it, too. I'd seen her like this in bullrush. No matter how badly the odds were stacked up against her she was never scared. Mrs Riddle could have hit Sheree all day and Sheree never would have apologised. And for a second it looked like Mrs Riddle was going to hit her again. Her raised arm just about came crashing down once more. But Mrs Riddle stopped herself and went back to rubbing her hand, then she strolled extremely calmly down the aisle to her desk.

'Stay sitting like that for the whole day,' she said to Sheree from the back of the room. 'If you so much as twitch I'm sending you to Mr Stringfellow. We'll see how cheeky you get to the headmaster.'

But Sheree never went to Mr Stringfellow. She sat dead still for the whole day, right through morning break, through lunch and little playtime. Mrs Riddle taught the class just like Sheree wasn't there and Sheree acted like she was a statue. I thought I should say something to Mrs Riddle but what could I say? She would probably hit me next. So I sat there and felt like a coward because I was such a scaredy-cat.

During Art I tried to say something. I made up my mind to tell Mrs Riddle that she hadn't been fair with Sheree. I even got up from the mosaic that we were making out of torn-up bits of magazines and went to where Mrs Riddle was sitting and almost said it. But I backed down when she looked at me and just made some useless comment about how I could bring in some more *Woman's Weekly*s from home.

Sheree didn't move a muscle until the final bell rang and then she stood up nobly and walked out of the classroom. Mrs Riddle didn't say anything to her. I listened carefully just in case she did, but she didn't. By the time I caught up with Sheree she was at the front gate, standing next to Eddie.

'I'm not apologising,' she said when I came close. 'Not to her. Not ever.' She smiled down to Ed. 'What's happening, Edster?'

Ed gave her a big goofy grin. 'I'm playing rugby. I'm on the wings.'

'That's good. What are you doing now, Kev?'

'Not much, why?'

'Just thought you might wanna play. I don't feel like going straight home.'

'I just need to chuck my stuff at my house and tell Mum where I am.'

'Do you wanna come, Eddie?'

No way did I want my little brother tagging along with us and I still hadn't forgiven him for all the stuff he'd stolen. 'He can't,' I said for him. 'He's . . . busy today . . . he promised to help Mum, didn't you, Ed?'

Ed nodded, wide-eyed. He had gotten way too easy to trick. Or perhaps, I thought, I had just gotten good at being a liar.

When we got to our gate I hooked my bag over Ed's shoulder, told him what to say to Mum about where I was, then pushed him down the driveway.

'What do you wanna do?' Sheree said as we watched him stumble towards the house.

'Don't know. What do you want to do?'

Sheree looked down towards the end of the street. 'That creepy old guy still live in that place across the road?'

'Mr Hill? Yeah, we don't want to go near him.' But she was already jogging towards the house and I had no choice but to follow.

She reached the part of the hedge that had tumbled down and crouched to the ground.

'We shouldn't be here,' I said.

'It's a free country.'

'The van's there. That means Mr Hill's home.'

'I don't care if he's on the other side of this hedge.'

'But there are stories about this place.'

'Like what?'

'About how he keeps his wife in a cage and how they eat kids.' Although the sun was shining on my back I was getting a distinct shiver up my spine, just as I had during the midnight walk.

'That's rot.'

'I don't know. No one has ever seen Mrs Hill. My brother Andrew thinks maybe Mr Hill keeps her in a dungeon. I think he might have murdered her but her ghost is still there.'

'Rot.'

'Why has no one ever seen her then? He's killed her, I bet.'

Sheree looked through the hedge at the house then turned to me with a sly smile. 'Maybe it's time to wake the dead then.' And before I could grab her she was off like a gust of wind.

She flung open the gate and bounded up the Hills' path, onto their porch. 'Wakey wakey!' she shouted and pounded on the door. 'Come on, Mrs Hill! Let us everyday people have a look at you!'

I watched in horror. Sheree knocked on the door like a mad girl again, then she sprinted back beside me and puffed out of breath.

'Did you see something?'

'No. You okay?'

'Of course. Didn't you see anything at all?'

'No!' I could see the front window from where we were. I was waiting for the curtains to move but they hung completely still.

'Maybe they didn't hear me,' Sheree said like she was disappointed. She got up to go again and I grabbed her arm.

'No, leave them alone.'

'What's your problem?' she said sulkily. She almost broke away from me but she stayed. 'Hell, you can be a sook sometimes, Kev.'

Sheree's remark hurt even more than a punch on the arm and I sat without speaking for a moment. She was quiet beside me. Then she stood up and knocked me lightly with her foot.

'You gonna mope all day?' she asked. 'If you do I won't take you to my secret place.' And again she was off. This time she ran the other way, past the Smith place, across the intersection. I shook my head and thought that she was a fool if she believed that I was going to run after her. But I was by her side within the minute.

We went into the bush from The Hollow. There was a path cut through the densely packed trees, but we avoided that and picked our way through the undergrowth like we were in an action movie. The sun flashed through the trees in solid rays all around us, each one buzzing with sandflies and what looked like some sort of smoky dust. The undergrowth was sparse to start with, but deeper in it got thicker — dead leaves, little curled-up ponga fronds and an obstacle course of fallen trees covered with slippery green moss.

I stumbled into a spider's web. 'How much further?' I said after I had spat it out of my mouth.

'Almost . . . almost . . .' Sheree said up ahead.

Somewhere in front of us was the sound of the river. It ran a pretty slow, straight course through Lumley, right under one end of the main street, but through the bush it dipped and curved, rushing more dangerously. Every Lumley child was told not to play in the river, but every summer half the kids in town swam in it.

'Almost there,' Sheree promised. 'You're lucky it's a nice day, this place can get as cold as a witch's tit when the sun's not shining.'

At last she stopped on top of a fallen tree trunk. The sound of water was very near now.

'It's over here and down a bit. You have to be careful.' She pointed to a rough vine dangling from the trees above. 'Grab this thing tight when you come. I'll go first.' She gripped the vine with both hands and started to lower herself down. She looked wobbly and unsure of herself though and even I could tell that her grip was clumsy, not half tight enough.

'Hell!' Her voice was brittle. 'Kevin!' she screamed and suddenly she vanished. I heard a crash behind the tree trunk. The sound echoed for a split second, then died.

'Sheree!' I leapt to the top of the trunk. 'Sheree?' I peered over. It was a steep drop. The river was below, closer than I had thought. It shimmered silvery through the trees. Sheree was nowhere to be seen. I called her name again, knowing that I had to go down after her.

'Are your gruds clean?' I heard in reply underneath me. 'I don't think so!'

Sheree's evil laugh filled my ears. Her head popped out from the side of the hill, only a few feet down from where I was standing. 'I bet you thought I fell. I bet you thought I'd cracked my head open or that I was floating down the river, huh? Hell, I practised that fall for ages.' She giggled a couple more times. 'Come on, Kev, don't be angry. I was having some fun with you, that's all.' She wobbled the vine to indicate I should join her. I grabbed it, testing it gingerly first, then slithered down until my feet touched solid ground.

From above, the hill looked like a dead drop down to the river, but right below the tree was a stony ledge that jutted out enough to be a landing pad. Sheree watched me closely. 'Well, what do you think?'

I was impressed. Directly underneath the tree trunk was a hole in the hill. It wasn't very wide or deep, being more of a hollow than a cave, and roots hung from the trunk so you had to crawl in, but it was exciting. Like something out of a fairytale or a Famous Five adventure.

'This is great! When did you find it?'

'Ages ago. I was climbing up the hill and I came across it. You can't see it from underneath until you're right in front. From the other side of the river it looks like just another bit of the hill. And of course you can't see it from up above.'

'Who else knows about it?'

'No one. You gotta swear not to tell anyone about it.'

'Cross my heart and hope to die, stick a needle in my eye.'

'You better not or I will.'

'Okay, okay . . .'

'I mean it!'

'Okay!' I changed the subject. 'How do you get out? Up the vine?'

'Nah, I just went that way for effect,' she said cheekily. 'You can squeeze out through the back. I usually come in that way too.' I looked to where she was pointing, but the exit, wherever it was, was well hidden. 'I even slept here one night.'

'Wasn't it cold?'

'Nope.'

'The ground must have been hard.'

'I didn't feel it.'

Sheree pulled out a sorry-looking packet of Juicy Fruit and asked me if I wanted a piece. I didn't. She took two bits for herself and stared straight across to the bush on the other side of the river, chewing the gum like an American.

'Maybe I should stay here tonight. I don't wanna tell my Mum about today.'

'Were you going to tell her? You didn't tell her about the note. I thought you'd just keep quiet about it.'

'Yeah, Mum'll just say it was my fault anyhow. She'll say I'm always mouthing off to people.'

'You weren't mouthing off to Mrs Riddle. She asked for it.'

'I thought I hated her before today, but now I really hate her.'

'You were brave today, I reckon.'

'You think so, Kev?'

'Braver than me. I should have said something to her. I should have told her what a cow she is.'

'Nah, that wouldn't have helped. She probably would have hit you too.'

'That's what I thought. But I still should have done something. I'm sorry.'

'Don't be sorry, Kev.'

'I could have at least said something.'

'Yeah, well no need to keep moaning about it, eh?'

I got what she meant. I did sound whiny. 'It must have hurt when she slapped you,' I said.

'Didn't hurt too much. Stung for a while. So what?' Sheree shrugged. 'You didn't think I was gutless for sitting there all day, did you?'

'No way! You hardly even blinked the whole time. I think that made Rabies-woman even madder.'

'Good. That's what I wanted to do. I just sat there and thought about nice things. Like being here or having a yak with my friends. She better not hit me again, that's for sure. If she does I won't sit there all nice like, I'll jump up and sock her back. Or maybe I'll run away and come and live here.'

The idea was exciting to me. 'I could bring you some food. Some of my lunch. Maybe I could steal some from our fridge?'

'I don't want you to get in trouble, Kev,' Sheree said as she tried to blow a bubble with the gum. 'You ever think about running away, proper like?'

'From school?'

'Nah, from Lumley.'

I thought about the boat and considered that Sheree didn't need to know about it. 'Not lately. Eddie and I tried to run away a couple of years ago.'

'What did you do?'

'We went one Saturday morning. It was winter, because I remember we had porridge for breakfast, then we sneaked out when no one was looking. It seemed to take us ages to walk into town and when we got there we had no idea where we were going. We passed by the fruit shop and one of the guys who worked in there and knew us called out hello. Then we reached the end of the shops and we had to go back and pass the fruit shop again and I was worried that they might think we had run away so I said loudly, "What else were we supposed to buy for Mum?" and Ed said, "Milk." '

Sheree grinned from ear to ear.

'Then we went along to the White Horse Hotel, the one in the middle of town with the fire escape, and wondered if we should get a room except Mum came along in the car with Kate and Andrew and drove us back home. That afternoon Kate and Andrew took us to *The Poseidon Adventure*. Ed got so scared when the boat turned over that he wet his pants.'

'That's a cool story.'

'How about you? Ever run away?'

'Nah.'

'What about the night you stayed here?'

'That was different. That was the night Dad left. I didn't wanna be in the house that night. I just wanted to be in my special place. Sometimes I think about running away but my mum needs help. If I went, she and my little brother would be on their own. It's not that I don't think about leaving Lumley, I'd love to get out of this dump.'

'Couldn't you go live with your dad?'

'Maybe, if my mum knew where he was. Maybe I'll go find him one day. And maybe I won't.'

I wondered what it was like to not have a father. I had sometimes thought it would make life easier. At least then Mum wouldn't have anyone to fight with. I wanted to ask Sheree how she felt about it but I stopped myself.

We didn't talk for a long time. It seemed the right thing to do. 'We'd better go now,' Sheree said finally. 'Mum needs me to babysit.'

We both stared one last time out at the bush.

'I like it here,' I told her.

'Yeah. This is my favourite place in the whole world. The bush is like my real home. Nothing can touch me when I'm here. You can come here any time you want, Kev.'

'When you bring me.'

'Nah. You can come any time you want to. I don't mind as long as you don't bring anyone else. Except Eddie, he can come if he wants to. He's a funny little bugger.'

'Maybe I'll just come by myself.'

'Suit yourself. But promise you're gonna come here if you feel like it. Any time you want to. Promise?'

'Cross my heart and hope to die.'

'Stick a needle in your eye.'

Chapter Seven

Mum called my name from the kitchen as soon as I closed the front door. It was only then I remembered what Sheree and I had done at Mr Hill's place. He might have spotted us leaving the scene of the crime and been round to complain about it. Mum stood at the bench, dropping spoonfuls of pink, brown and yellow cake mixture into a square tin. Marble cake. It was Dad's favourite and it didn't sit too bad with me either.

'Did you have fun with Sheree?' she asked me straight off.

'It wasn't too bad,' I said, guarded.

'Where did you go?'

'All over the place.' I knew she would have a heart attack if she learned I had been playing in the bush by the river.

'Not overflowing any more toilets, I hope.' Mum smiled wryly so that I knew she was kidding me. 'You like Sheree, don't you? Why don't you bring her in one day so I can meet her. Here, I saved you the beater.' The silver K-beater was laden with unscraped cake mix. I climbed up onto the bench and dangled my legs against the cupboard while I licked the beater clean. I guessed that Mr Hill hadn't seen us. That was good.

'Ed was funny this afternoon,' Mum said as she worked. 'He had the strangest idea that he was supposed to be helping me, but he couldn't remember what I'd asked him to do. I let him clean out the pot cupboard and now he's tuckered out on his bed.'

'That's weird,' I mumbled through the cake mixture.

'I got a letter from Nana today. She sends her love and wonders if we want to spend Christmas with her again this year. What do you think?'

I didn't think. We had made the six-hour car trip across to Nana's the year before and the most memorable thing about the journey was when Ed sicked up raspberry cordial all over me and Rachel. I loved Nana but I wasn't sure I wanted to go through another red vomit ordeal.

'It's still early days. We have months to think about that one. By the way, have you been playing with my pillowcases? The special ones Nana embroidered. I'm sure I washed them a while ago but I can't find them now. I think I can remember taking them off the line and putting them away, but I'm really not sure.'

I honestly knew nothing about the cases but Ed's name leapt to mind. I supposed that possibility had already occurred to Mum. She scraped the last bit of batter from the bowls and dropped it into the tin. Then she took a knife and made swirly patterns in the mixture.

'I have some bad news too. Your father let some more people go from work this afternoon. He had to do it, unfortunately. It's been a very hard day and I think it would be nice if you went down and met him before he came home.'

'Do I have to?'

'No, of course not. But I think it would be nice for your father if you did.'

'How am I supposed to get there, then?'

'Take Kate's bike. Your father can put it in the boot coming home.'

I pouted but felt selfish as I did. Mum asked me to open the oven door.

'What if I don't want to go?'

'Dad would like it if you did. So would I. Look, you go now and when you come home we can have this cake.' She smiled at me. Mum's smile was her biggest weapon. No one could resist her when

112

she smiled. I finished off the beater and jumped down from the bench.

'Put on your raincoat!' she called after me. 'I know it was sunny just before but I don't like the look of those clouds in the sky!'

Kate's bike was about two sizes too big for me. I had to perch in front of the seat and rock from side to side to work the pedals, although it was no trouble once I got into a rhythm. On the main street the store owners were shutting their doors and the light had begun to fade, painting everything with a shade of blue-grey. In the air above, Lumley's coming events were spelled out in a wire-netting strip strung across the street. I rode from one end of the stores to the other, then out towards the country. The town ended almost straight away. Shops and houses became fields and factories in just the blink of an eye. On one side was the concrete depot with dozens of tubs and troughs stacked on top of one another like building blocks. On the other side, the paddock where our family sometimes went to pick mushrooms. Beyond that was the tannery, a corrugated iron building with high rectangular windows. A terrible pong filled the air as you passed the tannery, like rotten eggs or burnt sulphur from Andrew's chemistry set. Some people complained that the smell was a town nuisance, but it wasn't that bad.

It began to spit as I turned into the driveway of the timber yard. I'd been in such a rush to go that I hadn't listened to Mum and had left my coat on its hook in the alcove under the stairs. But I knew I would be okay once I got inside because Dad was going to drive me home.

I expected to be able to ride straight into the yard but the big wooden gate was closed and someone had padlocked it. I supposed that Dad had shut the gate to keep out robbers and such people. Unfortunately it also kept me out. I skipped off the bike, lay it on the ground and shook the gates roughly.

The chain rattled noisily against the padlock. I waited and hoped that Dad or one of the men would hear the sound. The rain started falling even harder and the cold drops felt like little pins on my face and bare hands. When no one came I shook the gates again and shouted hello as loud as I could. I peered through the planks of the gate but I couldn't see any signs of life inside the yard. Then I walked up and down along the fence. I don't know why I did that but it took up some time and I couldn't think of anything else to do.

By now I was annoyed. I strode along the fence, stomping my feet hard against the gravel. When I got back to the gate I kicked Kate's bike except I misjudged and caught my ankle on one of the pedals. Then I was really angry.

'I didn't want to come!' I shouted. 'Mum made me! I wouldn't have come if she hadn't made me!'

I kicked the gate. It rattled another couple of times. And still no one came.

On the way back into town it rained more steadily and the smell of wet timber and rotten eggs hung in the air. I pedalled hard as I could and raced the drops, imagining I could dodge them as they fell. On the main street I steered the bike under the shelter of the shops but past the store fronts and awnings there was no protection. The rain soaked me through before I got even halfway home. Tiny streams of water ran from my scalp, over my cheeks, off my chin and even down my back. I held one hand over my face at first and shook my head, trying to flick the water away, but it soon got to the point where I was so wet I didn't care if I got any wetter. In a way it was fun, sort of like the Pots and Pans game had come to life and the world was about to be flooded. But the rain was so icy cold that I had begun to shiver. And I was worried that Mum would go crazy at me for not listening to her about the jacket.

Yet Mum had no bad words to say. Not one. When I dripped my way through the back door she made me strip there and then, and bustled me straight off for a steamy shower. I told her that the

114

yard had been locked, that no one had come when I called, and she apologised for making me go. She laid out some dry clothes on the folded seat of the toilet and fussed about in a way that made me feel special. The hot water took the chill off me and by the time I was dressed again I was feeling warm and tingly. I bounced down to the kitchen to keep Mum company. But I froze in the doorway when I heard her voice.

'I thought you'd like to see one of your sons. I didn't expect you'd make him cycle all the way home, in the pouring rain!'

'For . . . the . . . last . . . time, Meg, I didn't know he was coming. If I'd known I wouldn't have left. If you want someone to blame how about you? You sent him.'

'I thought you would be there!'

'I told you, I took a drive to calm down! I've had a hard day! Where is Kevin, anyway?'

'I made him take a shower. He was so cold his teeth were chattering. You should have seen him when he came in, he looked like a drowned rat.'

'Did you tell him about what happened at the yard?'

'Yes. That's why I sent him down to you.'

'Good.'

'Is that good because he knows or good because you didn't have to tell him about the layoffs?'

I heard the crash of a chair being overturned or slammed into the table. 'Do you think this is something I wanted? Do you think I wanted to be a failure?'

'I never said you were a failure, Bob.'

'No, but you're more than happy to remind me about how stupid I was to trust Adam Cleaver! This is where you say, I told you so.'

'I don't want to say that.'

'But it's what you think, what this whole bloody town thinks. Bob Garrick, the man who ran a perfectly good timber yard into the ground.'

'It wasn't you. It was Adam Cleaver.'

'And who let Cleaver walk all over him? Who listened to his plans for expansion? All that nonsense about new equipment and convincing me to lay off staff to pay for it!'

'But you've seen through that now!'

'And where did it get me today? I had to fire people, my friends, just so I can pay a bloody bank some interest!'

'We didn't have any choice.'

'You know what Cleaver's done, don't you? He's got me into debt and now he's going to tighten the screws. And I'm stuck. It's my bloody name on the bills.'

There was another loud sound. Another chair being turned over?

'Bob, calm down.'

'Who am I kidding? We were going under even before Cleaver turned up. We were going to lose the yard. He just made it happen sooner.'

The kitchen went quiet. I heard Mum walk across the floor.

'I got a letter from my mother today. She wants us to spend Christmas with her.'

Dad was bitter. 'The way things are going we won't have a choice.'

'Don't talk like that!'

'How should I talk?'

'Look, she sent us some money. She wants us to have it. She thought if she could just help us financially through the next few months we could pay her back or maybe not, I think it's a gift.'

'So now we're a charity case?'

'It's from my mother.'

'Send it back!'

'Bob, we need the money —'

The sound of Dad's fist pounding the table split the air. It was a sound I had come to know well. Dad shouted. Mum shouted. I couldn't listen any more. I just couldn't.

Ed had Horse of the Year scattered about the floor of our bedroom. I crouched beside him and rested my mouth on my knee so that my teeth made an indent in the skin.

'The horses have escaped and they're building a house,' said Eddie.

'Horses don't need houses.'

'I know. They're going to build a house for me to live in so I can stay with them forever.'

'Where is this house?'

'In the field. It's so big it takes up all of the field and the swamp. They were going to build me a garage but I told them not to, since I don't need a car. I can ride them instead.'

'What about a swimming pool?'

'They can build that too.'

'And a TV?'

'They'll buy that for me.' Ed made a couple of the horses parade around the sheepskin rug on our floor. 'You can live with us too if you want, Kevin.'

I picked up my favourite of the horses. He was jet black and had a white rein. 'What's this one's name?' Ed had told me before but I could never remember.

'Thunder. You can make him do jumps if you want.'

'No, you play with them.' I pushed Thunder towards him. 'I'll pretend to be a spectator.'

I sat against our dresser and watched him. He mouthed words and sentences as he moved the horses about. He liked to speak for each horse in turn. 'I'm tired,' he said after a time.

'Aren't you hungry?'

'No.' He was definite.

I helped him get ready for bed and then I did the same. Despite the shouting in the kitchen below I fell asleep quickly. It was dark outside and I pretended it was late.

'Wake up . . . wakey, wakey . . . Kevin, it's time to get up.'

117

My whole body cried 'stay asleep' but the voice was insistent. It drifted across the room then returned to me.

'Open your eyes, dear.'

'Mum?' I said tiredly.

'No, it's not Mum,' came back through the darkness. 'Your Mum is downstairs. I'm going to turn the light on now, okay boys?'

I tried to wake up but the blinding light stung and my lazy eye drooped shut. The owner of the voice turned out to be Mrs Lobb. Mum and Dad knew the Lobbs quite well. We had sometimes gone to their place for barbecues and the occasional birthday or anniversary party.

'We have to go on a special trip now,' Mrs Lobb explained. 'You're going to stop with us for tonight. You'll both need a change of clothes for tomorrow. Kevin, where would I find that?'

I wasn't sure whether this was real or just a strange dream so I sat on the edge of the bed and squinted at her through the white light and said nothing.

'Maybe they're in the drawer,' she said out loud. 'Don't bother getting dressed. You can stay in your pyjamas for now.'

I felt like I had hardly any control over my body but somehow I managed to force it over to Ed's side of the room. I shook him hard. Mrs Lobb looked over my shoulder. 'Don't be too rough.'

'He needs it,' I slurred. 'He's hard to wake up.' I shook him again and Ed's eyes snapped open like Frankenstein's monster being brought to life. He didn't say a word but rolled off the bed and started getting undressed.

'Keep your 'jamas on,' I told Ed.

'Where are your clothes, Kevin? Do you have dressing gowns? You'll need your schoolbags for tomorrow as well.'

Ed hadn't listened to me and stood naked by his bed like he did when he waited for Mum to dress him each morning. I stumbled across and helped him back into his pyjama top and bottoms. Mrs Lobb pulled clothes out of our drawer. 'Kevin, I want a bag to put some clothes in and your shoes. Where are they?'

I tackled her tasks one by one. I couldn't find a going-away bag so we stuffed the clothes and shoes into my school duffle bag. Neither Ed nor I had dressing gowns so Mrs Lobb made us get into our winter coats. Then she led the way downstairs. Every light was on but the house was ghostly empty.

'Where are Mum and Dad?' I asked when Mrs Lobb took us out the front door.

'They're around here somewhere. Don't worry, dear. We're taking you to our place.'

It was chilly and the porch steps were like blocks of ice against our bare feet. As we walked over the rough driveway I thought I heard talking in the front foyer. I tried to look back but Mrs Lobb jerked my hand and told me not to dawdle.

She pushed us into a strange car parked straight in front of Mum's Mini then returned inside. She didn't close the car door and the cold air sucked at us mercilessly. I decided Ed must be terrified and I tried to make him feel better. 'We're going to spend the night at the Lobbs,' I said in an excited voice. 'So we don't need to be scared of anything, do we?'

Ed murmured something about visiting a stable then slipped asleep against my shoulder. I butted him with my arm and tried to wake him up so he could keep me company but he was dead to the world. And despite the chilliness, and the feeling that something terrible was happening all around us, I headed that way too.

The next morning was a repeat of that whole dream. Someone shook me awake. A voice told me to wake up. Through the haze it asked me about clothes.

'Mum?' I repeated, sure that the night before had to have been my imagination. A hallucination. I couldn't remember ever having hallucinated before although when I was younger than Eddie I once thought I had seen the man in the moon waving at me.

'No, it's Mrs Lobb. Don't you remember last night?'

I opened my eyes. I was in an unfamiliar room. It was morning.

The air was cool, but there was a stream of warm, yellow sunlight coming into the room. Mrs Lobb flitted about, tidying as she went. 'You're in my house, Kevin. You came here in the middle of the night. It's time to go to school.'

'Where's Mum?' I asked, pushing back the covers slightly.

'She's in the middle room.'

'Where's Dad?'

'He's at your home, keeping the house safe.' Mrs Lobb started out the door. 'I've laid out clothes for both of you but you'll have to get a move on. Mr Lobb has to take you to school. Patrick wants to see you, too.'

We were in a sewing room. I was on a proper bed but Ed had a camp stretcher on the floor beside me. Like the night before I had to shake him before he would wake up. He didn't say anything as I helped him to dress but he glanced all around the room as if he was trying to figure out where we were. As soon as his clothes were on he grabbed my arm and hung on tight. He wouldn't let go, even when I said I needed to get changed. I dressed as quickly as I could with Ed clinging to me, then I straightened both the beds and we crept into the hall.

Most of the doors were open, but the door to the middle room was shut tight. I followed the sound of a conversation and found the kitchen. The Lobb family was sitting at the table, having breakfast.

'Here are the sleepy boys now,' Mrs Lobb beamed. She hopped up, zipped across to us and dragged us into the room proper. Her whole body twitched nervously as she moved. The way she skipped around reminded me of a little sparrow. She even looked a lot like a small bird.

'Hi men, how did you sleep?' Mr Lobb said. His face remained hidden in the paper, but he glanced our way long enough to give us a nod.

'I don't remember,' I said.

Mrs Lobb laughed. 'How about some breakfast? Patrick, make

room for the boys at that end of the squab.' Patrick obliged and we sat down in the window seat beside him. He stared at Ed and me like we smelled bad.

At first I avoided his gaze. He was the same age as Kate but neither she nor any of us Garricks had ever hit it off with him. Besides our parents being friends, we had nothing in common with Patrick. He was an only child and had gone to Lumley Main and then to Lumley High School. He and Andrew had traded punches on more than one occasion and I didn't like the thought of being in his house without my older brother around.

Ed was still holding my hand. He was looking straight down, with his chin just about resting on his chest. I looked back at Patrick suspiciously and he turned away.

Mrs Lobb hopped and bounced around the kitchen and I couldn't get the image of her pecking stale bread off our back lawn out of my head. I noticed that her hair was wound up tight at the back like a piece of fancy bread. The last time we had seen her it had been grey but now it was a motley brown colour which only made her look even more bird-like.

'Cornflakes or Weet-Bix?'

'Cornflakes.'

'And for you, Jerome?'

'He'll have cornflakes too.'

'I'd better make some toast,' Mrs Lobb added. 'And you should have something to drink.'

'I like tea. Ed will have cold water.'

'No, he has to have something hot.'

'He likes water.'

'But there's a heavy frost outside. I can't send him out with cold water in his stomach.'

'Ed likes cold water. He has it every morning.' I wasn't going to tell her that Ed was determined to be a horse and only drank what horses would drink. He would have probably only eaten hay and

121

apples and sugar cubes too but Mum had put her foot down there.

'Hugh, do you think Jerome should go out without something hot in his stomach?'

'If the boy wants water, he wants water.'

'Boiled water then from the kettle? Would you like that, Jerome?'

'He doesn't mind.'

'What's the matter?' Patrick said. 'Can't Jerome speak?'

'He can speak, can't you?' I replied, shaking Ed's hand in encouragement. 'And his name isn't Jerome, it's Ed.'

Mrs Lobb sighed as she placed the box of cornflakes on the table in front of us. 'No . . . no. I just can't do that to the poor boy. Jerome is such a pretty name. I've never liked your mother calling him by that other name. It's all right if I call you Jerome, isn't it Jerome?'

Ed still didn't reply.

'He likes Ed. We all call him Ed.'

Patrick was smirking at me. I tried to stare him away but he stuck out his tongue.

'Look at the time,' Mrs Lobb said in a fluster. 'You boys will be late for school. I don't think we have time for cornflakes.' She threw two pieces of barely brown bread from the toast rack onto our plates and started to butter one in a panic. Mr Lobb glanced up at the clock on the wall.

'We have to go now.'

'They can't leave without eating something! There's a thick frost out there.'

'And I can't take them to Lumley Primary and get to work on time unless we leave right away.'

Mrs Lobb was getting more stressed by the second. She thrust a piece of buttered toast at me. 'Eat this now!' she said desperately.

I waved her away and got up from the table. 'I'm not hungry,' I lied. In truth I was starving but at that second all I wanted to do was get out of that unfamiliar kitchen, away from smarmy Patrick, away from the yellow and white checks of the tablecloth, away from the overpowering smell of eggs and toast that was sitting in the air.

Mrs Lobb handed us our schoolbags. Ed stood where he was and stared at the ground. I grabbed his for him.

'I've put your lunches in there,' Mrs Lobb said as she pushed us down the hallway. 'I hope you like them.'

The door to the middle room was still closed.

'I want to see Mum before we go,' I said.

'You can't. She's sleeping. She needs some rest. You can see her after school, how about that?'

I didn't reply even though everything in my entire body screamed that something was horribly wrong. It was in Mrs Lobb's manner and the way Patrick stared at us.

Only one step outside the front door Ed dropped his silent treatment. 'Muuuuuummmmmm!' he wailed and refused to move any further. I tried to talk to him, to calm him down, but he just screamed louder. I jerked at his arm but he wouldn't move his feet. Mr Lobb was running the car on the road. A steamy cloud of exhaust puffed into the cold morning. He blasted the horn impatiently.

I jerked harder at Ed's arm.

'Jerome, Jerome,' said Mrs Lobb. 'You're going to school, Jerome. Won't you like that?'

'Muuuuuummmmmm!'

'Jerome, this isn't going to help anything.'

'For the last bloody time, his name's not Jerome!' I shouted at her. 'Shut up, Ed! Let's go to school!'

'You're not being a brave little man, are you *Jerome*?' Mrs Lobb said, giving me an evil look. 'Your mother wouldn't think much of this display.' She stood behind him and shoved him, softly at first but then harder and harder. Using all my strength I dragged Ed away from the porch, down the garden path and into Mr Lobb's car. We sat side by side on the back seat. Ed gripped my hand like he was going to suddenly cease to exist if he didn't hold on. I understood exactly how he felt.

It felt like the whole school was watching as the car pulled up. Mr Lobb tapped the steering wheel impatiently as Ed and I got out. He told me that Mrs Lobb would pick us up then he drove off, complaining that he was late for work. Some of the kids who saw us arrive wanted to know why we got dropped off when we always walked to school. I made up a story about spending the night with our aunt and uncle because our bedroom was being painted. Even Sheree believed me.

The news of more layoffs at Garrick and Son had gone round Standard Three even before I got to school. Most of the class didn't care. Some of them didn't know what 'layoff' meant. But Richard Street had plenty to say about it. He said that Dad was a scabby boss, that his dad was still mad at him. He threatened to beat me up after school. When I slipped Steve a note about it he promised to help. Richard and Steve had it out at morning play and by the time the bell rang Richard had been forced to apologise to me.

I met Ed at lunch time. Mrs Lobb had given us two peanut butter sandwiches each. Mum knew we hated peanut butter. I gave the sandwiches to Steve as a thank you for that morning and he gobbled them down gratefully. I took Ed for a walk around the far boundary. He had stopped holding my hand but he still kept his head down. I promised we would play A Hundred Pots and Pans when we got back to the Lobbs and maybe even the Black Beauty game, but I couldn't get one word out of him.

After school we waited for Mrs Lobb at the gate. She was half an hour late. She apologised and put on a smile as she asked us how our days went, but I could only manage one-word answers. Yes. No. Okay. She told us we could see Mum when we got home. At that point Ed started to whine 'Mum' again, not so loud as before, but enough to annoy me. I thought the ground should open up and swallow him. And me too.

Mum was still in the middle room. We walked in quietly and Mrs Lobb shut the door behind us. The curtains were drawn but it was light enough to see clearly. Mum was asleep. We stood at the end of the bed and I wondered if we should leave. But after a few seconds she opened her eyes.

'Hello, boys.'

Ed went to her, pulling me with him. We stood right by Mum's head and looked down at her.

'How are you?' she said in a weak voice. 'How was school?'

'The kids wanted to know why we came in a car,' I replied.

'Mr Lobb drove you. You're lucky.'

'Mrs Lobb was late picking us up and she gave us peanut butter for lunch.'

'Are you hungry? Ask her for something to eat.'

'She was late,' I repeated. 'Half an hour, I reckon.'

'She's doing her best, dear.'

'Are you sick?' I asked her. She certainly looked sick. Her eyes were puffy and tired. Her whole face was drawn. She looked older than I had ever seen her.

'I just need some rest and then I'll be better.' She swallowed and blinked slowly. 'Ed, are you okay?'

Ed sort of nodded but he looked like he was going to cry.

'He hasn't talked all day,' I said.

With that Mum looked like she was going to cry as well. Or maybe that's how she had looked the whole time. Ed let go of me and clung to her the same way he had clung to me in the car, as if his life depended on it. Mum winced but hugged him to her. As I watched I felt like someone was stabbing at my chest with a big knife, over and over and over. I backed away from the bed, so quiet that no one knew I had left, and went back to the sewing room.

I stayed there until it got dark. Eventually I could hear the sounds of Mrs Lobb preparing dinner. Then I heard her tell Patrick to fetch Kevin and Jerome. The door opened without anyone knocking first. Patrick didn't turn on the light but stood as a silhouette in the doorway.

'It's tea time,' he said and waited for a reply. 'Did you hear me?'

'Yeah, I heard.'

Patrick didn't leave.

'You don't even know what happened, do you? But I do. Do you want to know?'

'No.'

'Someone's gotta tell you.' Patrick coughed to clear his throat. 'You think you're so hot, you and the rest of your family, living in that big house, owning the timber yard. Dad says your sisters are the most uptight little bitches he's ever met. And your brother, little Eddie, is screwed in the head. Andrew isn't much better. And you're so stupid you don't even know what happened last night. We got woken up by the phone. Your mother was on the other end, crying and screaming. Your dad hit her. My dad didn't want to go but Mum insisted 'cause of you kids. I don't know why she bothered. My dad says your dad is a coward and that your mum should call the police and send him to jail. Its not like the timber yard would suffer if he did. Everyone knows he's practically bankrupt.'

Mrs Lobb called Patrick's name from the kitchen. He stared at me for a moment, like he wanted to say something else. Then his name was called again and he left, not bothering to close the door behind him.

I got up straight away and stood in the middle of the room, not knowing what to do or where to go. I considered running away, but I now understood what Sheree had meant when she said she couldn't leave her mother and her brother. I couldn't leave Mum and Ed behind. They needed me. Ed especially couldn't survive with Patrick and Mrs Lobb unless I was there to protect him.

I paced the floor, thinking up other plans. Perhaps I could go to the timber yard and find Dad? Maybe he could explain what was going on. Maybe I could take Mum and Ed to Sheree's secret place or perhaps we could even catch the bus to Auckland and stay with the girls? None of the ideas made sense.

I walked into the hall, stopped midway down and slipped to the floor with my back against one of the closed doors. There was a spooky glow coming from the kitchen end of the house. Mrs Lobb was talking to Mr Lobb. Mrs Lobb said if she was Meg she would have been out of bed by now. Mr Lobb said he was sick of cleaning up other people's messes and he didn't want us to stay another night. Patrick's hollow cough punched through their conversation a couple of times. I squeezed my eyes shut so that the glow became fainter and fainter but even when I shut my eyes completely the light still somehow got through under my eyelids. I heard pots clanging in the kitchen. A motorcycle powered past in the street outside. There was the sound of the television from the lounge. And in the middle room Ed was crying that he wanted to go home and Mum was whispering so softly I could hardly hear her.

'It's going to be all right. It's going to be all right.'

Chapter Eight

We had to stay at the Lobbs for that night, and one more. Mum never left her bed although by the final evening she was well on the mend, enough so Ed and I could spend the night top-and-tailing on the camp stretcher that Mr Lobb set up beside her bed. It felt better just to sleep alongside her. Then, on the very next day, Mum picked us up from school and drove us home like it was an ordinary afternoon. Like nothing was different. It was just as if those couple of days hadn't happened. Dad arrived home after work and the two of them had their usual conversation. How was your day? What's for dinner? They were uneasy with each other and neither of them smiled the entire meal but they didn't fight. They talked. They discussed the yard. They spoke about money problems. But there were no shouts or screams. Not like before.

Even though there was peace outside me, inside my head it was another matter. Should I believe what Patrick told me? Could Dad really have hit Mum? Was he capable of such a thing? How should I feel about Dad? Did I hate him? Did Mum hate him? Did he hate her and me and Ed? If so, why? Would this happen again? Could I stop it next time?

Mum and Dad didn't help. They were cautious with each other and play-acted their conversations. Neither of them was one hundred per cent there. When you added in Ed, who at times made even Aunt Erin look normal, I felt like a character in a science fiction story. My real family had been replaced by robots, or maybe

I had fallen into a parallel dimension and these people who looked identical to my family were actually strangers. It was a heavy coat for me to wear.

So it was almost a relief when, exactly a week after we went back home, Mum and Dad announced they were going on a snap holiday. They needed to be away together and since the school holidays were coming they would travel down south, then pick up Andrew in time for the May break. Ed and I were to stay in Lumley. For a scary moment I had us back at the Lobbs. But Mum said she'd arranged for Mrs Yoxall to look after us and straight away everything was okay.

Mrs Yoxall was a roly-poly ball of a woman with pure white hair who had a house across the road from Lumley Primary. She had looked after Andrew, Eddie and me several times before, a night here, a weekend there, but never for two whole weeks. Her house always smelled like cooking; roast dinners were her specialty. She had a toy cannon which fired matches. You weren't supposed to fire them at the cat, though. She also had a goldfish pond covered with chicken wire so that same cat couldn't get at the orange fish. She cooked porridge every morning, even in summer, and after breakfast Ed and I got to take the pot outside to feed the fish the leftovers. They would bob up and down for it, their little mouths opened in tiny 'o's to suck in the food. Bits of porridge often stuck to the wire and you had to push them through. I always used a stick because I was scared the fish would bite off my fingers.

Mrs Yoxall didn't have a husband or any kids. Mum had said we weren't supposed to ask her about it. Andrew told us she had been married with two sons but her family had been killed in an encounter with a land mine during the war. Mrs Yoxall sort of waddled, favouring one leg, and Andrew's story was that she also stood on the mine, but her fat legs saved her.

Mum and Dad dropped us off on a Friday evening. There were hugs and kisses from Mum and 'hurry up' looks from Dad. I struggled in with the bag that held our clothes and put it down to wave goodbye. Both Ed and I promised to be good. I made sure to tell Mum I would take care of Eddie. Ed said a special goodbye to Dad but I couldn't bring myself to do the same. I hadn't figured out how I felt about him. In many ways he had become a villain to me. If he was the monster Patrick had described then I didn't want him as a father. I judged it best to keep my distance until I was sure.

Mrs Yoxall waved goodbye along with us then ushered us gently inside. 'Dinner is just about ready now. You can leave the bag by the door, Kevin, we'll sort it out later. Now, hold out your hands so I can see how clean they are.' She checked us one at a time. 'Ed, you seem fine, but Kevin, your hands are filthy. Go wash up.'

I was well used to the 'your hands are filthy' routine. My hands weren't filthy or even dirty but Mrs Yoxall felt secure knowing she had checked us for germs and it made her feel even better if at least one of us was sent to drown those supposed germs in the wash-basin. I didn't mind the whole thing. Mum hardly ever asked us to wash our hands before dinner so Mrs Yoxall's concern was a treat.

I remembered the bathroom was the third door down on the left, except I remembered wrong. It wasn't a bathroom, it was a bedroom, and sitting in the bedroom was Mr Harris, the schoolteacher. He had his back to me, hunched over a small desk in a corner of the room. The desktop was piled with paper and there was paper on the floor, in the rubbish bin beside the desk, even all over the bed. Mr Harris turned as he heard the door open and stared at me with more than a touch of surprise. I stared back, equally shocked.

'I . . . I . . . um . . . this isn't the bathroom'. My face began to burn. Mr Harris stood up and his surprise melted into a grin. 'Next door down on this side, sport. You're Kevin.' He extended his hand. 'I've seen you around school. Esther's class.'

'Mrs Riddle.'

'Sorry. Mrs Riddle.'

'What are you doing here?' I asked, then realised how rude it sounded when it was out of my mouth.

'I live here, have all year. Moved in about January. Molly — Mrs Yoxall — is my landlady. She says you're staying with us for a fortnight.'

I nodded dumbly, not quite able to look at Mr Harris when he spoke. I was still embarrassed. He must have thought I was looking at the paper all around the room. 'Don't mind the mess, sport, I'm just catching up on some marking. Anyway, I'd get a move on if I were you. You don't want to be late for Friday night roast lamb and mint sauce.'

I washed my hands a bit longer than necessary and before I went back to the dining room I made sure that my face had gone back to its normal colour. Mr Harris gave me a sly wink when Mrs Yoxall introduced us formally. She explained that he was boarding with her and had been since early that year. Mr Harris played along completely and shook my hand for the second time, giving a polite 'Nice to meet you' that was so utterly convincing it almost fooled me. He carried the pretence so far as to ask me what class I was in and this time corrected himself with Mrs Riddle's name.

'. . . Esther's class, sorry — Mrs Riddle. I forgot that unwritten golden rule. You're not allowed to use a teacher's first name in front of children. Isn't that right . . . Molly?' Mr Harris clamped his hand over his mouth in mock shock. 'Am I allowed to call her Molly in front of you, Kevin?'

'Of course,' I said, all wriggly and embarrassed.

'No, no. I don't want to break your unwritten code. I know technically that rule has to do with teachers, but I suspect it extends to all adults. Am I right? Molly, just to be on the safe side, I'll call you Mrs Y while our two guests are here,' he said seriously.

'Oh, no,' Mrs Yoxall replied. 'Mrs Y makes me sound like a question. I'll be waiting for Mrs What, Mrs When . . .'

'Mrs Who,' I said, getting the joke.

'Doctor Who's wife,' Mr Harris added.

Everyone except Ed laughed.

'I guess you boys will be looking forward to the school holidays, won't you?' Mr Harris said as he passed over the potatoes. 'What do you have planned?'

'Nothing much. All the other kids come home so Ed and I will probably just play with them.'

'You have how many brothers and sisters?'

'Three sisters and two brothers, including Eddie.'

Mr Harris looked to the quiet little boy sitting beside me. 'You're pretty wordless there, Eddie old son. Anything wrong?'

'Nope,' Eddie replied with a full mouth. 'I'm just digesting my food.'

Everyone started laughing again, including Eddie. He looked so happy for the first time in over a week that I wanted to hug him. But I resisted. We were at the dinner table, after all.

Mrs Yoxall was a Presbyterian, or a Pressbutton as Kate called them, so she couldn't take us to Mass. She didn't think we would go to Hell if we all missed church once or twice so we slept in and had a communal brunch of her famous porridge followed by toast followed by Eddie and me feeding the goldfish. I had to hold his hand all the time by the pond because Mrs Yoxall said he'd fall in and drown otherwise. Mr Harris came out with us and talked about the fish. Ed informed him wisely that his favourite type of fish was sea horses. I explained about Eddie's obsession with horses, and how Ed got his name, and Mr Harris impressed us with his horse knowledge. He knew a lot about those animals, even for a teacher. He went so far as to play the Adventures of Black Beauty game for Ed. You had to admire the man for that.

Mr Harris was so nice and friendly all weekend that the first thing I told Sheree when I saw her was that we had been more than just unlucky not to get him as our teacher, we had been robbed blind. I didn't want her to tell anyone else that I was staying with Mr Harris but she blabbed it all around the class and soon enough all of the girls and some of the boys pumped me for information. Annette Luney was the worst. She acted jealous towards me, as if she wanted to be in my position, which of course she did. It was fun to be the object of so much attention and envy but I was disappointed at the same time. I had wanted Mr Harris to be my special hero but with so many other kids stuck on him, he became less special. Common, even.

The news spread even wider than Standard Three. At lunchtime, Julie Dwyer hunted me down when Sheree and I were playing on the painted map of New Zealand outside the school office. We had a game in which you ran from the tip of the North Island to the bottom of the South. You could leap across the tiny Cook Strait with ease. The game had some point but it had long been forgotten. Julie was with her flock of bashful friends, girls so bland that I didn't even know half their names. Sheree eyeballed Julie suspiciously and our game ground to a halt.

'Is it true that you're staying in the same house as Mr Harris?' said Julie.

'Yes, he's really nice.' I hoped that would be enough.

'I know that, silly,' Julie laughed, then fell silent when she caught Sheree's look. 'But I want to know what he does at night.'

'He has dinner.'

'What else?'

'He finishes dinner.'

Julie laughed again and ignored Sheree obviously this time. 'It's for them.' She pointed towards her friends. 'Kim and Terry and Cheryl all said when they grow up they want to marry him. I quite like him too,' she said shyly and held me in a cutesy, bashful gaze. 'Just a little bit. So they want to know what sort of things he likes to do. And eat. Like what his favourite foods are, things like that.' She stared at me with her Barbie doll eyes until I replied.

'He likes Mrs Yoxall's roast lamb and mint sauce . . . chocolate chip biscuits . . . coffee . . . and he eats porridge.'

'All at the same time?'

'No!' I howled. 'He has porridge for breakfast and the other things for dinner.'

'Anything else?'

'We've only been there a few nights.'

'I'll come and ask you again, then. Tomorrow.' Julie gave me another lingering look. 'I think Mr Harris is nice, but I think you're nice too.' She smiled sweetly, returned Sheree's cold stare and skipped back to her whispering, pointing friends.

'Oh Kevin,' Sheree mimicked as Julie left. 'You're soooooo nice!'

'What's your problem?'

'Nothing wrong with me.'

'You look like you sucked on a lemon.'

'She's a cow.'

'She's okay.'

'So you do like her!'

I remembered the sore arm I had got the last time we had discussed this topic. 'Of course I don't! Cross my heart, I don't.'

'Then why are you so sweet to her?'

'I am not sweet!'

'You talk to her like she's your girlfriend.'

'I was just being friendly.'

'She was doing all that eye-batting stuff. Made me sick.'

'I hate that stupid eye stuff, you know that.'

'Well I want you to hate her too, Kev. She's no good. She and her friends don't deserve to be alive.'

'They're not that bad.'

'You're wrong! Promise you won't be nice to her. Promise you don't like her!'

'I can't be horrible to her for no reason.'

'Course you can.' Sheree stared straight at me, like she was searching for something in my face. I half shook my head because I didn't understand what she wanted to see.

'Stuff you then.' She spat onto the ground beside my feet then ran off. She wouldn't talk to me later in class and ignored me after school when I asked if she wanted to come to Mrs Yoxall's and see the goldfish.

I guessed that Sheree, like every girl in school, had a crush on Mr Harris and saw Julie as a challenger for his heart. Another explanation played at the back of my mind, but I didn't let myself think too much about that. It couldn't have been that. Not *that*. And when I sat across from Mr Harris at the dinner table it was easy to see why the girls would want to fight over him. I wondered if he had any idea he was so loved. I wanted to ask him but it sounded stupid when I practised it inside my head, so I kept the question to myself.

Since Mrs Yoxall didn't own a TV we spent each evening at her house doing something different. One night it was cards. Snap and Fish. Eddie had some trouble keeping up so we played by his rules which changed constantly, always in his favour. On another night we used the cards to build a tower. But we couldn't get more than three levels no matter how careful we were. On another Ed and I fired matches and chewed-up bits of paper out of the toy cannon. Mrs Yoxall was worried we might shoot out our eyes so while she was in the room we had to be careful. But as soon as she left Ed and I took turns 'killing' each other.

On yet another night Mrs Yoxall told us, without any prompting, the story of her life. She described how she met Mr Yoxall when she went to a dance. She hadn't wanted to go but her best friend made her and she met Mr Yoxall not on the dance floor, but standing in line for refreshments. He stood on her foot and when he turned to apologise it was love at first sight. They got married and had two sons, Colin and Roy. During World War II London was bombed, and Mrs Yoxall described how she and her family got buried under their house when it collapsed. The dust cleared and she crawled out from the rubble but Mr Yoxall, Colin and Roy were still trapped. By the time the rescuers dug them out they were all dead. Mrs Yoxall's legs were hurt by the bomb and she had never fully recovered. I thought it scary how close Andrew's land mine story had come to the truth.

Mrs Yoxall talked about what it was like after the war when she sailed to New Zealand on a big boat and how excited she was to come to Lumley which was so different from London. She showed us her photo album. There were pictures of her in a nurse's uniform outside a hospital and one of Lumley Primary just after it had been built. The classrooms looked just as they did today, but the playing fields were an expanse of dirt. And there was no assembly hall. Ed wanted to see some pictures of London but Mrs Yoxall said she had lost them when her house was bombed. Then she had to leave the room.

Back at school, Sheree kept me at arm's length. For days I tried to talk to her but she pretended I wasn't alive. Julie, unfortunately, kept her word and asked for more on Mr Harris. In a way Sheree was right. I should have just told Julie to go away because I really didn't like her and I was only nice to her out of politeness. Julie was happy to see that I wasn't with Sheree and talked to me for as long as possible. While Julie batted her eyes and her friends giggled I caught Sheree spying on us. She ducked behind the Primers block when I looked her way. I was uncomfortably stuck between the two of them and I thought I was pretty dumb for getting caught in such a tricky bind. Then finally, much like one of the bombs that hit Mrs Yoxall's house, the whole situation exploded.

I had spent the lunch-time hour all by myself on the steps in front of the staff room. I was feeling particularly sorry for myself that day and had laid waste to a whole infantry of ants simply out of spite. I squashed a couple to start with then let the other ants collect the dead bodies. I followed them along the step to the nest then sat outside their front door and killed every second ant that came out. Soon there were far more little still bodies than live ones and the survivors scuttled around the step in a panic. I heard some shouts and cries somewhere in the school grounds but thought nothing of it at first. A roar swept through the sky. Then another roar, far too loud to ignore. It was the noise of a playground fight. Nothing else sounded quite like it. I ran to check it out and saw a huge crowd forming on the netball courts. Kingsley Helms was on the outer edge.

'What's happening?' I asked him.

'It's Sheree and Julie Dwyer, they're having a scrap.'

'Shoot!' I tried to push my way through but the kids were packed so tight it was impossible. 'How did it happen?'

'Someone said that Sheree told Julie she was ugly.'

'That's not how I heard it,' Donna Luney, Annette's older sister, told me. 'Julie said that Sheree smelled. Sheree was gonna walk away but Julie said her mother had said that Sheree's mother was the town mattress.'

'Nah, they're fighting over some guy,' a Form Two boy turned and explained. 'I heard them both scream about him as they went down on the concrete.' He looked at me closely. 'You hang around with Sheree don't you? *And* I've seen you with Julie.' He grabbed the arm of my jersey. 'Hey, maybe they're scratching their eyes out over you.'

The crowd in front of me pushed forward and the Form Two guy let go. Kids shouted things like 'Get her!' and 'Hit her again!' but it was impossible to work out who their shouts were for. In the centre other kids chanted something jumbled. From where I was it sounded like 'goatery, goatery, goatery'. I circled the group and jumped up and down to catch some of the action but I wasn't tall enough. Then I got on my hands and knees to crawl my way through, but there were too many legs in the way. The Form Two boy turned to me again.

'You must be something if you've got two chicks after you. Maybe you should keep them both.'

'They're not scrapping over him,' Donna Luney laughed.

'I heard some guy's name.'

'It's probably Mr Harris,' I chipped in. 'They both fancy him.'
'Is that right?' said Donna, interested.

The Form Two boy pointed across the courts. 'Well if it is Harris, we're gonna find out soon enough 'cause here he comes.'

Mr Harris and Miss Joyce hurtled towards the crowd of kids and Mr Harris cleared a path through the group with huge, strong sweeps. The chants and cheers went silent and a huge 'Ooooooooo' swept around the circle. Above the group Mr Harris waved the onlookers away with a loud, 'Get out of here!' No one moved at first but he continued to shout and one by one the kids in the crowd walked away. Some of them groaned, 'I didn't see anything,' and, 'It was just getting good.' I fought my way past them but by the time I got to the front everyone had gone. Sheree kicked and screamed as Mr Harris pulled her across the courts. He hoisted her off the ground and tucked her under his arm without missing his stride. Miss Joyce was right behind them with a sobbing Julie cradled in her arms.

Steve slapped me on the back. 'That has to be the best thing I've seen all year.'

'What happened?'

'Dwyer really asked for it. She said some mean things about Sheree's mother. Sheree ignored her for a second then went off her tree. Dwyer didn't stand a chance.'

'Sheree beat her up?'

'Hell yes. I don't blame her. If someone said my mother was the town mattress I'd probably lose it too. God knows what Dwyer was thinking when she did it. Even I wouldn't take on Sheree!'

'Did you hear them say anything else?' I asked him tentatively.

'Like what?'

'Like . . . did they yell about anything . . . else?'

'I didn't listen that close. I was too busy studying Sheree's technique.'

The end-of-lunch bell rang. There was nothing I could do for Sheree now. I tried not to think about her because I knew I would only worry myself sick. But we heard nothing official about the fight from Mrs Riddle and Sheree's desk was empty all afternoon. I couldn't help but think I was to blame for the fight. I didn't know what I found more alarming. That Sheree might be in big trouble, or that she and Julie Dwyer had actually been scrapping over me.

When Eddie and I got back to Mrs Yoxall's after school she beckoned us into the kitchen with a floury hand.

'What are you cooking?' Ed asked her.

'Scones, lovey. Now you go outside and play. I want to talk to Kevin alone.' She dropped some raisins into his hand and Eddie skipped out the back door. 'Remember, stay away from that fish pond!'

Mrs Yoxall cut the scone mixture and placed the doughy squares on a baking tray. 'Are you okay? I heard one of your friends got into a fight with Monica Dwyer's girl.'

'Sheree Humphries. Mr Harris took her to the staff room and she didn't come back to class. I don't know what happened to her after that.'

'I thought that might be the case. Mr Harris popped back to tell me what happened, in case you were worried.'

'Really?' The man was an angel, there was no doubt about it. A saint. I canonised him on the spot and pictured him bathed in celestial light like my other favourite saints, George and Sebastian; George because he fought a dragon and won, and Sebastian because we had a book on the lives of saints at home and there was a drawing of him in it. He had been shot in the chest with arrows yet he still managed to look up to heaven with a holy smile. It was the bravest thing I'd ever seen. Mr Harris wasn't a Catholic but I didn't think he would mind if I worshipped him.

'He took Sheree home, so he could talk to her mother about the fight.'

'Is he there now?' I wondered if I should race to The Hollow and catch him there.

139

'That was a little while ago. I daresay he's at school somewhere. He probably won't be back until dinner now.'

'I'll ask him about it as soon as he walks in the door.'

'It seems that Sheree gave the Dwyer girl a good pasting. No blood or broken bones but it sounds as if it was a cakewalk. I can't say I'm surprised. The Dwyers are the most spineless family I've ever been acquainted with. Not that I approve of everything April Humphries has done, mind you. But you've got to applaud any woman who can raise two children on her own.'

'Sheree's neat.'

'Mr Harris says that was his impression of her too. A bit wild, but decent.'

'She can flip her eyelids upside down.'

'That's nice,' Mrs Yoxall smiled then peered out the window. 'Now go and look after your brother. We'll have to dredge him up from the bottom of my fish pond if you don't.'

Mr Harris appeared during dinner. He muttered an apology and took his seat. Mrs Yoxall gave him a sharp look and he apologised once more, with a waggish grin, and got up to wash his hands.

'What a day!' he puffed on his return. 'But you'd know all about that, wouldn't you Kevin?'

'Is Sheree okay?'

'She's fine. She'll be at school tomorrow. I talked to her and her mother. Mrs Dwyer's just been down at the school too. Everything's sorted out.'

'Is Sheree in trouble?'

'For the fight?' He shook his head. 'I think it was a bit of both of their faults. Mrs Dwyer didn't want to see it like that, but I talked her round.'

'What were they fighting about?' Mrs Yoxall asked.

'Hard to say. Seems Julie made some unsavoury remarks about Mrs Humphries.'

I took a deep breath. 'They didn't mention . . . me at all, did they?'

'No, sport. Should they have?'

'No,' I replied, breathing out. 'No.'

'I spoke to Mrs Riddle as well and she understands.'

I couldn't imagine Mrs Riddle understanding anything. 'Julie should get in trouble, since she started it.'

'It doesn't matter who threw the first punch, or the first insult, now. It's sorted out.'

Mr Harris was right, of course, and once more he rose in my estimation. I had a vision of him as our father. Not Our Father, like God, I saw Mr Harris as our dad. Unlike our real dad, Mr Harris wasn't the sort of man who would work on weekends or smoke smelly cigars with big fat men or drive Bernadette out of the house or make his family spend three nights at the Lobbs'. Mr Harris was young and handsome. He told jokes and he never raised his voice angrily. I wished that he would adopt me and take me to live with him. And Eddie too. I felt guilty for even imagining such a thing, but I still turned the idea over in my mind.

'How are you finding your class, Kevin?' Mr Harris said, right out of the blue.

'It's okay.'

Mr Harris ahemed to clear his throat. 'I asked because when I spoke to Esther Riddle after school, she mentioned you were her most difficult pupil.'

'That doesn't sound like the Kevin I know,' Mrs Yoxall commented.

Mr Harris agreed. 'It was such a surprise I had to confirm it was you she meant. But she did. She said you were rude, Kevin.'

'Are you rude at school?' Mrs Yoxall asked me directly.

'No.' It was all I could manage. I was completely shocked. Rude. That word had come back to haunt me. It wasn't that terrible a word. Heaps of kids wouldn't have cared a fig if some Rabies-

141

teacher called them rude. But it stung me because I knew it wasn't true. I wasn't rude and I had spent months trying to show Mrs Riddle that.

Mr Harris ahemed again. 'Don't take this the wrong way, Kevin. I just found it strange because I know you. Then again, maybe you're different in class? Maybe you and Sheree muck around a bit?'

'No.'

'You're sure?' Mr Harris looked around the table. I don't think he had wanted to get so involved with Mrs Yoxall and my brother around, but he'd got in too deep now and had to continue. 'Esther told me you play up all the time.'

'That's not true.'

'She's at her wits' end trying to cope with you and Sheree.'

'But I've been good for ages. And Sheree doesn't play up. Not much.'

Mr Harris cast his eye over me and sighed. 'Then how about the dental clinic thing? I already knew about it, of course. You two were infamous in the staff room for that trick. Esther said you're both like that all the time.'

'We're not!' I shouted.

'Then how about when you tried to steal that money?'

'What money?'

'Esther said she caught you stealing money out of her desk. The school photograph money. She came into the room at lunch time and caught you taking it.'

'I never did that!'

'Out of the goodness of her heart she didn't tell anyone. That's more than I would have done.'

'She's lying! I didn't do it! I never took any money!' I was almost crying, I was so disappointed.

'She told me you did, Kevin. Now one of you has to be wrong. Could it be you?'

'It's her! It's her!'

'Are you sure? Kevin, look at it this way, why would Esther lie about something like this?'

My mouth fell open. I wanted to yell again that I hadn't done it but nothing would come out. I gritted my teeth and bit together so hard my head started to shake. Mrs Yoxall reached over the table and grabbed my hand. 'Calm down sweetie. Mr Harris is just asking questions. Now look, your dinner's getting cold. Finish that, and I have some special apple and peach crumble for after. Mr Harris won't say anything else about school, will he?'

'Ah yeah . . . sorry, sport. End of conversation. I shouldn't bring work home.'

I shook my head slowly, but I couldn't look at him. My rosy visions of life with Mr Harris disintegrated. He would never adopt me now. I was damaged goods. I glanced over to Ed who was in his own world, totally involved in his dinner. I wished I could be like that. I wished I could just escape and not think about things. Not worry. But unlike him I could never shut off. The problems gnawed away at my brain. They chained me to the real world then danced around a bonfire in my head and chanted like demons with twisted faces made even more ugly by the reddish light of the roaring fire. No matter how hard I tried to shut them out, the demons stayed with me. All the time. I heard them chant all through dinner and I could still hear them later when I closed my eyes to go to sleep. Sleep that didn't happen for hours and hours and hours.

Sheree came to school the next day just as Mr Harris had promised. Before the first bell she ran up to me and whacked me on the shoulder and called me Kev. She didn't talk about her fight or how she had snobbed me but she looked pleased with herself. Julie hobbled around school like a scared rabbit. Sheree only had to glance in Julie's direction to make her wince and crawl away.

I felt uneasy with Sheree at first but then I guessed she was like Eddie, able to shut off and forget. As we walked into class I punched her arm.

143

Sheree looked at me in utter shock. 'You haven't ever done that before.'

'I have now,' I replied and raced her inside. She won. But I let her.

I tried not to have bad thoughts about Mrs Riddle but it was hard because I knew she only had lies to say about me. Despite that, I was still determined to change her opinion of me. That day gave me another chance to turn her around. We had a big spelling test that morning, one that would put us up a spelling grade or keep us where we were. I was sure this time I would shoot up to Grade Seven with Annette Luney and Richard Street. Some of the class were permanently stuck in Grades Three and Four. I was in Grade Five although I knew I could do better than that. I had worked hard on my spelling and even had Mrs Yoxall quiz me during the weekend on the lists of words. I desperately wanted to do well in that test. Mrs Riddle wouldn't say cruel things about me if I was one of her best spellers. I knew she wouldn't.

Late in the morning Mrs Riddle read out the words for the various grades and when we finished, collected the tests. She would mark them during lunch then write our new grades, or our same old ones if we hadn't done well, on the top of the page. She was late back in the afternoon and we all assumed she was busy marking. We tried to read silently while we waited. There would be hell to pay if the class was anything but quiet when she returned.

One and a half school readers later Mrs Riddle came through the door and immediately wandered down the rows, handing the tests back. I waited eagerly. I knew I had gotten all the words right. I expected a page of neat red ticks and a new grade number. Six or Seven. Maybe even an Eight, although I didn't want to get my hopes up. The tension grew as the pile of paper in Mrs Riddle's hand got smaller and smaller.

All the dumbos got their tests back first. The best students were always on the bottom. When there was just one page left, I knew I had outdone even my own expectations. Mrs Riddle walked down the row towards me. I put out my hand, which fairly shook from the expected pleasure. But she kept walking, straight past me, and laid the page on Annette's desk.

I stared at my empty hand then looked around the room like I was in a dream. Mrs Riddle had no more papers. I glanced over to Steve. His page was full of ticks and crosses, mostly crosses. There was a '4' on the top of it. Sheree mouthed 'five' at me. She raised her eyebrows as if to ask me what I got. I shrugged.

'Right, class,' Mrs Riddle announced. 'I was disappointed, I have to say. Spelling is very important and yet most of you haven't improved since we last had a grading test. Annette and Richard did very well. I've put both of them up another grade. The rest of you need to try harder.'

I thought my test must have got misplaced. I raised my hand. Mrs Riddle ignored me for a moment but I held it in the air until she had to call on me.

'I think there's been a mistake,' I said.

'How so, Kevin?'

'I haven't got my test.'

'Really?' Her heels clicked on the classroom floor as she walked down the aisle. 'I remember marking it. You're not just ashamed of your grade are you, pretending you've lost it so you can try again?'

'No,' I said uncomfortably. 'I didn't get it back.'

'It's true,' Steve stuck up for me. 'You didn't give it to him.'

'Is that right, Steven Armstrong?' Mrs Riddle gave him a look so ugly that it made him shrink in his seat and Steve wasn't the sort of kid to scare easily. 'I do remember marking it, Kevin. You're sure you didn't get it?'

'Yes.'

'I must have lost it but I wouldn't worry. It was a particularly unremarkable test. You didn't change grades, in case you're worried.' She turned her back on me. 'Take out your quad books, everybody.'

It was like I was in a dream again. All of the class dug in their desks for their quad books except me. My arm went up like it had a life of its own. The sound of desks opening and closing filled the room. Steve whispered something but I didn't hear him over the din. Mrs Riddle finally noticed me.

'Yes, Kevin?'

'Mrs Riddle, I'm sure I did better on my test than you said.'

'Well then you're wrong.'

'I want to see my test.'

'I lost it! We're doing Maths now, not Spelling. Get out your quad book right away.'

She wrote on the blackboard. I looked down into my lap and thought again about my test. I was sure I had got them all right. Absolutely positive that I had. I almost gave up. Kevin the Coward. But I forced myself to be brave. Once more my hand went up. Steve whispered again. I heard him this time. He said, 'Don't be stupid.' It was an eternity before Mrs Riddle faced the class again. Her eyes narrowed when she saw me. She shook her head.

'I'm not interested, Kevin! Your test is lost! That's the last I want to say about this! Take your quad book out now!' She went back to the dark grey face of the blackboard.

I looked at the back of her head then put my hand up one more time.

'Mrs Riddle?'

'You really don't know when to give up, do you, Kevin Garrick?' she said without bothering to turn around. And she said it like she didn't want an answer. But I gave her one.

'No, I don't.'

The class went silent.

Mrs Riddle said, 'Pardon?' and looked over her shoulder at me.

'I want my test.'

'I don't know why you're so concerned. You hardly got any words right.'

'I don't believe you,' I said sourly. 'Give me back my test so I can see for myself!'

'You silly boy. I can't be bothered arguing with you anymore.'

'Give me back my test you . . . ugly . . . old . . . cow!'

The room had been quiet before but now there was a deathly hush all around me. I glared at Mrs Riddle so that she knew I meant what I said. Her face was like a statue. Her eyes were wintry. She stared at me. Stared and stared. I stared back. She stared. I stared. While she stared, she fumed. Fumed and fumed. We were evenly matched for a second. Her coldness versus my hot anger. But as she stared at me and fumed I felt my fires begin to cool. I wasn't someone who could keep anger going for very long. I always prided myself on being nice. It was hard being mad. I thought about what I had just said to Mrs Riddle. It was a dumb thing to say to your teacher, even if she was an ugly old cow. I remembered how Mrs Riddle had hit Sheree. I didn't like pain. In fact, I was scared of it. Mrs Riddle clenched her fists tightly.

'Kevin, come up here.'

I didn't move.

'Come up, or I will drag you up here myself.'

I stood up reluctantly and walked towards her. When I reached the front of the class I was careful to keep my back to the other kids but Mrs Riddle dug her fingers into my shoulders and spun me around.

'Children, I want you to look carefully. This is something you should remember for the rest of your lives. As you get older you will come up against a lot of nasty people. There will be people who let you down. People who cheat you. People who mistreat you. But the nastiest people you will meet are the liars. And standing in front of you right now is a little liar.' She shook me angrily and her nails pressed harder into my shoulder. 'Isn't that right, Kevin?'

I shook my head, trying not to look at the classroom, but she held me under the chin and forced me to stare at the sea of blank faces.

'Oh, but it is true. A stinking filthy little tattle-tale liar.' I tried to squirm out of her grip but she held me tighter. I felt tears, hot and salty, welling up behind my eyes.

'One thing I will not stand is a liar. Especially not one who doesn't know when enough is too much. Class, Kevin Garrick not only just accused me of hiding his test, as if I would bother myself with something so trivial, but he told lies about me to another teacher. Did he come to me and talk to me about these things? No, he told lies. Not forgivable white lies. Or even a lie to protect someone else. But big, black, dirty lies. Lies that I had repeated to me at lunch time today. You know what you said, don't you Kevin?'

I shook my head again. The whole scene blurred like a finger painting. I didn't want to cry, not in front of my friends. I tried to escape. I tried to lose myself in my head. But the classroom wouldn't disappear. The demons danced around the fire. I heard them chanting.

'You disappoint me, Kevin. Someone who thinks he is such a good speller with such a marvellous memory, and he can't even remember something he said last night? Let me remind you. You told Mr Harris that I was a liar! Isn't that right?' She spun me back around to face her and crouched down. 'That's what you said, isn't it! Isn't it! Why would I bother lying about you? Why would I waste my time? You, young man, are nothing but a fibbing toad. What are you?'

I shook my head.

'A fibbing toad! What are you?'

I wouldn't say it.

'Repeat after me! My name is Kevin Garrick and I am a fibbing toad!'

My head was shaking, sort of wobbling from side to side, like it was on a spring.

'Say it! Say it!'

'No!' I shouted. 'Leave me alone!' I saw a flash of bright red and

148

my anger swelled up again. The very touch of her hands and the closeness of her to my face made me sick. I wanted her far away from me. I pushed out with everything I had. The force of my shove caught her by surprise. She lost her balance and sprawled backwards. A voice came from somewhere deep and told me to run. Run, Kevin, run. So I ran. I ran out the back door, down the deserted cloakroom corridor, out to the playground, across the sports fields and through the trees behind the school. I ran so fast that the demons couldn't keep up. I let the afternoon swallow me. I had escaped at last.

I ran like a bat out of Hell, except why should a bat leave Hell so fast? I imagined bats were pretty happy in Hell. I was more like a cheetah leaving Hell, bounding away from Mrs Riddle's five-days-a-week Hell. Or maybe I *was* a bat because I was running blind, without direction or plan. I didn't look back but I was sure Mrs Riddle would be straight after me.

I streaked past a woman with a pram. And a paddock with nothing in it but some old car tyres. I felt like I could run forever. But as what I had done began to dawn on me, I slowed down gradually from a sprint to a jog to a walk. Then it finally hit me. I had run away from school. Not only that, I had pushed Mrs Riddle over. Perhaps I could go back, I thought to myself. Maybe no one would notice if I sneaked in the back and sat down. I realised that was so unlikely as to be ridiculous. Perhaps Mrs Riddle would accept an apology? Maybe I could still win her over. Perhaps, maybe, perhaps, maybe. A man came out of a driveway up ahead and saw me. He walked my way. I realised Mrs Riddle could have phoned on ahead. The entire town was probably on the lookout for a small boy running away from Lumley Primary. What could I do to throw him off my scent? I had to make him think I wasn't the boy he had been warned about. He came closer. I remembered the trick that had worked the time Eddie and I had run away.

'Now what was I supposed to tell Mrs Luney?' I said out loud as we passed. 'That Annette is sick and she has to come and get her? Yeah, that's right.'

The man looked down at me strangely and kept walking. For a second I expected to feel a hand on my shoulder, but his steady footsteps sounded into the distance. When I had put enough room between us I picked up my pace again. He hadn't been on the lookout for me, but there were bound to be others. I had to hide.

The swamp changed in winter. The mud level crept up the side of some of the fallen trees and the dried parts, like a hard brown puzzle during summer, were sealed smooth. The cicadas were silent and there were long shadows everywhere. It was a far-from-friendly place. I sat down by the edge of the wet part, just through the trees, and stared at the brown muck. I tucked my knees up under my chin then wrapped my arms around my legs. I wanted to cry now, but all I could do was look at the ground and listen for sirens. The police would be called in by now. They would comb the countryside for me, talk to Mrs Yoxall, check out our house. The swamp was the only safe place. Ed might guess I had come here but I doubted the police officers would get a coherent sentence out of him.

To keep myself busy and warm I set about building a raised track through the swamp. I dragged all the large wood I could find from under the trees and dumped it into the gooey bits. The wood didn't sink but sat on top of the mud and it was secure enough to support my weight. I worked quickly, trying to concentrate completely on my mission. But I kept an ear out too. I knew I would be easy prey for the police if I dropped my guard even for a moment.

By the time I decided I had done enough, a fairly decent path lay on top of the marshy ground and the shadows had stretched until they could lengthen no more, merging into a dense, dark slab. The swamp was murky now, even less friendly. In the spooky light I felt an instant chill and looked around nervously. When I remembered the scene in the classroom a new fear rose up in me. What if I had hurt Mrs Riddle when I pushed her? What if I had killed her? She could have hit her head on a desk and bled to death over the floor. I was suddenly sure that was exactly what happened. The police weren't just looking for a bad boy then, they were hunting down a murderer. I tried to swallow but I choked instead. Andrew had once trapped me under a blanket and pulled it tight around my face so I couldn't breathe. I couldn't even scream for help. I kicked and struggled but he held me down, so long I thought I was going to die. I felt just like that in the swamp except this time there was no Andrew to take the blanket away at the last second.

In a panic I darted through the trees, into the open field. There, the afternoon struggled with night in a sky sunk so low with dismal-looking clouds that it seemed like it would collapse upon itself. The harsh wind blew into my face and stung my eyes. A hard cow-pat gave way as I ran over it but I was going so fast I didn't get any poop on my foot. I reached the edge of the field and to my horror found myself beside the Hill place. If Mr Hill found me today he could take me and no one would know. They'd all think I'd run away from Lumley. Then he would carve me into pieces and feed me to Mrs Hill. Even a murderer didn't deserve such a fate.

Through the sparse parts of the hedge I could see their washing line, heavy with rows of freshly washed linen. Large billowy sheets and smaller pillowcases breathed in and out with the wind. I found a space under the hedge, the same space Ed and I had ducked under when we followed the mysterious figure, and ran down the street, then into our driveway. I sprinted up to the porch and threw myself at the front door.

'Let me in!' I hammered at the door like it would give way if I hit hard enough. I put my finger on the bell and held it down, keeping watch in case I should be ambushed from behind. By some miracle I hoped Mum and Dad had returned early. They would

151

open up and let me inside. Everything would be sorted out. I would be happy.

When no one appeared I ran around the side to the kitchen window. The cloth and pot scrubber were neatly placed on the sink bench. The rest of the kitchen looked sad and unlived in. There was a soft glow of light behind me. Mrs Aston-Peach's back door was open. I thought about going over. I could pretend it was a social call. Maybe I could even persuade her to give me something to eat and hide me. I felt hungry, like I had never eaten in my life. But I decided against the visit. Mrs Aston-Peach had horrible grandchildren who recited dirty rhymes. She couldn't be trusted.

As a last resort I ran to our back door and peered inside. Everything looked as it usually did. There were boxes and old newspapers piled up against one of the walls. The door to the washhouse was open. I could just make out the hazy white edges of the washing machine and chest freezer. I saw my reflection in the glass panel of the door. A scared boy with wild eyes stared back at me.

It finally sunk in. This was an empty house. There was no one home. There was nowhere else left to run. I had no more places to hide. I left the back door, followed the path round the side of the house and began the long walk down the driveway.

Mrs Yoxall was beside herself when I tapped at her patio door.

'We called the police,' she flustered, more worried than angry. 'I thought you might have drowned yourself in the river. Or worse.' She didn't explain the worse. 'The police told me I should give you another few hours before I got upset. They didn't even seem concerned.'

My hands were white and numb and I had lost the feeling in my toes, they were so cold. She felt my frozen fingers and ordered me into the bathroom. Ed bounced around her as she ran me a shower. He rabbited on about me being buried alive or something. He was a little confused about the whole thing but it was nice to see him because he made the place feel a little more like home. I asked Mrs Yoxall whether the police would take me to jail when I had finished in the bathroom.

'What are you talking about? No one's taking you anywhere.'

'What about Mrs Riddle?'

'She's the last thing you should be worrying about now.'

The hot shower turned my hands and feet back to their ordinary colour. I stayed in for far longer than usual because it was so lovely and warm. Mrs Yoxall knocked on the door to make sure I hadn't fallen asleep; she was obsessed about me drowning, even in the shower. I heard her on the phone when I finally turned the water off. 'He's back now,' she said. 'He'll be fine, I'll take care of him.'

Mr Harris couldn't apologise enough for what had happened. He said he never should have mentioned anything to Mrs Riddle. The whole mess was entirely his fault. Mrs Riddle hadn't been killed by her fall although she had been stinking angry. She wanted me expelled. My heart fluttered when I heard that. But Mr Harris had managed to calm her down. He had also talked to Mr Stringfellow who'd said I was welcome back at school. The whole story about the money and the desk came out. Mr Stringfellow wondered if Mrs Riddle had got it wrong somehow. He knew Mum and Dad and was sure I was an honest boy. Mrs Riddle wouldn't listen to him and stormed out of his office but not before Mr Stringfellow made her promise that she would forget about what had happened that afternoon. Mrs Yoxall said that Mrs Riddle should never have used what Mr Harris had said against me. She wouldn't be surprised if Mrs Riddle *had* lied because she was sure I wasn't a liar. Mr Harris did think the whole situation was strange. Mrs Riddle had been off her rocker in the headmaster's office. He'd never seen that side of her before.

Mrs Yoxall made crumbed schnitzel for tea and it was the best thing I had ever tasted. Mr Harris felt so cut up about what he had done that after we finished dinner he drove me to the Milk Bar, his treat. He wouldn't stop apologising. 'I'm so sorry,' he said. 'It was a stupid thing to do. Mates again?'

I wasn't sure and kept him hanging. I told him where I had gone that afternoon. He said the dark swamp sounded scary and he wanted to know all about Mrs Aston-Peach's grandkids when I mentioned them. My story of the lemon war had him in fits. Then I told him about the boat Eddie and I tried to build. And about our stay at the Lobbs. It didn't seem so bad when I talked about it. Mr Harris told me what it was like for him when he had come to Lumley at the start of the year. He'd been lonely at first but gradually he'd come to like the town. He thought Lumley was a good place to settle down and raise a family. We talked about heaps of stuff and from time to time Mr Harris would order another round of goodies until I was so bloated I could hardly move. It took two ice-cream sodas, a banana split, and a triple-decker chocolate sundae, but I finally forgave him.

Chapter Nine

'Boy, did you miss the best part of the afternoon,' Steve said as soon as he spotted me walk into the Lumley Primary grounds. I was hoping to slip quietly back into school but that was a high hope. I knew I'd be in for some attention from the other kids. I would have enjoyed it too, if I hadn't known that I had to face Mrs Riddle at the end of it.

'When you pushed Mrs Riddle and ran out the door she fell backwards. No, fell isn't the right word. She sorta rolled back on her heels and, no not rolled . . . rocked backwards . . . that's it, she rocked backwards, so far that she slipped, no, not slipped . . . toppled . . . she toppled back onto the floor with her feet up in the air. Her dress flew up and the whole class saw her gruds. Honest to God. Horrible old white ones they were too. Probably had skid marks on the insides. Paul says he saw a bit more, if you know what I mean, but I think he's been in the cowshed too long.'

I felt dreadful. Mr Harris hadn't mentioned this part.

'She was screaming something disgusting. Annette Luney tried to help her up but Mrs Riddle just screamed her head off and wouldn't let anyone touch her. Got up all by herself. Then half the other teachers came to see what was happening.'

By then I felt sick. Pushing another kid was one thing, but pushing your teacher, there was an unwritten rule against it. I wouldn't have been surprised if it was the eleventh commandment. Thou shalt not push thy teacher.

'Mrs Riddle disappeared for ages. That woman from Mr Stringfellow's office came down to look after us. We had to read quietly. Then Sheree got her talking about what it was like when she was at school and that took up most of the afternoon. When Mrs Riddle came back Sheree asked where you were and Mrs Riddle said she'd informed the authorities that you'd run away. Where'd you go?'

'Home.'

Steve seemed very disappointed with that news. 'Well, did the police find you?'

I didn't have the heart to tell him that not only had the police not found me, they hadn't even left the station to search.

'No. I must have dodged them.'

'Good going!'

'What else did Mrs Riddle say about me?'

'Nothing. We had Maths like normal then we went home.'

'Hey, Garrick, where were you?' I heard behind me. It was Kingsley Helms.

'None of your business,' I answered under my breath. A circle of kids crowded around me.

'It's Kevin!'

'Hi, Kevin. No one knew where you had gone.'

'I knew he wouldn't get kicked out of school.'

'Long time, no see.'

'Its SuperKev!'

Sheree saw me and hung back for a second. Maybe she was waiting for me to go to her or maybe she thought the crowd would part to let her through. But it became clear that neither of those things was going to happen so she pushed the other kids out of the way and took me to one side.

'Where did you go yesterday? I thought you would have gone to my . . . secret place,' she whispered. 'I checked it out but you weren't there.'

'I didn't think about that. If I'd remembered I would have gone.'

156

'Next time, eh? I would have hid you.'

'Next time,' I promised.

'I was worried about you. Rabies-woman made it sound like she'd got the police onto you. Are you in trouble?'

'I don't think so.'

Sheree liked hearing that. 'I told you before, Kev. You're too lucky. No one else could have called her an old cow and got away with it!'

The other kids had been eavesdropping and they joined our conversation. Everyone tried to talk at once. I heard the words 'old cow' repeated all over the place. 'Rabies-woman' got mentioned too. I felt a bit bad about it since I was responsible for making both phrases so popular. The Street gang kept their distance but I could tell even they were talking about me.

'Boy, you've got nerve,' Steve told me. 'My dad would say you've got a backbone like a black bull.'

'My dad'd say something different,' Paul added.

'Something dirty, probably,' Steve replied.

'You're just jealous 'cause you didn't see what I saw.'

Sheree punched Paul on the shoulder. I was glad that for once it wasn't me at the other end of her fist. 'You didn't see anything, you bloody liar.'

'I did so! I'm telling you Kevin, it was the first time all year I was glad the old cow put me up the front of the class.'

We heard three sharp claps, Mrs Riddle's sign for attention. The din died instantly. She stood in the door of the classroom, her face as grim as a barracuda's. All of us kids wondered the same thing. Had she heard me call her an old cow? Did she hear me say 'Rabies-woman'? Paul sweated potatoes beside me. I was just glad I'd had my mouth shut when she appeared.

Mrs Riddle pointed inside the room and we filed in one by one. I expected something terrible to happen to me. Despite Mr Harris's promise that it was all sorted out, I was sure Mrs Riddle would do something. Pull me out of line and drag me back in front of the class, maybe. Or slap me on the back of the head as I passed her in the doorway. But I got to my desk safely and sat down. Mrs Riddle unlatched the door and pulled it shut, then walked to the back of the room and fished out the roll from her desk. While she did that Sheree turned around to face me. She had her eyelids flipped over. I smiled nervously at her and wondered if things really were going to be okay.

Mrs Riddle started the morning, as she did every day, by marking off the attendance register. Greg Adams . . . Steven Armstrong . . . Tara Cooke . . . Mrs Riddle glanced at each kid in turn as she called out their name. The kid was expected to nod back or say 'Here' then Mrs Riddle would move on. I thought the world would stop when she spoke my name. I waited for her to give me a personal dose of her death-stare. Mrs Riddle said . . . Kevin Garrick . . . and looked in my direction with a watery expression. I nodded back but Mrs Riddle looked straight through me. At first I thought she hadn't seen me or she had some dust in her eye. She moved on . . . Adam Gipps . . . Kingsley Helms . . . Sheree Humphries . . . and glanced at each of those kids.

The same thing happened when she looked at me later that morning. Her eyes glazed over, like a wall had sprung up when she turned my way. Then it happened once more, then all morning, then for the rest of that day and then every day. Each time she had to look at me it was as if she was staring at an empty desk. She also never called on me to answer a question. She never noticed my outstretched arm when I raised it, no matter what the reason. She didn't ask me to help around the classroom, or to come to the front of the class and write my Maths answers on the board. She didn't even say my name, except for when she had to take the roll. Inside that classroom, to her, I became a non-person, a nothing in her eyes. And I didn't mind at all. Not one bit. Being ignored like I didn't exist was far better than being treated badly for no reason.

Mum and Dad returned along with Andrew. The telephone rang

the first Saturday of the May holidays to say they had arrived home and Mrs Yoxall suggested she bring us boys around after dinner, so that Mum and Dad had some time to unpack and freshen up. Mr Harris wasn't there for our last dinner. He was out with a friend of his, some woman who worked at the bookstore. Before he left he told me and Ed goodbye. It seemed a bit odd, since we'd see him around school all the time. He shook my hand and gave us both a wink as he went out the door. Ed tried to wink back but he could only close both eyes at the same time so he did that instead.

Mrs Yoxall cooked one final delicious roast dinner then drove us home. I thought she was going to cry when we gave her a goodbye hug. Mum thanked her and insisted she take something for her trouble but Mrs Yoxall said she'd adopt us if she had the chance. She talked to Mum quietly out by the car. I was certain they were talking about me but Mum never said a thing about what happened with Mrs Riddle which made me think I was wrong about that. She would have at least mentioned it to me, I was sure.

I raced Eddie upstairs to see Andrew and we burst through his door unannounced. Bad idea. Andrew was getting changed.

'Get out!' he shouted, struggling to pull on his shirt quickly.

'We wanted to say hello,' I told him.

'Hi!' Eddie added.

'I told you to get out!' Andrew yelled again. 'Didn't you see the door was closed? Are you two blind or just terminally stupid? Get out! Go on, move it! And shut the door behind you!'

'Andrew's in a bad mood,' Ed said as we headed back down the stairs. 'He must be sick. I'm gonna tell Mum he's sick.'

'No, don't,' I advised. 'Just leave him.' Something told me Andrew wasn't sick. He was just getting older. I had seen the same thing happen to the girls when they went to boarding school. One second they were happy to have you splash around in the bath with them and the next they screamed if you so much as tapped on the bathroom door while they were inside. My worst fears for Andrew were confirmed when he came down for dinner and I got my first proper look at him. He was different. He looked taller and more solid. His voice was deeper. His hair darker, maybe. He had changed.

The girls arrived the next day and Mum, Ed and I met them at the bus station. I was worried that they too would be even more different than before. Who was to say that this change thing didn't happen every time they went away? What if they came back even more screamy and less fun to play with? How would Ed and I survive the experience?

But they looked almost the same when they stepped off the bus, although Rachel's usual shoulder-length hair was now further down her back, and straight away Kate picked up Eddie and swung him round just as she always did. They both gabbled to Mum at the same time . . . the trip was okay . . . Kate made the hockey team . . . hasn't Rachel's hair grown . . . and more. Mum beamed from ear to ear. She looked so proud. Ed and I each hauled a bag off the platform. Kate had to help Ed, but I got the larger of Rachel's two cases all the way to the Holden although I banged it against my ankles about a million times.

Andrew was full of how wonderful boarding school was and how he was the most popular kid in his year. By the second day he had complained to Dad that he was bored senseless sitting around the house with the 'children' so Dad set him to work preparing his room to be wallpapered. Andrew's room had the oldest, mouldiest paper in the house. His walls carried the reminders of several events. Charley the cat had used more than one patch as a scratching post. In places the floral paper was ripped to the scrim. There was also a portion with black splatters where Andrew had chucked an ink bottle at Kate. The top came off in mid-flight and it stained Andrew's bedspread and the carpet as well as the wall. Then there were the more recent scribbles from last year where Ed had practised writing his name. I'd laughed at him because he could only print his 'e's backwards.

Andrew moved out all his furniture and stripped the room. The floral paper practically fell off the walls, that's how old it was. Then

Dad helped him to paste up the new wallpaper. The new design had a plain line to it, nothing flash, but nothing particularly horrible either. In the second week they tackled the main bedroom. Mum chose a softer design that time, something with roses on it. And finally they repapered the den, using the same paper as in Andrew's room. The best thing to come out of all this redecorating was that Andrew thought he lost his Little Traveller orienteering compass in all the mess. I kept my mouth shut while he turned his room upside down trying to locate it. No way would I tell him I had lost it. Andrew finally theorised that he had thrown it out with the old wallpaper and now that the set was broken he passed the pen-torch on to me to, as he dramatically put it, 'continue the Garrick legacy'.

By comparison I hardly saw Rachel and Kate all holidays. They attended an endless round of parties and evening get-togethers at the Milk Bar. Mum thought Kate was a little young to be out but Rachel said she was looking after her and Kate was pretty sensible anyway. During the days the girls would hole up in Rachel's room and play their Abba and Seals and Crofts albums. Rachel bought 'Love to Love You Baby' by Donna Summer and Mum got upset when the girls mimicked the rude breathy bits at the end of the song. The girls also dragged the upstairs phone in with them and held it hostage for hours at a time until Mum got tired of them tying up the line.

One day they took Ed and me to a variety show held at the War Memorial Hall. The host invited children up on stage to sing a song then the audience clapped for who they liked best. I wanted to go up but I hummed and ha-ed too long and missed out. All us Garricks clapped hardest for a little girl, younger than Eddie, who had sung 'Twinkle Twinkle Little Star', but a teenage girl who sang some boring religious song received the loudest applause from the audience as a whole.

Since most of the kids were home Mum decided we should take a trip to Aunt Erin's. Andrew moaned about it.

'I just travelled all the way up from Wellington. I don't want to sit in the car for half the holidays!'

He had no choice in the matter, however, and he joined Mum, Rachel, Kate and me on the day trip. We left Eddie with Mrs Yoxall. You should have seen how happy she was to have him back.

Good Samaritan looked just the same. The big mound of dirt hadn't changed a bit, it was as bare as ever. Mum left us kids in the waiting room like always. Rachel and I searched for the Fuzzy Felts but the box was gone.

'What a dump!' said Andrew.

'I thought Mum told you to leave that sort of talk in the car,' Rachel reminded him. Mum had given Andrew the hard word several times on the way down, warning him not to misbehave in the hospital or else she'd leave him there. It was an empty threat although the thought of Andrew trapped in the Nut House appealed to me.

'Well, this place gives me the creeps.'

'Keep your voice down. The nurses'll hear you.'

'I don't care. I didn't want to come anyway.'

'Why don't you say something new?' Kate remarked.

'Well I didn't! Just because we've got a whacko aunt doesn't mean we have to visit her all the time. It's not like she even knows we come.'

'Mum talked to her last time,' I told him.

'Yeah? Maybe she should check in here as well. She's been pretty crazy lately herself.'

'Andy!'

'She has! You didn't hear her in the car coming up from Wellington. She went on about how she loved the family being together . . . like I care.'

'It's been a rough year for her, and Dad,' Rachel replied.

'Well, Mum must have been pretty looped out if Dad had to slap her back to the real world.'

Rachel closed the waiting room door. 'That's not what happened.'

'Sure it is.'

'No it's not,' Kate said. 'Dad beat Mum up. He was in a bad mood and he took it out on her.'

'You're both wrong,' Rachel argued. 'Dad just lost it for a second. He didn't mean to do it.'

'Why are you sticking up for him?'

'It's not Dad's fault, it's Mum's. She's always complaining about money!'

'You're a chauvinist pig!'

'Both of you shut up!'

The three of them were so busy with their argument that they didn't notice when I slunk out of the waiting room. I just suddenly felt like being with Mum. I walked by open doorways and in the back of my mind I worried that I might get grabbed by some patient and hauled inside, never to be seen again. I was relieved when I found the right room.

'Kevin?' Mum said in surprise.

'I got bored waiting.'

For some reason I had expected Aunt Erin to be seated in bed, talking to Mum. Probably because that's what happened on our last visit. But Aunt Erin was flat on the bed, the way she always was. She looked like she hadn't moved a muscle since I had last been there.

'Did you talk to her?'

'Not this time. The doctor said she hasn't been lucid . . . awake . . . for a month or so.'

'I thought she was getting better.'

'She was . . . for a while. Come here.' Mum held out her arms and I sat on her lap. 'Why don't we just stay for a while and talk to her anyway?'

'Why? She can't talk back.'

163

'I know. But sometimes, when people are like this, they can hear everything that goes on. They just can't talk themselves.'

'So if we talk to her she might hear us?'

'Shall we give it a try? Why don't you start?'

I felt a bit stupid but Mum was keen and there was no one else about so I began.

'Hi, Aunt Erin. It's Kevin. I came to see you last time as well. It's the school holidays at the moment so most of the kids are home. Andrew's being a big pain. He wouldn't stop grizzling all the way down here, would he Mum? He's my least favourite brother. He might come and see you later, then you can judge for yourself. Kate and Rachel are here too. Ed didn't come, he's at Mrs Yoxall's. We just stayed with her. Her and Mr Harris. I think you'd like both of them, they're nice.'

There was another change of season during those holidays. The frosty mornings became bitter. The chilly evenings froze solid. The perfect days, when it was cold but sunny, were swept away in the rain and hail and wind. Ed and I took up A Hundred Pots and Pans again; no longer did we have to fake any of the weather effects. Ed also turned the upstairs landing into a horse sanctuary which was fine until Andrew stood on Thunder and broke off all of his legs. Ed bawled so much Andrew had to stick the legs back on which was also fine except he put the back legs on the front and the front legs on the back. Eddie cried once more when he saw the new Thunder and I tried to pull the legs off but the glue had set fast. After that Thunder was so deformed that he lost much of his appeal, and all of his galloping ability, and Ed hardly ever took him out of the box again.

The holidays, like every holiday, ended too soon for my liking and two weeks after they arrived, Rachel, Kate and Andrew all departed. The girls were sad to leave home but Andrew said he couldn't wait to get back. Dad, Ed and I drove them all to the station and saw them off. Mum stayed in bed because she had a cold that day. She couldn't even kiss them goodbye in case she passed on some of her germs.

The first day back at school was miserable and the rain didn't let up once. The start of the second term was always the worst time of the year because you weren't even halfway towards the Christmas break yet and you had also lost those autumn days with the pretty leaves and mild weather when you could still play outside and you knew that it was going to get worse and worse and colder and colder and that none of it was even going to begin to let up until spring, which was months and months and months and months away. That was why Lumley Primary had its yearly trip up the mountain at the start of the second term, so that the onset of the bad weather was offset by the prospect of trekking through the snowy bush.

The whole school didn't get to go, only Standard Two and older. And the classes didn't all go at once. Standard Two had planned their trip since before the holidays and went during the first week back. Standard Four were going the week after, and the older kids in Forms One and Two were going to Remihana Dairy Factory instead this year. Mrs Riddle announced that our class would be going up the mountain in three weeks' time. She handed out the permission forms, with their purple meths-smelling writing, and explained that we needed at least six parents to go with us, otherwise the trip was off. I made Eddie sprint home with me so I could make Mum volunteer for it.

I burst into the living room and ran smack into a strange man in the doorway.

'Why hello there,' he said in a friendly voice.

'Hi,' I said suspiciously.

Ed hid behind me. The stranger glanced at the family photo he had been admiring. 'You must be . . . Andrew,' he guessed and tapped my picture. 'Quite a squint you've got there!'

'It's my lazy eye. And I'm not Andrew, I'm Kevin.'

'Sorry, your mum rattled off your six names so quickly I didn't get a chance to match them with the faces. Kevin it is.'

'Where is Mum?'

'Visiting the little girl's room.' The stranger rolled gently back and forth on his heels. He had hollow cheeks and silver-framed glasses. He seemed okay. At least he didn't smoke a cigar like that other visitor.

'Who are you?' I asked him and caught him off guard.

'I-er-I'm —'

'Kevin!' Mum said as she came through the door. 'What sort of question is that?'

'No,' the stranger said. 'It's a valid question. It was just expressed very . . . straightforwardly.'

'Kevin is nothing if not straightforward, sometimes determinedly so. Kevin, Eddie, this is Mr Sanderson. This is Kevin and behind him is Eddie. Ed, come on out so we can see you properly.' Ed wouldn't budge. 'Mr Sanderson is having a look around our house. He likes looking at houses.'

I had the permission form unfolded in my hand. I pushed it at Mum. 'What is it?' she asked but didn't take it from me.

'It's a form to say I can go up the mountain and that you want to look after the kids.' I flapped the page in the air hoping she would grab it off me.

'Not now, honey. I need to show Mr Sanderson the upstairs.'

'But we have to have it back at school this week!'

'Then I'm sure I can look at it later. Right now, I'm busy.' Mum smiled sweetly to our visitor.

'But we have to have six parents or else we don't get to go.'

'Kevin . . .'

Mr Sanderson piped up from the other side of the room. 'Why don't you handle it, Margaret? I can show myself upstairs.'

'Oh no, Kevin can wait.'

Mr Sanderson insisted though and vanished up the stairs. Mum finally took the form from me. 'That was not a very nice thing to do. I don't want you doing that to our other guests.'

'What other guests?'

'No one,' Mum answered vaguely. 'Just in case we have other guests . . . now what does this form say?'

I leaned against her while she read. With Mr Sanderson out of the room Eddie relaxed and took up a position on Mum's other side. But he kept one eye firmly on the door for when Mr Sanderson would return.

Mum passed the form back to me when she was finished. 'You can go, of course, and I'm happy to volunteer. But I think your father might like to help out for a change. Why don't you ask him at dinner tonight?'

'Don't you want to do it?'

'I want you to ask Dad first. He'd enjoy the trip up the mountain.'

I pushed the form at Mum again. 'Why don't you just do it?' I said. 'You can sign it now.'

'Ask Dad first,' she ordered and left the room briskly. Eddie followed her like a puppy. She didn't understand at all, I thought. I couldn't ask Dad. I didn't want to ask Dad. I certainly didn't want him to help out on the trip. I could just see Richard Street's smarmy face when Dad turned up at school. I would never live it down. It wasn't like Dad had come on any school trip before, so why did I have to get lumbered with him now? The more I thought about it, the angrier I became. I wasn't going to ask him, I decided. If questioned about it I would pretend to know nothing. Trip? What trip? No, Dad, you're not needed for any trip. It would be so embarrassing Mum wouldn't have any choice but to come herself. I left the paper on her chair as a silent protest.

The form reappeared in my place at the dinner table, completely filled out and signed, by Dad. He had also printed his name on the dotted line beside where it said 'Parent Assisting'. Neither he nor Mum discussed it during dinner, which put me in a bind. I didn't want to raise the topic with Mum because I knew she wouldn't listen any more. But I couldn't hand in the form. I couldn't have Dad there. I just couldn't.

But if I didn't hand in the form I wouldn't be able to go. I lay awake for hours and imagined how the other kids would laugh at me when Dad arrived at school, how I wouldn't want to be seen with him on the mountain. In the depths of the night I considered all sorts of mad possibilities. I could get sick. Dad could get sick. I could run away. Again. The mountain could erupt and spew lava down its slopes. The entire class could get amnesia and forget about the trip. I prayed for such a miracle when I handed in the form the next day.

At the end of the week Mrs Riddle passed out sealed envelopes with instructions to all those kids whose parents had promised to assist. She said there had been a good response; eight parents had volunteered. I hoped that meant Dad wasn't needed, but one of the envelopes had his name neatly typed on the outside. I threw the hateful thing into my desk. I was really stuck now. But even then a plan began to form in my mind. Dad was going to come . . . unless something happened to the envelope . . . unless I 'accidentally' left it at school, then told Dad they had enough parents and he didn't need to come. If he never saw the envelope he wouldn't be any the wiser. And then at school a couple of days before the trip I could say that Dad was unable to make it. 'He's busy at work and sends his deepest apologies.' The trip could still go ahead with the other seven parents. It was a devious plan; I was getting more crooked as the year went by. I felt a spike of guilt when I told Dad he wasn't needed, although he didn't seem worried about not going. I made that mean that he hadn't cared about the trip in the first place.

For the next couple of weeks that envelope scorched a hole in my conscience. It burned fiercely with guilt and anxiety. In case Mrs Riddle spotted the envelope I transferred it from my desk to my bag, and then under my mattress. I couldn't bring myself to throw it away. The envelope sat underneath me every night and the thought of it lying there with Dad's name typed so perfectly on the outside kept me wide awake. I felt like the princess who had the pea under her mattress except this was worse because she didn't know about the pea, but I was all too aware of the envelope and exactly what I had done. I might have avoided having Dad on the trip, but I made myself pay for it.

It got worse and worse as the days, and nights, went by. Come the week of the trip I was a nervous wreck. Several mornings before we were due to go I padded into the kitchen, rubbing my eyes, barely awake after another restless sleep. Mum placed a bowl of Weet-Bix with hot milk, an alternative to porridge in winter, in front of me and joined me at the table. I mushed the biscuits into a thick gooey paste then sprinkled on lots of sugar. 'I heard about something quite disturbing this morning,' she said seriously as she picked her way over the front page of the newspaper. I had a sinking feeling that someone had talked to her about our trip. I almost confessed on the spot. It was just as well I had a mouthful of Weet-Bix.

'Mrs Aston-Peach phoned to say that her washing line was stripped of clothes last night. Fortunately she'd only washed some old golfing gear the night before, so whoever it was didn't get much.'

I didn't look at Mum but the way I slowly stirred my cereal gave away what I was thinking.

'I've already checked the attic. It wasn't Eddie. Maybe he's found a new hiding place but there's no way he could have reached Mrs Aston-Peach's line. And he wouldn't go out at night. Not unless you two have had another of your midnight excursions?'

'Of course not.'

'I know. I mean, I know it wasn't you, Kevin. I know you're honest.'

My stomach sank again. I felt like such a rat about that stupid envelope.

'Whoever took Mrs Aston-Peach's gear left all her pegs on the back stoop. That doesn't sound like something Ed would do.' Mum turned a page. 'I'm wondering if there's a thief in the neighbourhood. I've been thinking the same way ever since our pillowcases disappeared. The ones from Nana. I've turned this house upside down but I still can't find them. I assumed Eddie took them, but now I'm sure he didn't. I think they were stolen from the line.'

The word 'pillowcases' sat in my head all day. I knew I had seen pillowcases somewhere recently but I struggled to remember where. It wasn't until Eddie and I walked home from school and I glanced across at the Hill house that it hit me. There had been pillowcases on the Hill's washing line! I had seen them the day I ran away from Mrs Riddle! I began to piece the jigsaw together. Some robber had made midnight raids on the neighbourhood. Ed and I had followed a mysterious figure in a nightdress one night. Our pillowcases had gone missing. I had seen lots of pillowcases on a certain washing line. One name came to mind: Mrs Hill. It was her that Ed and I followed that strange night. The things missing from our washing line, Mrs Aston-Peach's golfing gear, all our lost tools and even the Smiths' letterbox were probably her work too.

Ed had stolen some stuff but Mrs Hill was even more twisted and deranged. Who knew where she would stop? How far would she go? Someone had to halt her black-hearted progress and I was the boy to do it. I would free our pillowcases and whatever else I could find from Mrs Hill's evil clutches and become a hero. The Hill house was the last place I wanted to set foot, but this was my chance to do penance for my guilty conscience. The bad thing I had done to Dad seemed like nothing compared to the overpowering evil of Mrs Hill.

I decided to sneak to the Hills' back door, creep inside, throw the stolen gear out of a window, then pick it up from the lawn. I put the Little Traveller pen-torch into my pocket, in case any parts of the house were dark, and put on my oilskin, in case I had to go down to the damp cellar. I also wrote Mum a note with the word 'Hill' and left it in the biscuit tin just in case I was captured. Mum and Dad had tea and bikkies every night after dinner so I knew the note would be uncovered if the worst came to the worst.

Once outside, in the field, I was glad to see that Mr Hill's van was not parked in the driveway. I made my way along the hedge. Then I heard a rustling noise behind me. Ed poked his head through a gap.

'What are you doing?' he said in a voice so loud you could have probably heard it clear across Lumley.

'Go away,' I whispered and walked away from him.

Ed followed. 'Why do you have your coat on?'

'Because it might rain. Now get lost!' I started jogging in circles, trying to get him to leave me alone.

'I want to play with you. Let's go to the swamp.' Ed tried to run after me but he fell over on the muddy ground and landed awkwardly on his side. His face shattered like a broken mirror. His bottom lip began to quiver the way it always did before he cried his eyes out.

'Ed . . . gee . . . don't . . .' I pulled him off the ground and hugged him hard. 'Don't cry . . . Eddie . . . come on . . . I'm sorry . . . okay?' I checked his arm and rubbed off the dirt. 'Look, there's hardly any mud on your jumper. Does your arm hurt?'

'No,' he said in a tiny voice.

'See, there's nothing wrong. Now go home and play.'

'Where are you going?'

I knew I wouldn't get rid of him until I told him. 'I'm going to the Hills' place, okay?'

'No! Mrs Hill is there!'

'Ed . . . just leave me alone.'

'I'm gonna tell Mum!' He tried to duck through the hedge but I yanked him back and plonked him down on the ground, hoping my rough treatment would act as sufficient warning. 'She's gonna eat you!' he insisted.

'Don't be stupid.'

'Andrew said she would.'

'She's locked in the cellar.'

'But what if she gets out? I'm telling on you.'

'Well you can tell Mum if you like,' I challenged. 'I'm going and that's it!'

I picked my way along the hedge to the gate at the back of the Hills' place, thinking Ed would disappear through the hole. Instead he scurried like a spider after me.

'You stay here!' I ordered.

Eddie nodded soberly. I swallowed hard then sprinted through the Hills' gate, across the lawn, and dived against the back wall. I waited for the world to end, expecting fire and brimstone to fall from the sky or flaming pits of acid to open up underneath me. But nothing changed. The world looked just the same from this side of the hedge. With a quick glance at my escape route, I inched along to the back door. It was a big ugly brute, with rusted hinges and peeling paint. The handle was high. I took a huge breath and stretched up to open it. The door swung inwards with a creak right out of a spooky movie. I leaned on the door jamb and listened but the house was still. I took one last glance at Eddie who was crouched down like a small mouse, peeking through the slats of the gate with a scared look on his face. I gave him a Mr Harris-style wink. Ed blinked back. And then I went inside. Inside the Hill house.

I pushed the door almost closed then tip-toed forward. I found myself in a kitchen. It looked grey in the afternoon light. The smell of burning greeted me. It was an old smell like it was ingrained in the walls and the floor and the ceiling. There was a half-finished apple browning on the kitchen bench and someone had left the fridge door ajar. I debated closing it but I knew that spies and detectives never left any sign of their entry so I didn't touch it.

I looked around for a likely place to keep stolen pillowcases. In our house the hot-water cupboard was on one side of the kitchen, but there were hardly any cupboards in this place. One by one I peered inside all of them. There were plates, cups and glasses, some boxes and tins, pots, dishwashing liquid, but no pillowcases.

There were two doors leading out of the kitchen. I was faced with my first choice. One door was slightly open, one was fully closed. I chose the open one and found myself in the washhouse. Bingo. The room had a stone floor like in our laundry. But where Mum had a new automatic washer, against the wall here was a well worn wringer machine. And more cupboards with doors. There was also a pile of unfolded clothes on the floor. The pillowcases weren't in the pile. They weren't inside the machine either. Or in any of the cupboards. The backs of the shelves were dark and I had to use the pen torch to see all the way inside. I almost died when I shone the light at the back of one shelf and saw a can marked with a chilling red 'X' and the word 'Poison'.

I walked back to the kitchen and opened the closed door. A long hallway with six doorways stretched out before me. At the end, ruby-coloured glass in the front door spilled blood-red light onto the carpet. There was a different smell here. A musty odour, like that of an old coat that someone had worn while walking through the rain. Each of the doors was shut. I would have to try them one at a time.

I listened closely again. I knew I couldn't be too careful here. Mr Hill might arrive home any moment and any of these doors could be the one to the cellar. I forced myself to be extra-aware as I went to the first door and turned the knob. It didn't open. It was locked. I cursed silently and padded to door number two, still looking all around. But it was locked as well. The third door I tried was the same. And the fourth. I cursed once again. On the wall was a strange picture. I couldn't tell whether it was a painting or a photograph. It had an orange sky and there was a long black smudge on the bottom that could have been a road, or a beach. I saw what looked like a person walking on the black smudge. I would have looked more closely to see who or what it was but I felt I had no time to waste.

I approached the last two doors with a pounding in my ears. As I reached out for the knob of the fifth door I heard a click from the far end of the hall. But when I turned to look, the hall was empty. The click echoed ever so slightly and died. I had imagined it, I told myself. I was freaking, hearing noises that weren't real. I reached for the knob again. It was locked. There was only one door left, the door to the front room. The room where the curtains had flung open by themselves. The pounding had become almost deafening by now. Boom, boom, boom, boom was everywhere around me. I stood in front of the door and tried to make the sound stop. Unlike the other doors, this one had a handle instead of a knob. I wondered if this was significant as I stretched out my hand. The handle was cool to touch and gave as I pushed down. The door opened a crack. I paused. I had expected this door to be locked as well. I didn't know what to do next.

'Kevin?' I heard suddenly behind me.

I jumped a mile. Eddie was at the other end of the hall, just inside the door. I'd never seen him look more afraid or more lost. There was pure terror all over his face.

'What are you doing here?' I whispered.

'You took too long.' He was talking loudly again.

'Go away.' I wanted to pick him up and rush him out of the house but my hand was stuck to that handle. It wouldn't let me go.

'I'm scared. I want to go home.'

'Eddie, go back!' The door beckoned to me, begged me to go inside.

Ed took a couple of steps forward. 'Let's go home, Kevin.'

'Come here, then.' I motioned furiously with my free hand.

'I don't like it here. It pongs funny.'

'Yeah, yeah . . . hurry up.'

Eddie took another step towards me. He was looking all around the hall just as I had done before. I hated him for coming and I hated myself for being the reason he was there.

'Where is the cellar?'

'I don't know, Eddie! Just come to this end of the hall, then we'll go.'

'Maybe we should try and find it.' Ed stopped and looked at that weird picture on the wall. 'What's that?'

'How should I know?'

'The sky is the wrong colour.'

As he stood staring at that picture the door beside him opened a crack.

'Ed! Look out!' I shouted.

Ed turned but he was too late. An old, wizened hand, curved inwards like a claw, reached out, grabbed one of his arms and tugged at it. Ed's eyes bulged wide. 'Kevinnnn!' he screamed. The hand dragged him back, towards the room. 'Kevinnnnnn! Kevinnnnnnnnn!' Ed scrabbled for a hold against the wall, knocking the picture wildly crooked. He caught the door frame and held on. I was at his side in a second. I grabbed his free arm and pulled. The force on the other end was fantastic. Ed was screaming like a banshee.

'Help meeeee!'

'Hang on, Ed! Hang on as hard as you can!'

The tug-of-war lasted infinite seconds. The hand jerked back and forth like it was trying to shake Ed loose. I hung on to Ed's arm for dear life. Then the hand lost its grip, or maybe it let go, I didn't see. Ed and I lost our balance and fell in a heap to the floor. Ed landed squarely on top of me but I was first to my feet. I hadn't let go of his arm for one second. I winged it down that hallway, dragging Ed behind me so fast that he hardly touched the floor. I fumbled with the complicated latch on the front door. Ed was still screaming something crazy like 'Please don't eat meeeee!'. I kept turning around in case the owner of the hand appeared. The latch finally slid across and we ran down the steps, sprinted along the street and up our driveway, coming to a stop by the back door. We leaned against the house and panted hard.

175

'You okay?' I asked Ed when I had finally caught my breath enough to speak.

His eyes were still wide with fright, but he nodded.

'Not a word to Mum or Dad!' I noticed there was blood on his sleeve. 'Shoot, Ed! You're bleeding.'

'I am?' his voice started to crack.

The wound wasn't deep, just a couple of scratches, the sort made by fingernails. 'It's okay. You're not going to die.'

'It hurts.' Ed's lip quivered.

I didn't want Mum to hear him crying so I patted him on the back. 'You were really brave, Eddie.'

'I was?' he sniffed.

'Heck yes! You went into the Hill house all by yourself! Even Andrew hasn't done that.'

'He hasn't?

'Only you and me.'

Eddie smiled. 'You saved me.'

I tried to act humble, although I was actually bursting with pride. I had tussled with a monster for the life of my little brother, and won. I was invincible. Immortal.

'Who was it who had me?' Ed asked.

'I don't know,' I told him. But I knew all right. We both knew.

Chapter Ten

The morning of the trip dawned a perfect day. I knew it would be fine weather because the sky the night before had been a rose colour. Red sky at night, shepherd's delight, red sky in the morning, shepherd's warning. Mum packed me a special lunch including a thermos of her soup and made sure all my cold-weather gear was in my duffle bag. She told me not to fall down any crevices or to wander off by myself. She thought it was a shame Dad hadn't been needed but hoped I had a fun trip anyway.

There were parents already waiting in the classroom when I got there. I joined Steve and his father. Sheree had been sitting at her desk and she came over as well. Mr Armstrong was a grown-up version of Steve, tall and thick-set with short blond hair and deep-set crystal-blue eyes. He had represented the province in rugby as a young man and you could see the front row forward still in him.

'They've divided up the kids to go in cars,' Steve explained to me. 'We asked for you, Paul and some of the other guys.'

'What about Sheree?'

'She's a girl.'

'Isn't she coming with us?'

'She's a girl!' Steve repeated. 'It's too late anyhow. All the cars have been filled. You're going with someone else, aren't you, Sheree?'

'Kingsley Helms,' Sheree replied. She looked hurt. She could hide her feelings, but not that well.

'Maybe I can swap cars, so we can go together,' I told her.

'Go with her then!' Steve said. 'We'll have a better trip without you.' He turned his back on me. Mr Armstrong, who had been talking to Mrs Riddle, noticed what was going on.

'What's happening, boys?' he said. He had a distinctive accent, with a broad country twang to it.

Steve explained the situation. 'I don't want any girls,' he added at the end.

'Sheree's different from other girls,' I argued in her defence.

'I don't see a problem, Stevie,' Mr Armstrong said. 'I've got the Landrover. I'm sure we can squeeze one more in the back.'

'But it was gonna be just boys.'

'Sheree's as strong as any boy,' I threw in. 'Stronger.'

Mr Armstrong laughed. 'Sounds just like your mother, Stevie.'

Steve folded his arms and turned his back on me again. I pushed Sheree at Mr Armstrong.

'This is Sheree. As you can see, she's not that big. She won't take up much room.'

'Pleased to meet you, Sheree.'

'I don't wanna be any trouble,' Sheree replied.

Mr Armstrong tapped Mrs Riddle on the shoulder. 'I understand Sheree here has been put into another vehicle. I was wondering if I could take her with me in the Landrover.'

Mrs Riddle screwed up her mouth. 'No, I'm afraid that's not possible. I've already drawn up the roster.'

'Any chance we could tweak it a bit?'

'It would disrupt everything!'

Mr Armstrong chuckled. 'If one little girl goes with someone different? Look, I'll take Sheree with me and if it disrupts anything, anything at all, you can tell me off later.'

'That is simply not acceptable!' Mrs Riddle drew Mr Armstrong aside and spoke to him privately.

'What sort of bull do you think she's spinning?' Sheree asked me.

'Who knows? But don't worry. I'm not going in the Landrover unless you come too.'

The two adults talked for a moment then Mr Armstrong came back to us. He looked pleased with himself. 'It's all sorted out. Sheree, you're with us!'

When Steve heard that he strode out of the classroom in a huff. Mr Armstrong followed, to tell him off no doubt. I hadn't seen Steve throw a tantrum before. As far as Garrick tantrums went, it was tiny, but for him it was a big deal. I couldn't understand his reaction to Sheree coming along. If nothing else, having three older sisters had taught me that there wasn't much difference between girls and boys, except for the obvious things, like that girls wore dresses and boys played rough sports and Sheree had even blurred those lines, being so good at bullrush and all.

Steve finally stopped pouting and his father made him apologise to Sheree. He muttered that he was sorry and quick as a flash, Sheree slugged him a friendly one in the stomach. 'Don't you ever leave me out of anything again.'

Then we all climbed into the Landrover and the convoy of cars left the school. I peered out the windows anxiously as we pulled away from the gutter. Sheree asked me what I was looking so worried about. I couldn't let her know that I was having final regrets about tricking Mum and Dad. Instead I told her I got carsick on long trips and she made me promise to say if I wanted to chuck so she could open the window for me. I had to wonder why Steve ever thought Sheree was something less than a boy.

During the drive up Mr Armstrong led a multi-verse round of 'Old McDonald Had a Farm' with each of us being one of the animals. I did my expert dog bark which Mr Armstrong thought was very life-like. I figured he knew what he was talking about because he had three dogs of his own. When the song died, the boys gathered around Mr Armstrong for stories about his rugby days while Sheree and I stared out the back window of the Landrover, watching the ground whip out underneath the back of the vehicle, and pulled faces at Annette Luney, whose mother was driving the car behind us.

'I thought your dad was coming,' Sheree said, pressing her face against the glass.

Great, I thought, another reminder of what I had done.

'He couldn't make it. He's busy at work. Didn't you hear me tell Mrs Riddle that?'

'I haven't listened to anything in her class since she hit me.'

'Same for me, since I pushed her.'

'She hasn't liked either of us all year.'

'I tried to make her like me.'

'That wasn't ever gonna work.'

Sheree motioned for me to come in close. She didn't want anyone else to hear what we were talking about. The other passengers in the Landrover were all totally engrossed with Mr Armstrong, his tips on how to play better rugby and his stories of famous players, nail-biting games and changing-room jokes, but Sheree and I whispered anyway.

'Mum says if someone hates you, there's nothing you can do to change it. She wanted to know what I'd done to Rabies-woman to make her be so mean to me and I couldn't think of anything special. That got me thinking, why does Rabies-woman hate us?'

'If I knew that I could make her like me.'

'Well it's not right to hate someone without a reason. Mum thinks Rabies-woman's a bit sick. Thinks she's had one too many falls off the back of a horse, if you know what I mean. Mum also said I'm always talking about you, but that she's never met you. That's my fault . . . sorry . . . anyhow I told her how you pushed the old cow and she said she don't care what you'd done, if you were my friend then that was good enough for her and that you sound real nice and that you could come over whenever you want. You could come tomorrow, if you like.'

'I'll have to ask Mum, but I think I can.'

It wasn't long before the Landrover plunged into the bush at the base of the mountain. Sheree became instantly transfixed. She stared out at the bush like it was a huge pile of Christmas presents and her eyes sparkled as we climbed the hill towards the plateau. There was snow down even this far, lying in grey-white blobs along the roadway. Mr Armstrong had to slow down because of ice on the road. Sheree looked at me with a serene expression. I remembered she had told me how much she loved the bush. It was plainly obvious.

Mr Armstrong parked the Landrover at the chalet, which was at the end of the mountain road, and opened up the back to let us out. The chilly mountain air swirled around us and it was a shock after the warmth of the Landrover. I put on my winter coat straight away.

'Cold enough for you?' Mr Armstrong grinned. 'You'd better throw something else on, Sheree. You're liable to catch something if you don't.' There was an uncomfortable silence. None of us boys said a word. We all knew Sheree didn't have a coat.

'I'm not cold,' Sheree replied at last.

'Still . . . even hardy types like you need to keep warm,' Mr Armstrong said. He picked up a bush shirt from the front seat and lobbed it underarm to Sheree. 'Try this for size.'

'If you insist.'

'I do. If that doesn't keep the chills off, nothing will. Colour suits you as well.'

The bush shirt was more like a dress on Sheree and we had to roll up the sleeves to stop them flopping over her hands, but at least she looked warm.

Mrs Riddle stood on the steps of the chalet with a brown woollen scarf tied around her head. She looked like the pictures I'd seen of the Queen on the news, sort of hoity-toity and proper. Steve and Paul started a play fight in the parking lot. They ducked and dodged among the gathering crowd, attempting to cram snow down each other's backs. I noticed that Mrs Street was standing in the crowd. Richard sneered at me when I looked over and he pointed me out to her. I pretended to ignore them but their eyes burned a hole in the back of my head.

Mrs Riddle made the boys stop their snow war then explained that we weren't going to the top of the mountain even though she had promised at the start of term that was what we would do on this trip. It was too cold, she said, and the weather report predicted a storm. Ignoring the disappointed groan from the class she called out the itinerary. A long bush walk to begin, to Hardy Falls. Lunch by the Falls, then the shorter, more direct route back to the chalet for a tour and talk, then home. In Mrs Riddle's voice, it all sounded like a death march through Hell.

But the hike down to the Falls was so pretty and so peaceful that not even Mrs Riddle's introduction, or her presence, could spoil it. I walked between Sheree and Mr Armstrong. Steve went on ahead with the other boys from the Landrover but his father was content to stroll at our gentle pace, enjoying the scenery with Sheree and me. The winter bush was damp, but not wet; the ground soft, but not slippery. Dappled sunlight played on our heads. Cheeky fantails followed us part of the way, chatting shrilly to each of us in turn. Underneath the birdsong was the roar of Hardy Falls, becoming more distinct as we closed in on it. At one point early on we caught a peek of the Falls through a clearing. Even from a distance you could see its power and its beauty.

The waterfall was even more fantastic close up. The whole base of the cliff where it plunged down was misted with spray. The sound of water hitting rock was so loud you had to shout to be heard. Mrs Riddle apologised to the parents, she hadn't realised how wet it was at the Falls. She had also miscalculated the length of the trip down and it was well past midday when we arrived. We had two choices, we could lay our coats down and eat lunch there or press back towards the chalet, an hour's walk away. Despite Mrs

Riddle making a strong argument for moving on, immediate lunch got the vote.

The trek back was just as pretty, though spoiled because Doug Llewellyn and Richard Street walked behind me and Sheree and we watched our backs the whole way. Halfway up we all had to stop because Paul slipped off the path and hurt his ankle. He and Steve had been horsing around, jumping at each other from behind trees. He hobbled in front of the class and we all had to walk even more slowly because of it. Sheree complained that the bush shirt itched her legs. She told Mr Armstrong she was grateful for the loan of it but she didn't understand why it had to be made of such a prickly material.

We came out of the bush just above the chalet and I told Sheree it was as close to perfect as a day at school could be.

'We should come up here every day,' Sheree agreed.

'We could have all our classes in the chalet.'

'And we could eat our lunch in the bush. Maybe we should talk to Mr Stringfellow about it.'

'I don't think they're going to —' I stopped mid-sentence. Our station-wagon was in the parking lot.

'Are you okay?' Sheree asked me.

Dad got out of the car and began to walk towards us.

'Who's that?' Sheree asked me.

I swallowed. 'My dad.'

'I thought you said he couldn't come.'

I had nothing to say to that. It was a lie which was about to come crashing down around me.

Dad zeroed in like a heat-seeking missile. Richard Street muttered some rude words behind me. Mrs Street was talking too. She didn't swear but there was a similar venom in her voice. Dad grabbed my wrist and pulled me off the deck of the chalet.

'What the hell did you think you were going to accomplish by this one, eh? What the hell were you thinking? You have done

some stupid things in your life, but this more than takes the cake!'
The entire Standard Three class and seven parents stared at us.
'Your mother found the letter when she stripped your bed this
morning. Perhaps next time you'll try a better hiding place.' Dad
twisted my arm and made me wince. 'Are you ashamed of being
seen with me? Is that it? Your mother told me you didn't want me
to come today. Is that why you hid the letter?'

His anger became disappointment when he looked into my eyes
and realised he had guessed right. I was ashamed of him. He fell
silent, just in time for Mrs Riddle to appear behind me.

'Is there a problem?' she oozed in her sweetest voice. 'I'm Esther
Riddle, the boy's teacher.'

'Bob Garrick. As you know, I was supposed to have chaperoned
on this trip.'

'Yes, your son brought the form back to school. But when you
didn't turn up this morning I presumed you were a non-shower. So
many parents over-commit themselves for things like this and then
simply bail out without a word on the day. There was certainly no
need for you to come all this way to apologise for not turning up.'

'I didn't come to apologise,' Dad replied.

Mrs Riddle feigned surprise. 'Really? Since your son didn't say
anything I simply assumed you couldn't be bothered coming.'

Dad held me in a bitter stare. 'What, you couldn't even lie for
me?'

'I told her you couldn't come.'

'Just like you told me about the envelope?' Dad said.

'This isn't the first time he's lied,' Mrs Riddle whispered at him.
'Mr Garrick, I think I need to have a talk to you about your son.'

'Well talk then, I'm listening.'

'Surely it's obvious to you that the boy has no sense of what's
right and wrong? It's been a full-time job keeping him in line this
year. In fact, I can't recall having any other student who's ever given
me such trouble. He clearly needs better guidance where

responsibility is concerned. This whole debacle is an example of that.'

I wanted Dad to defend me. To defend himself. Surely he could see she was a lying snake? Dad nodded lightly in agreement. Mrs Riddle smiled to herself.

'I'll take care of it,' Dad said. 'What's happening now?'

'We're about to tour around the chalet, then one of the rangers will give a talk about mountain rescue. You don't have to stay for that.'

'We'll see. Kevin, get in the car.'

'No . . . Dad.'

'We'll sort this out in the car!'

Dad steered me towards the parking lot. I kept protesting. 'Dad, she's lying! I did tell her you couldn't come, I mean it! This is the truth!'

'Who can believe the truth from him?' Mrs Riddle said after us. 'There have been so many lies.'

I struggled in Dad's hands. 'Don't listen to her.'

'Kevin, I've had just about enough. Get into the car!'

'But she hates me!'

'Look at that!' Mrs Riddle shouted. 'A liar to the end. You have to admire his consistency.' I couldn't see her but I imagined she was smirking to the other children. 'As you sow, Kevin Garrick, so shall you reap.'

Dad came to a sudden stop. He literally stopped in his tracks. He slowly turned and walked back towards Mrs Riddle.

'What is it?' she frowned.

Dad kept walking until he was right in her face. He spoke in a low growl. 'You know, I don't mind learning my son is trouble. I can deal with that. What I really hate is having my face rubbed in it.'

'Excuse me, but I wasn't —'

'Of course you were. Any decent person would have known when to stop. You were just out to hurt the boy then.'

185

'I meant nothing like that!'

'I know what I heard. You might frighten ten-year-olds but you don't scare me.'

'I have never been so insulted!'

'And give up that surprise act. It makes you look like a fool. Makes me want to believe the boy. Come on, son.' Dad left her and guided to me to the car. Mrs Riddle had no comeback.

The people on the deck watched in an equally stunned silence. I was torn. I wanted to cheer because someone had finally rendered Mrs Riddle speechless. Not just someone, my dad! But I was still in trouble. I still had to face up to what I had done. I saw Sheree in the crowd. We connected, just for a second. She managed to give me a wave, and a grin, before she was carried into the chalet by the push of kids going inside.

Without a word Dad got into the driver's seat and unlocked the passenger door. I climbed in cautiously. We sat in silence. I waited for Dad to speak. He most likely was waiting for me to do the same.

'Are we going home?' I asked at last.

'I don't drive when I'm angry,' was the answer.

'She *is* lying, Dad. I told her you couldn't come. I said you were busy with work.'

'And that would make it better? I don't care about some trip up a mountain. And I don't care what your prissy teacher in the chalet over there thinks of me. If I lived my life by what people thought I wouldn't leave the house every morning. I'm not ashamed to be me, but I won't have you ashamed to be my son. You have no right to be ashamed. Do you understand that?'

'Yes,' I said softly.

'I used to be ashamed. Remember the day of the swimming sports? I turned up to watch you that day.'

'I didn't see you.'

'I was running late. I got there as you were about to dive in. I heard your mother defending me to Marge Street. I wanted to go in

186

and join her, but I couldn't face that crowd. So I let my wife fight my battles for me. I waited outside the wire fence and watched you all drive away.

'Then, there was what happened with your mother. I just wanted to hide after I did that. I took the phone off the hook and sat on the stairs and stayed there and tried to work it all out. I tried to work out how I had managed to screw things up so badly. How I had managed to destroy my father's business. How I had hurt your mother and you kids. Then I realised I couldn't hide any more. No matter what I'd done or what the future might bring, I had to face it. I've made mistakes Kevin, and I'll keep on making them. Life's not perfect. My biggest mistake is that I thought it was.'

'I am sorry about today, Dad.'

'What you did was very stupid. I came up here to tell you that. I didn't come to punish you, just to say that. You can go back with the others now. I'll wait here till you're finished.'

I had no desire to join the group again.

'Go on. I won't come in. You don't have to be seen with me.'

I didn't move.

'I also have some news which your mother and I have been saving for another time, but since all the other secrets are out of the bag, we should drag this one kicking and screaming from its hiding place. We're leaving Lumley.'

'No, Dad . . .'

'The timber yard is up for sale. The house is on the market. As soon as they both sell, we're going.'

'Why?'

'We don't have a choice. The business is going under. I have to get out now, cut my losses.'

'But our house . . . ?'

'The house is a big asset. At the moment, I need the money from the sale to offset my debts with the timber yard.'

'Where will we go?'

'At this point we're thinking of Remihana. I'll buy another business, something a lot smaller. I'm sorry, Kevin, but we really don't have a choice.'

I was too stunned to speak.

'Maybe you should join your friends now,' Dad suggested. I nodded numbly and got out of the car. Leaving Lumley? I didn't want to believe it. I wandered across the parking lot in shock. Remihana? We'd visited it several times. It was a town bigger than Lumley. It had a pedestrian mall in the middle of the shopping centre. I'd found fifty cents there, beside a phone box. Remihana was only about half an hour away from Lumley, but at that moment it might as well have been the far side of Neptune. We're leaving Lumley. Dad's words circled around inside my mind. I staggered towards the chalet in a trance. I almost lurched into Annette Luney.

'Get out of my way, Kevin!! What's the matter with you?'

'We're leaving,' I said distantly.

She looked me up and down like I had two heads, then scuttled away quickly. Other people came off the chalet deck and also stared at me. I walked through them, bumped back and forth by their unfriendly shoulders until Mr Armstrong rescued me and pulled me to one side.

'Hold your horses, little man. Where's your dad?'

'In the car. Where is everyone going?'

'We're heading back to school,' Steve griped. 'The ranger's too busy to give the talk. This is so slack.'

I looked for Sheree but didn't see her. I wanted to tell her we were leaving. She would make me laugh and forget about how bad I felt.

Paul limped out of the chalet doorway. 'Where's Sheree?' I asked him.

He had scored himself a handful of leaflets. 'Dunno. I haven't seen her since we went inside.'

'Maybe she's in the loo,' Steve suggested. I wondered if she had managed to turn the chalet toilet into another mini-replica of Hardy Falls.

Mrs Helms was sent into the Ladies but returned shrugging her shoulders. A quick search around the chalet failed to locate Sheree, but Mr Armstrong's bush shirt was found underneath one of the couches. Mrs Riddle was immediately brought in on the hunt.

'I hope this isn't some little game. Sheree and — Kevin —' she practically choked on my name, '— are well known for pulling pranks. This is right up their alley.'

'No one has seen her for at least twenty minutes. Kevin has been with his father all that time.' Mr Armstrong raised his eyebrows to make a point.

'She may be outside already,' Mrs Helms suggested. 'Let's try the parking lot.'

We did. Sheree wasn't there. Steve and I checked the viewing platform beside the chalet. Sheree was not on it.

'What's the matter?' my father asked, getting out of the car when it became clear something was wrong.

'Sheree's missing,' I explained.

'One of the girls in the class has gone,' Mr Armstrong added. 'Dan Armstrong,' he said and Dad introduced himself as they shook hands. 'We think she may have snuck out of the chalet.'

Dad was quick to become involved. 'She can't have come this way. We would have seen her otherwise.'

'She must have gone back into the bush then,' Mr Armstrong deduced. 'We walked down to the Falls today. She's probably run back down the path.'

'When was she last seen?'

'About half an hour ago.' Mr Armstrong held up the bush shirt. 'She's left this behind.'

'What else is she wearing?'

'Just some flimsy cotton dress.'

Dad looked up at the sky. 'The weather looks like it might close in. The temperature's dropping already.'

'Have you got a coat?'

Dad made me fetch his jacket from the back seat of the car.

There was a seriousness to the cut of his jaw now. He and Mr Armstrong cornered Mrs Riddle. Dad zipped up his jacket as he spoke. 'We're going to look for the missing girl. I suggest you try and get some help.'

'What about the other children?' Mrs Riddle said, dismayed.

Dad looked at her like she was an idiot. 'Cram them into the cars and get them home.'

'I don't see why we should panic just because one little girl is playing some silly joke on us.'

'I suggest you get a move on,' Mr Armstrong told her.

Mrs Riddle stood there like she was paralysed. 'I'll take care of it.' Mrs Helms replied. 'And I'll tell the ranger what's happening.'

She raced off to do that and returned only moments later with the harassed looking ranger in tow. Dad and Mr Armstrong explained that they were going to start searching and the ranger agreed it was a good idea. He said he would put the rescue services on alert. If Sheree wasn't found within the next few hours then teams of searchers would be brought in. Mrs Riddle wondered whether that was necessary but the ranger explained it was procedure. The mountain was brutal, especially in winter. After conferring with the ranger, Dad and Mr Armstrong started off towards the bush. I ran after them, leaving Mrs Riddle in my wake.

'You can't come, Kevin,' Dad told me. 'You go back to town with the others.'

'I want to help look.'

'You'll slow us down.'

'It's another pair of eyes,' Mr Armstrong said plainly. 'We can't hurry too much anyway. Got to go slowly.'

Dad nodded his agreement.

'Steve should come as well,' Mr Armstrong added. He called Steve over and the four of us pressed into the bush, just as the clouds moved in overhead, turning the perfect afternoon dark and foreboding.

I don't remember much of what I was thinking while we

searched. I was thinking about lots of things, and yet I was thinking about nothing. Everything had happened too fast for me to take it all in. I glanced up at my dad who was walking beside me. He was surveying the bush with every step. Mr Armstrong was just behind him, doing the same thing. I mimicked them, but in the back of my mind I wasn't really worried. Sheree could handle herself. Most likely she had gone back for another look at Hardy Falls. Or maybe she had just wanted to be in the bush again. We would probably run into her coming back up the path. She'd get in trouble for scaring us then we'd take her home.

But hours later I began to think twice. Sheree didn't know this bush like she knew the area around her secret place. What if she had wandered off the path and couldn't find her way back? It was getting cold, even for someone as rugged as her. We walked at a slow pace and called out for her. 'Sheree! Shereeee! Where are you? Where are you Sheree?' We made it down to Hardy Falls and scouted around down there. Mr Armstrong thought we should head back to the chalet. We would need torches soon, and wet-weather gear. Dad suggested that he retrace our steps up the long route while Mr Armstrong took us boys back the shorter way. It was agreed. I didn't even get a chance to say goodbye to Dad before we started back up the hill towards the chalet. I heard his shouts over the noise of the Falls for a while, but then I lost him. I had two people to worry about now. Sheree all by herself somewhere in the bush and Dad, walking alone up the path. When the light faded completely Mr Armstrong made Steve and me hold his hands. He was worried about losing us too. His palm was rough and his hand so big it completely enclosed mine.

Things were very different back at the chalet when we returned. The chalet was lit up, looking like one of those little plastic cabins that came on Christmas cakes. The lights pierced into the thick mountain darkness but barely dented it. There were a lot of men both inside and outside the building. Mr Armstrong talked to some

191

men in orange jackets and told them where Dad was. They said they would go down to him, with a torch and a big black oilskin so he could continue the search. They were worried that Sheree hadn't kept to the path. She could have gone anywhere. Mr Armstrong volunteered to go with them. The men in orange jackets said that they had to leave now, before the rain started. There was a lot of bush to cover.

'You boys stay here, okay?' Mr Armstrong said, crouching down beside us. 'That's an order.'

Neither of us put up a fight. We were tired and cold and I knew the search would only be hindered if we came along now. Mr Armstrong left with his group. At least, I told myself, Dad would be okay. A stocky man, with square shoulders and a bushy ginger moustache, ushered us to the back of the busy chalet and led us to a long sofa by the miniature display of the mountain. We sank into the warm cushions and Steve fell asleep almost immediately. I sat up, fighting my tiredness. The man handed me hot tomato soup in a paper cup. I burned my tongue with the first mouthful then blew on it until it was cool enough to sip down. I heard the rain begin. It pounded against the roof like a hundred hammers.

'Heavy front,' the man said in his deep voice. 'Once it settles it'll stay all night.'

He kept talking to me as I drank, asked me where I went to school, what my favourite TV show was, that sort of guff. I knew what he was doing, trying to keep my mind occupied so I didn't think about Sheree. When I had drained the cup he took it off me and plumped up the pillows. 'Try and get some sleep,' he said kindly.

I told him that I should get up and check whether my dad was back yet but the man was sure he wasn't and promised to wake me if anything happened. I was too tired to work out whether that was a real promise or just a pretend one, so I snuggled down and closed my eyes. I was so worried about Sheree that I thought I wouldn't be able to sleep but I drifted off with ease.

When I woke up I heard talking in the background. My head hurt and my mouth was sticky where I had dribbled into the cushion. Steve was still asleep on the other end of the long couch. I looked across the chalet and saw Dad and Mr Armstrong warming their hands at a glowing bar heater. They looked weary. It was light outside, but it was still raining. Dad realised I was awake and walked over to me.

'The man was supposed to wake me up,' I said grouchily.

Dad leaned down beside the couch. 'I thought I should let you sleep.'

'Did you find Sheree?'

'One search party came across her just before dawn.'

'Well, where is she?' I said, looking all around the chalet. 'Is she okay?'

Dad didn't say anything. He stared at me with a pained look in his eyes. He breathed out, a heavy kind of sigh. Then he slowly shook his head from side to side.

Chapter Eleven

Sheree's funeral was held in the Lumley Primary school hall. The day was so cold that the little puddles of ice that Ed and I used to smash with our heels on the way to school, that had usually turned into water when we walked home, didn't melt at all. But inside the hall, once the place filled up and the doors were closed, the cold outside became a distant memory.

All the school and lots of people from town turned up to say goodbye to Sheree, even some people who had never met her. They all milled around the back of the hall before the funeral began, talking stiffly. And wasn't it the coldest day you could remember and what a waste of a young life. I stood in the corner holding Mum's hand while Ed hung off her other arm. Mrs Yoxall stood with us and told me several times to visit soon, she missed me. Mr Harris caught my eye from across the hall. I could see he wanted to say something to me, but he didn't come over. The woman from the egg shop was there. So were most of the parents who had come up the mountain, including Mr Armstrong who brought Mrs Armstrong with him. The principal, Mr Stringfellow, worked his way through the crowd, shaking hands and nodding his head. Yes, how sad. Yes, a tragedy.

All the time, Mrs Humphries sat in the front row of the hall and Sheree's baby brother played on the ground by her feet. Sheree's coffin was on the stage, and Mrs Humphries gazed at it like it was the only thing she could see. I didn't think it was very fair that the rest of us should stand in a group while she was alone so I let go of Mum and I joined Mrs Humphries on the school form. We sat in silence for a moment. Then I figured she might not know who I was so I said, 'Hello, I'm Kevin.' She didn't turn and look, but she put her arm around me and hugged my head under her arm. It seemed odd, having a woman I had never met hold me like she knew me well and yet I didn't feel uncomfortable at all.

A man in a costume like a priest's, except different, welcomed everyone and thanked them from Mrs Humphries for coming. Then Mr Stringfellow made a speech about how it is a tragedy when a child dies and even more of a tragedy when one as full of life as Sheree dies. Mr Harris also spoke saying that he had only recently met Sheree but that he wished he had known her better. Some other people also got up and said things. Miss Miles, the dental nurse, said that Sheree was one of the sweetest children she'd ever come across. Then the man in the costume read some stuff from the Bible which I didn't catch much of because Mrs Humphries started to cry and instead of listening to the man all I could hear was the echoey sound of her sobs and her uneven breath, coming in fits and starts like hiccups. There were tears rolling down her cheeks, one after the other. She didn't wipe them away and some of them dripped into my hair. When the man finished reading, Sheree's coffin got carried out the side door to the same big black car that had brought it. Dad took up one of the handles. So did Mr Armstrong and Mr Harris. And some man I didn't know. Next to the men the coffin was tiny, almost too small to fit Sheree inside.

Then everyone milled around the back of the hall again. The man in costume said that Mrs Humphries had asked that it only be family at the cemetery and invited everyone to stay in the hall for a cup of tea. The hatch to the kitchen flew up and a kettle whistled over the crowd. Mrs Humphries stayed sitting at the front of the hall, still staring at the space where the coffin had been. She didn't let go of me once nor did she say anything to me and I had to sit there with her until Mr Harris came over and led her and Sheree's little brother away out the side door. People who I hadn't even met before came up to me, asking me how I was, and said that I shouldn't feel sad because Sheree had gone to a better place. But the thing was I didn't feel sad. I didn't feel anything at all, except a bit tired. Sheree wasn't there. That was all. It was like a day when she was away from school, when she wagged or was sick. Sheree wasn't in the place that I was, but I felt she was still out there somewhere. I half-expected her to come bounding through the crowd any minute, calling my name, ready to punch me playfully on the arm. 'How are you, Kev? Why are all these people here, eh?' I tried to imagine what it was like being dead, but the best I could come up with was Ed asleep, without the snoring. Then I tried to imagine what it was like in heaven with the angels and archangels, whatever they were, and Jesus and God and white light. But I got confused wondering whether you were up in the sky or somewhere in space with the stars. I settled on it being in the sky because whenever you saw pictures of heaven you saw lots of light and clouds and there were no clouds in space, and sometimes in the late afternoon when the sun was shining through the clouds it would come in hard, blinding shafts of light that looked just like the light in those pictures. When she saw that sort of light Kate always said, 'That's God coming down to Earth.'

The crowd started to leave the hall. Mr Stringfellow called off school for the rest of the day. The long line of cars parked on both sides of the road outside school pulled away one by one. Dad went back to work. Eddie and I went home with Mum. She fed us lunch, tomato sandwiches and a raspberry bun washed down with a Spaceman drink, and watched me closely, so much that I told her no holds barred to leave me be. But I said it in a nice way so that it didn't come out all moody, something like, 'Don't worry Mum, I'm all right.' She seemed to understand. Eddie and I dragged his Horse of the Year game into the kitchen and played with it on the lino next to the wood fire, while Mum sat at the kitchen table, reading.

Her name was Sheree. She was my friend. One day she walked into the bush and got lost among the trees.

Mum didn't want me to go to school the next day. She thought she should be around me in case I felt sad, but I wanted to go straight back, I didn't want things to be any different. If I had hung around home I would feel strange because I'd think I was supposed to be at school, but I wouldn't be at school so I'd know something was wrong and then I'd think about Sheree and remember what had happened on the mountain. I argued so hard that Mum had to let me go in the end.

When I got there, all the kids were super-friendly. No one was horrible to me, not even any of the bullies. Steve and Paul wanted to spend all their free time with me. Annette Luney gave me a card with 'Sympathy' written in silver letters on the front that found its way to the bottom of my bag at faster than light speed. I thanked her nicely for it, of course, but the card was ugly. Not the card itself, that was plain-looking. It was just that Annette had never liked either me or Sheree so her sympathy was hollow, it came out of nowhere and that made the card ugly. Yet apart from that card and the kids being nice around me, nothing at school was different, just like I had hoped. Except for Mrs Riddle.

I hadn't seen her at the funeral. That didn't mean she wasn't there, but I hadn't spotted her. She turned up late to class the day after, rushing in the side door with a murmured apology. She bustled around her desk and instructed us to take out our Language books while she strode to the front of the room and wrote a whole lot of sentences on the blackboard. Nothing was out of the ordinary. Then Mrs Riddle turned around and looked at us, or more specifically looked at Sheree's empty desk, and suddenly her eyes went all wonky. She walked right up to the desk, sat down at it, laid her head in her hands, and started to cry. Everybody in class stared at each other. No one knew what to do. Steve whispered to me that we should offer her a hanky or at least say something. I didn't think so.

Mrs Riddle kept crying all through what should have been our Language lesson and beyond. At times she pulled herself together, but then as soon as she got up from Sheree's desk and looked back at it, she would fall apart again. Some of the kids crowded around her, told her not to worry and not to be sad, yet none of them could get a reply out of her. I didn't comfort her once. Sheree wouldn't have wanted me to. I knew that as surely as I knew Sheree herself would never sit in that desk again. I had this vision of her somewhere in heaven, looking down at our classroom and laughing at Mrs Riddle. It was a mean, unkind thought but that didn't stop me having it. Mrs Riddle cried until morning play when Mr Stringfellow came into the class and led her away. She never returned.

It was about this time that people started turning up to view the house. A 'For Sale' sign was hitched to the front gate and word that the Garricks were leaving Lumley was passed through the town. The kids at school asked me question after question about when we were moving and where we were going to live. Even the teachers were interested.

'I've heard you're leaving,' Mr Harris said, catching Eddie and me at the school gates one morning. 'When?'

'Soon, we don't know exactly yet.'

'That's a shame. I was looking forward to teaching you next year. I haven't been teaching that long.' He counted to himself. 'This is my fifth year, but I've already come to realise that there are kids that you never think of again. Kids who make no impact on you at all. And then there are children who you remember for some special reason, names you will never forget. Sheree was like that. There was something about her, a toughness and a softness both at the same time. I'll remember you too, Kevin, for different reasons.' He gently touched my hair and I felt a warm tingle run from my scalp, down my back. I imagined this was how the lepers must have felt when Jesus healed them. New. Important.

I didn't know quite why I liked Mr Harris so much, why all the kids liked him. He was tall and good-looking, with a handsome smile, and it was easy to like him because of those things. But I think I liked him most because he wasn't afraid to say how he felt about something and because he had listened when it mattered, when it mattered to me.

The 'For Sale' sign stirred up a pile of interest and we soon played host to visitors from Lumley, and outsiders who had seen the advertisement in the district newspaper. Most of them rang before they came. Ed and I soon dreaded the sound of the telephone because it meant another group of people would troop through our house and we would become circus attractions once again; smiling, performing children. We were put on our best behaviour from day one and were kept in check each time with promises that perhaps this was the family who would buy the house. But a seemingly endless stream of bodies tramped up and down our stairs, poked their noses into our linen cupboard and measured the den wondering whether their desk would fit in there, yet the house remained unsold.

Not everybody telephoned. One school morning we were disturbed at the breakfast table by three sharp raps at the door. Mum thought it was Mrs Smith calling for another cup of something and sent Eddie to let her in. He returned in moments, with two strange adults in tow. I ignored them at first. Mum was standing guard over the toaster and didn't see them until the woman cleared her throat loudly. Mum turned in surprise and quickly wiped her hands on a tea towel when she realised they were special 'house' visitors, as opposed to the common neighbourhood variety.

'Hello,' she managed. 'You're here to view the house?'

'We are,' the woman answered. 'You're not ready for us.'

'Did you phone first?'

'It doesn't say to phone first in the ad,' the man pointed out.

199

The woman glanced around the kitchen which looked pretty dismal considering Ed and I got dressed down here in winter right beside the fire, so there were two sets of pyjamas lying on the floor. Horse of the Year was still around too and the contents of my schoolbag had been strewn halfway out the door to the wash-house in a failed effort to locate a missing library book due back today. Annette's sympathy card had been found instead and was immediately torn into several pieces and scattered over the hearth.

The woman stuck her nose in the air. 'I don't like to be expected. I feel you get a better view of the house. People are inclined to cover up its defects when they know you're coming, wouldn't you say?'

'I wouldn't,' Mum said politely. 'Kevin, look after your brother. I'll take . . . I'm sorry, I didn't catch your names.'

The couple were Mr and Mrs Haughey from Remihana. They were not impressed when Mum told them that's where we were headed, though they reserved any specific comment on the town. They picked their way through the kitchen and laundry then they disappeared into the rest of the house. Ed went on like nothing had happened, but I followed their voices, moving from the living room to the den then up the stairs.

Ed was fidgety and restless. 'Kevin . . .'

'Shhh.' I hissed. I could hear footsteps above us and thought that if my brother shut his trap for a second I could make out what was being said. Ed took that as a cue to start singing.

'I'm a little fire engine, Flick is my name. They won't let me put out fires, isn't that a shame?'

'Shut up, Ed.'

'But I want to be a fire engine, to put out the fire.'

'What fire?'

'The one in the toaster.'

I finally saw the trail of thick black smoke that was pouring out of the toaster.

'Heck, Ed! You could have said something!' I leapt up from the table and banged my thigh so hard I gave myself a dead leg. I limped across the floor. 'Only a stupid kid would let the toast burn.' I jiggled the lever until the two slices of bread, that now resembled a couple of pieces of square charcoal, popped out the top.

'I want butter and honey on my toast.'

'There is no toast.'

'But you just cooked some.'

'Thanks to you, it's burned. What did you think all that smoke was?'

Ed finally grasped the situation and contented himself with humming the Flick song quietly. I opened up the back door to try and clear some of the stinking smoke. No sooner did I do that, than the front door slammed shut. Fearful that more visitors had turned up unannounced I ran to the hall and caught sight of Mr and Mrs Haughey walking back to their car, which was parked crookedly halfway down the driveway.

I found Mum in the master bedroom, furiously making the bed.

'Grab that side,' she told me. 'Where's your brother? In the kitchen, burning himself on the toaster I suppose.'

I held my tongue. Mum snapped her side of the bottom sheet tight over the mattress and waited impatiently for me to do the same.

'Those people left,' I said, in case she didn't already know.

'How much sheet do you have?' Mum checked over my side of the bed before I had a chance to reply. She shimmied the sheet across her way a bit, we tucked it in neatly, then picked up the top sheet and the blankets. We smoothed down that layer, laid the fluffy duvet over the top and put the pillows in place, all without a word but in short, sharp movements. Mum was angry and I knew it wasn't at me, but it didn't make me want to stay in the room with her The finished bed gave me an escape. I almost ran from the bedroom back to the kitchen.

Ed hadn't moved. 'I want some toast,' he demanded.

'Okay, okay.' I slotted two more slices into the machine.

'I want butter and honey on it.'

'You already told me that.'

'I thought maybe you forgot, dummy.'

'Don't call me a dummy.'

'Stupid dummy!!'

'Shut your face, Ed, or I'll smack it in!'

'Stupid stup—'

'Stop it, you two!' Mum was in the doorway. 'Just stop it!' she screamed full blast.

Ed got such a fright that he started crying, instant tears. Her anger forgotten, Mum dashed across the room and hugged him like he was a little stuffed toy.

'Eddie, I'm sorry. You shouldn't have been shouting at one another like that!' Mum began to cry. She looked just like Ed, all small and helpless and hurt. I cried too. The tears flowed out of me. I couldn't have stopped them if I had wanted to.

'I'm sorry,' Mum sobbed. 'I'm just so sorry.'

'I don't want to leave Lumley,' I said through my tears.

'I know, honey.'

'Me neither,' Ed wailed.

Mum rocked us both gently. 'I know, I know. But you two have to be strong now. You have to be my brave little boys. I have to be braver too.' She half laughed. 'I can't let one silly woman's comment about an unmade bed upset me. I might be showing people an unmade bed every day. Yours, probably, Eddie.' She hugged him tight and he sniffed back his nose rudely. Being the gentleman of the two of us I wiped mine carefully on the sleeve of my jersey.

'Come on,' Mum urged. 'You'll be late for school if you don't get a move on.' But that wasn't good enough for me. Mum felt sad and I wanted to do something to cheer her up. An idea hit me that was so brilliant I almost fell to the ground. I dashed upstairs and returned with my hands cupped behind my back.

'What are you doing, Kevin?' Mum said, looking at my mysterious grin. 'What are you holding?'

'It's a surprise.'

'Do I have to guess?'

'Nah.' I held out my hands carefully. The small black cat pepper-shaker was shiny in the bright kitchen lights.

Mum took it gently and studied it closely. 'It's a cat.' she said softly. 'For pepper?'

I nodded. 'I bought it for your Christmas present, but you can have it now.' Mum stared at the cat strangely. I thought she was going to start crying again. But she didn't. She looked and it and looked at it and looked at it and looked at it.

'This is so special,' she whispered at last. 'This is so . . . special, I'm going to put it in the china cabinet with the other special things. This is the best, and the earliest Christmas present I've ever had. Thank you, Kevin.' Then she looked at me, so beautifully that I thought I was going to start crying again, until Ed began to sing loudly, and terribly out of tune, in the background.

'I'm a little fire engine, Flick is my name. They won't let me put out fires, isn't that a shame?'

Mum sniffed the air. 'I can smell smoke.'

The toaster was never the same after that morning and we took to putting bread under the grill in the oven instead. It took a lot longer but Mum didn't think the kitchen could cope being smoked out so often. I experimented by grilling bread and butter with sugar sprinkled on it. The sugar went runny in the heat and turned into a sort of toffee when it cooled down. It was just the thing for the freezing cold mornings.

Winter had a stranglehold on Lumley and was choking us for all we were worth. Jack Frost was working overtime, Miss Bourke, our new teacher, told us. He would nip at our ears and pinch our toes until chased away by the lambs of spring. He had a particularly cold spell brewed up for us this year. Miss Bourke had once taken a trip to Iceland and had come all the way from the bottom of the South Island to teach at our school so we figured she knew exactly what she was talking about.

One afternoon, as we sat dreading the moment when we had to leave the warm classroom, she made an exciting prediction.

'I think we're in for snow. Mr Mountain is ready to shake that white stuff from his head any day now.'

I asked Mum whether that could be true. She couldn't remember a colder winter in Lumley and she had lived in the town since she married Dad. If we were really lucky it might snow before we left. After that I was terrified that we would be gone before the snow fell. But I only got in two good days of fretting before all the cold nights, and all the frosty mornings and all the numb fingers, not to mention toes, and all the drippy noses and the sniffles and the windburn and the blown-inside-out umbrellas were suddenly worth it. It snowed in Lumley.

'You got your wish, look out the window,' Mum said with a smile when she woke us up. She drew the curtains apart. I jumped out of bed and rubbed the misted-up window clear. The world outside had been transformed into a scene from a Christmas card. A couple of pine trees, some deer and Santa Claus would have been right at home on our front lawn. The snow had filled up the gutters in the roof and covered the driveway. Nothing was moving. It all looked peaceful and magical.

'It's been falling steadily all night. The man on the radio said it's the first time it's snowed on the town in over 40 years. Come on, Ed, you don't want to miss the snow, do you?'

I certainly didn't. I threw on the first clothes that I pulled out of my drawer then raced down to the kitchen.

'You're lucky,' Dad told me as I wolfed down my breakfast. 'When it snowed here last I was too young to remember it.'

'Just be careful. We don't want you getting frostbite,' Mum added.

'I won't,' I mumbled with my mouth full.

She placed two pieces of toast on my plate and handed me a huge cup of hot milk and Milo. I swore that she could read my mind. Something about the excitement of the snow, or maybe it was just the extreme cold, had turned me into an eating machine. The Milo and toast were delicious, especially when you mixed them up together in your mouth.

Ed finally staggered into the kitchen looking like the walking dead. He shut his eyes against the lights and found his seat almost by instinct. Mum gave him his breakfast, then did a double take when she looked at him properly.

'You feeling okay, Eddie?'

'I want to play in the snow. I want to build a snowman.' He yawned like a hippopotamus showing off his tonsils.

Mum felt his forehead and pursed her lips, concerned.

'You're burning up, and your cheeks are flushed. You're going back to bed right now. I'll be up to take your temperature.'

'I want to play in the snow.'

'Want and doing are two different things. Back to bed, now.'

Ed was on the verge of throwing a wobbly or maybe bursting into a well-timed bout of tears. Then Dad looked sternly out from over the newspaper.

'Do what your mother says.'

The order was obeyed and Ed dragged himself up the stairs, lingering on every step. He looked so disappointed I actually felt sorry for him. The snow wasn't something to be missed. If I had been Ed I would have been shattered. Then again, if I had been Ed I wouldn't have got sick at such a stupid time.

The snow was the event of the year at school. Standard Four issued a general challenge to the other years and the battle lines for a snowball war, timetabled for lunch, were drawn. Steve, Paul and I found ourselves, strangely, on the same team as the Street gang. We discussed strategy before the first bell and immediately disagreed about where we should attack from and, more importantly, who would lead the troops. Steve and Richard both wanted the job and it got hairy for a moment until Steve reminded Richard just how hard he could punch and he was elected commander-in-chief unanimously.

Then an announcement came up at a special morning assembly that the snow was off-limits. Snowball fights were especially banned. A huge groan of disappointment washed around the hall. Mr Stringfellow said he understood how we felt but that this was the best for all concerned. Back in our room Miss Bourke explained that the school was worried about children getting cold and sick. The snow was wetter than probably any of us realised. Our body heat would melt the snow and we would get wet and if we ran around in the freezing cold all damp we were sure to come down with something. When she told us that snow was actually frozen water I almost didn't believe her. Feeling it on my hands on the way to school it had seemed dry, like washing powder. I wasn't sure what I had thought it was made of, but it certainly wasn't water.

Miss Bourke repeated Mr Stringfellow's order. No playing in the snow. At morning play and lunch time the whole school stood on the concrete areas that had been cleared by some unseen caretaker and stared like hungry wolves at the forbidden white stuff.

Finally set free at the end of the day, I sprinted home as best I could on the slippery footpaths. Ed was lying in bed with his colouring books scattered grumpily about him.

'Are you gonna play in the snow? You can't play 'cause I want to play as well.'

'I'll tell you what,' I replied. I didn't want to waste a precious second of 'snow time', so I threw off my schoolbag and emptied the junk from my pockets as I spoke. 'I'll make a snowman just for you.'

Ed was not amused. As soon as I was out in the snow I saw him watching from our window with a familiar hungry expression on his face. I waved to him to be nice, but I couldn't help being grateful that it was him who was stuck in our room and not me.

Miss Bourke was right, the snow was wet and in the end there wasn't that much of it. Enough to cover the ground and sit like clumps of sickly white icing on the branches of some of the trees, but not enough for a full-fledged snowman. My attempts to roll a small snowball into the bottom-part-of-a-snowman failed miserably and instead the starter ball formed a large Swiss roll shape, perfectly round but hopelessly thin. It was more like a wheel than a ball. I tried to pat some snow onto the sides of the wheel but it wouldn't stick, no matter how hard I pushed down. I resigned myself to making a skinny snowman and gave it a similar Swiss roll chest and head. I had to admit it looked nothing like what I had been dreaming of all day but when I added some rocks for eyes, some sticks for arms and carved it a mouth, it took on its own personality. I named my snowman Ronn Karr, who was this character in the Legion of Super-Heroes who could turn himself paper-thin. That way it would seem like I had meant to make it so skinny.

Ed wasted no time in judging the poor thing. He had grizzled to Mum so much that she brought him down to the den. He watched me carefully all afternoon and even rapped on the window to tell me to get a move on or say when he didn't like what I was doing.

'My snowman looks strange.'

'That's because it's a super-snowman.'

'What does he do?'

'He turns paper-thin.'

'That's a dumb super-power. Can he fly? Does he have heat vision? If he did he could disappear all the snow in the night and you wouldn't be able to play in it tomorrow.'

'He doesn't have heat vision.'

'Then maybe I'll use my heat vision tonight when you're asleep and there'll be no snow left when you wake up.' Ed took himself back to bed, satisfied that he had ruined my afternoon as much as possible in his current state. I had no doubt that if he had really been gifted with heat vision he would have carried out his threat.

Both Mum and Dad were far more enthusiastic about Ronn Karr. Mum said the snowman looked nice. Dad made a special effort to have a look at it, even though it was night by the time he got home and he had to go and check it out with a torch. He told me it was a fine piece of work, a bit skinny, but fine nonetheless. He felt bad about Ed missing out on all the fun so after dinner we scooped up an ice-cream container of snow from the far corner of the lawn, where it was whitest and purest, and took it upstairs. The first thing Ed did was stuff some into his mouth. All this time that's what he'd really wanted to do, eat it! Then he put some of his horses onto it and gave them a skiing lesson and fell asleep with the melted snow in the container leaking onto his duvet.

Later, Mum and Dad and I watched television in the living room. *Good Heavens* was on with a man called Mr Angel who really was an angel and who granted three wishes to people who had done a good deed. Three wishes! I thought that I had been very kind to Ed that day, having not teased him for being sick, and deserved at least one, so I wished for everyone in our family to just be happy. I was rewarded with a knock on the door. Dad ignored it until Mum threw telepathic hints across the room. She had some knitting unravelled over her lap, down to the floor, and no way did she want to disturb it. Perhaps she also thought it was another Mr and Mrs Haughey.

She and I listened as Dad opened the door. We recognised the voice that said hello. The knitting forgotten, Mum got up and told me to stay where I was but I followed her to the hall. Dad stood squarely in the doorway. Past him was someone I hadn't seen or even heard mentioned for months.

Bernadette, the prodigal daughter, had returned.

Chapter Twelve

There was a stunned silence. We were all shocked, paralysed. No one moved. No one so much as blinked or breathed. Bernadette looked like she wanted the porch floor to open up and swallow her but that would have only got her a couple of feet down so she would have still felt the same and she would have been under the house where it was dirty and Andrew had once found a dog's skeleton.

'Can I come in?' she said at last.

She tried to come in the doorway but Dad blocked her path. Bernadette looked at him with a mixture of resentment and surprise and he wavered enough for Mum to get in beside him and usher the new arrival through to the lounge. Bernadette left her bulging suitcase on the porch and Dad complained to himself as he brought it inside to the bottom of the stairs. Then we joined the women.

Bernadette had taken up a spot on the sofa. Dad paced the floor a couple of times then settled in his chair in the corner, watching the whole proceedings suspiciously.

'How are you?' Mum asked Bernadette. It sounded like such a silly question, the sort of thing you say to a stranger, not family. 'You look tired.'

'I'm working too hard. And I think I have a cold. There's a virus going around campus, everybody's had it.'

Bernadette seemed smaller than I remembered. Her shoulders were hunched together and she sat with her legs crossed and her hands placed one on top of the other on her lap. Mum was right, she looked tired. There were harsh lines under her eyes and her hair, which usually fell softly around her face, was pulled back sharply in a baby ponytail.

'You have to watch those viruses,' Mum replied. 'They can get serious if you don't look after yourself. I heard about a man who caught a strange virus just like a cold who was dead within three days.'

Mum's story didn't make either Bernadette or Dad any cheerier. Bernadette and Mum shared a couple more exchanges, just like that first one, then Bernadette yawned. 'I'm really exhausted. I think I'll go up to bed.'

Mum offered to make the bed but Bernadette held up her hand. 'I can do it, thanks. Kevin might want to help me up the stairs with my bag, though.'

Bernadette said goodnight to both Mum and Dad. Only Mum replied, then I followed her up the stairs, half-carrying, half-dragging her heavy case to the top landing.

'Thanks, Kevin,' she said and gave me a clumsy sisterly hug. 'I missed you, kiddo. We'll have a talk tomorrow.' She let me go and carried her bag into her room where she closed the door.

Eddie was already asleep in our room so I couldn't tell him the news. His cold had settled on his chest and his heavy breathing sounded like a saw slowly working its way through plywood, interrupted only by loud, hacking coughs. It wasn't so bad when he lay on his side but on his back the sound was unbearable and it woke me up several times during the night.

In the morning the door to Bernadette's room was ajar. Her bag was opened out on the floor and her bed was made. But she wasn't down at breakfast where Dad was buried in the morning paper and Mum was carefully grilling toast. I took my seat in the quiet kitchen, wondering if I should speak and break the silence. I hadn't heard any raised voices the night before, but Mum and Dad were so careful around each other that they had clearly spoken, and disagreed.

Bernadette entered, dressed in her old quilted dressing gown, her hair wet and smelling of crisp green apples.

'What a wonderful morning!' she yawned. 'This snow is so pretty.'

'You certainly picked the right time to come down. How are you?' Mum asked her. The question didn't sound as silly as it had last night.

'Fine. How did you sleep?'

'Like a top.' The remark warranted a slight flick of the newspaper from Dad. Bernadette poured herself a cup of tea. 'Poor little Eddie. I could hear him last night all the way from my room. He sounded terrible.'

You should try sleeping in the same room as him, I thought to myself.

'I had an idea last night,' Bernadette continued, stirring her tea. 'I thought I might walk with Kevin to school. Get some fresh air, see the town with the snow.'

'That sounds lovely, dear,' Mum replied. 'Not in your dressing gown, of course.'

'No, Mum,' was the cheery answer. 'How soon do you have to go, Kevin?'

'I have to finish eating, then I brush my teeth and then I go.'

Bernadette downed a couple of mouthfuls of tea and hurried back upstairs so she had plenty of time to dress. To her, fashion was far more important than food. And then once again it was the silent trio in the kitchen with nothing to say and no one saying it.

By the end of the driveway it became painfully obvious why Bernadette had decided to walk with me to school. Painful because the wind glancing off the snow nipped at my cheeks and chin, and obvious because Bernadette was hardly subtle about what she wanted to know.

'Do Mum and Dad ever fight about me?'

'Not really. They used to fight heaps. Before they had their holiday.'

'Yeah, Mum mentioned that. But what about me? What did they say?'

'Mum once talked to me about you in the attic. But Dad . . .' I shook my head. 'No one's really mentioned you since you ran away.'

'I didn't run away,' Bernadette said like I had offended her. 'Running away is what kids do when they're your age. I left home. Mum and Dad just have to get used to that.'

We crunched along the footpath. It was pretty much clear of snow now, as was the road. Gullies of a drab white sludgy mixture lay in the gutters.

'They didn't say anything else?'

'No. They've been talking about other things.'

'Like us leaving Lumley?'

Her remark surprised me. It hadn't crossed my mind that she would know about that, but when I thought about it all the older kids had probably been told long before me. Official news always started at the top of the family and worked its way down. That was the Garrick pecking order and even though Bernadette had been out in the cold for a while she most likely knew more about the move than I did.

'I don't want to go,' I told her.

'Who does, kiddo.' I hated the way she said 'kiddo' to me. 'Don't worry about it. This town is a hole, anyway. Remihana isn't much better but at least it's a change. Auckland, that's where it's all happening. There's so much up there.'

'I'd rather stay here,' I said, defending my town.

'It's so big up there. You can only imagine how big it is. They have more than one picture theatre, and places where you can go and buy 40 flavours of ice-cream, and buses that go down the main street hanging onto electrical wires.'

'We've got a picture theatre! And there's the Milk Bar!'

'It's not the same.'

I grew annoyed at her for putting down Lumley. She had grown up here. She should have been more loyal. But I couldn't help being intrigued by the buses that hung on wire, and the 40 ice-cream flavours sounded like a treat.

'How is school?'

'It's okay. We had a horrible teacher but she's gone now.'

'Mum told me in a letter about your friend Sheree. That's really sad.'

We made it to Mrs Rocher's dairy and Bernadette stopped. 'You can go the rest of the way by yourself. I'll see you after school.' She headed back the way we had come and again I felt annoyed at her. She'd said she wanted to walk to school with me but she hadn't even come halfway. I hoped she wouldn't tick Dad off the same way she had ticked me off or else we were in for fireworks.

Dinner was another quiet affair. Eddie was down for it. He was feeling better but his cough was still wet-sounding and Mum had him bundled up in his thickest pyjamas and one of Andrew's old dressing gowns. Dad barely spoke and he chewed his food mechanically, like a robot would, with his bottom jaw as frozen as the water trapped in the snow outside.

Several times Bernadette tried to start a conversation with him. She would make a remark that usually Dad would have talked at length about. Not a bite. She then tried to converse with Mum but Mum was obviously uncomfortable talking if Dad was going to be so withdrawn. And with Eddie sick and content to just sit and sniff, there was no one to make silly off-the-cuff comments which had absolutely nothing to do with anything, but which were good icebreakers and were at least funny. So the table was silent.

When Dad retired to the living room with his cup of tea, the rest of us stayed in the kitchen. Bernadette helped Mum with the dishes while I cleared the table. Ed basically just stayed out of our way.

'This can't go on forever, can it?' Bernadette said as she scraped one of the plates into the waste disposal.

Mum put her finger to her lips and pointed towards the living room. She walked across to the door and closed it carefully.

'I don't see why we have to sneak around and talk like spies,' Bernadette said. 'It's our house as much as his.'

'Try and be a little more understanding. This is hard for your father. He's still dealing with the way you left.'

'He's had months.'

'And he may take more months. You know he deals with things in his own time. You turning up unannounced didn't help.'

'I thought it would be better if I surprised you.'

'You certainly managed that. You have to try and be more patient.'

Bernadette frowned but promised that she would try. Mum placed another plate in the rack, ready to drain. 'How long are you planning to stay?'

'Just a week.'

'For a holiday?'

'Yes,' Bernadette said tentatively. She must have heard the same odd tone in Mum's voice as I had. 'Why?'

'It is just for a holiday, isn't it?'

'Yes, Mum.'

'You would tell me if there was something else happening?'

'What are you trying to say?'

'Well, there was an article in the *Woman's Weekly* last week about young women and . . . babies and I thought . . .'

'Mum!' Bernadette said aghast. 'Are you saying you think I'm pregnant?'

'Shhhh,' Mum said, looking around at me and Ed.

Bernadette was laughing. 'What do you think I'm doing in Auckland?'

'You're grown up and living by yourself. I'm not as unworldly as you might think.'

'I don't believe I'm hearing this from you! No, I am not pregnant. I think there's something I would need to do to get in that state and I intend to wait until I'm married for that!'

Bernadette put her arm around Mum's shoulders and gave her a squishy squeeze. At that moment Dad walked through from the living room. Bernadette and Mum broke apart as he crossed the kitchen floor and placed his cup and saucer on the sink bench. Bernadette spoke to him as he started to go.

'By the way Dad, do you need any help at the timber yard? In the office maybe?'

'No,' Dad grunted and kept walking.

'You could at least be polite. I deserve that much,' Bernadette threw back.

Dad spun around and stared straight at her. 'I don't think you deserve that much at all.'

'Why? What have I done that's so bad?'

'You walk out of this house, disobey your mother and me, embarrass us with the Palmers who were planning on you to board with them, then we don't hear from you for months and you expect to walk back in here and be treated like Lady Muck. It doesn't work that way.'

'It's not like I did this to embarrass you.'

'But you did, and then we don't get one word of apology. Not one word to hear of how you were.'

'I wrote letters!' Bernadette shouted back. 'I wrote lots of letters!' She cupped her hand to her mouth, realising she had said something she shouldn't have.

Dad looked shocked for a second then turned his anger on Mum.

'What do you know about this, Meg?'

'Bob . . . I . . . she's right . . . you were so . . .'

'I don't want to hear it!' Dad yelled. He stormed from the room and charged up the stairs, then a door slammed somewhere.

'I'm sorry, Mum,' Bernadette said. 'It just came out.'

'Don't worry,' Mum sighed.

'I don't believe him! He was the one who didn't want to talk about me leaving. He was the one who didn't want to know. He has no right to be so angry now.'

'Do you really think so? How would you feel if you suddenly found out someone was keeping secrets behind your back? It's partly my fault. I should have told him but I didn't want to worry him. And there never seemed a perfect time. I'll go take care of it.' She dried her hands and followed Dad.

Bernadette finished the dishes and wiped down the bench. She tried to make idle chat with me about the snow, Ronn Karr in particular, but she wasn't really interested, she was just trying to fill in time, fill in the silence. There was some shouting upstairs, but it didn't last long. Mum and Dad were back in the living room within the half hour. Bernadette stayed out of Dad's way. It was all she could do.

It wasn't as cold the next morning and the snow showed the first signs of melting. Miss Bourke told us that now the temperature had gone up slightly, it wouldn't be cold enough to keep the water turned into snow. She advised us to make the most of the snow while it was there. I resolved to give Ronn Karr some much-needed attention as soon as school finished, maybe even give him some friends if there was enough snow. But when the time came Bernadette was waiting at the school gate for me.

She suggested I might like to walk into town with her to do some window-shopping. I got the feeling she really wanted me to come so we wandered to the shops together and walked up and down the chilly main street. On the way there Mr Harris drove past. He beeped his horn and stuck his hand out the window to wave at me.

'What a heart-throb!' Bernadette exclaimed. 'Who's he?'

I explained that he was the teacher who taught the Standard Four kids and boarded with Mrs Yoxall.

'You stayed with him for two weeks?' She was impressed. It wasn't often that I impressed Bernadette.

We passed the Hollywood Cinema.

'What do you say we go to a movie tonight?'

I'd never been to the pictures at night and the idea sounded tremendously exciting.

'*Jaws* is on.' Bernadette said after checking the posters in the glass box outside the theatre. 'It was in Auckland ages ago. It's a bit scary for you, kiddo.'

I tried to hide my disappointment. Bernadette must have noticed because she grabbed my hand and started swinging it playfully up and down as we walked. 'It's no great shakes, believe me. Just a big fish and some spooky music. I think its an R anyway so I doubt we could sneak you in.'

'What's the pictures like at night?' I asked her.

'What a strange question! The same as during the day. You think something different happens there?'

I tried to explain myself but 'I don't know' was all I could manage.

'It is a little bit different. You have adults there, rather than grotty kids, so no one throws Jaffas or giggles in the seat behind you. The theatre's grander-looking, it's far more swish. The staircase, you know, the curved one you go up, well that looks like gold under the lights.'

'It's wood painted gold.'

'Yeah, but it looks like real gold at night.'

We stopped in front of Wheeler's Footwear and Bernadette peered into the window at the display.

'If I can't take you to the movies I'm going to buy you some new shoes. How about it?'

She seemed really excited by that so I went along with it and we left the cold street for the heat of the store. We both knew Mr Wheeler who owned the shop and he helped us pick out a pair of shiny brown lace-ups with rubber soles. Bernadette insisted I wear them out of the shop and so Mr Wheeler packed my old shoes into the box and I tucked it under my arm. I walked carefully along the street, not wanting to ruin the soles before I got home.

'You're walking like Donald Duck,' Bernadette grinned at me. She tried to walk the same way and we got a lot of stares from people passing by. We must have looked ridiculous, the two of us, with our silly walk and big grins on our faces.

On the way home we cut through the park, which was deserted except for some sparrows hopping their way through the snowy grass. As we passed the slide Bernadette got excited again and insisted that I have a turn.

'I don't really want to,' I said, finally tiring of doing things to please her.

'No, go on.'

I just wanted to go home but Bernadette held out her hand for the box and I supposed that one slide couldn't hurt. I climbed up the ladder and whooshed down. It wasn't bad, but it wasn't the highlight of my life either. When I got to the bottom I felt a sudden cold wetness around the seat of my pants. I stood up awkwardly.

'What's wrong?' Bernadette asked me.

'The bottom of the slide was wet.'

'Let me have a look. Oh, you're soaking.' She started brushing my trousers, like that was going to dry the dark wet patch. 'It looks like you peed your pants, on the wrong side. I didn't know —' Bernadette broke off and cradled her face in her hands. Her body shook slightly and small sobs were coming from her hidden mouth.

'I'm okay, honestly,' I told her. 'I'm not even cold. I didn't get my new shoes wet either.' That didn't seem to make any difference.

'I'm sorry, Kevin,' she said in fits and starts.

'I don't mind.'

'We'll go home in a second . . . I'm sorry . . . it's just that it's not easy being back here and Dad's not making it any easier. I'm working so hard up there, trying to make ends meet, trying to keep

218

up with my study and my part-time job. I thought if I could come home and have a rest, everything would be okay.'

As I watched her I thought that all anybody did in our family any more was cry. I stood beside Bernadette and waited. It felt like she was never going to stop. A woman walking a collie dog crossed the park but I don't think she saw us.

We walked the rest of the way home talking about the new shoes and some of the movies Bernadette had seen in Auckland. She insisted we stop at a dairy and buy Eddie a bag of lollies, in case he got jealous about the shoes. I told Bernadette they were the nicest shoes I could remember owning. I would make sure I only wore them on special occasions so that I didn't ruin them.

The wind was icy on the wet bit of my pants but I didn't complain in case it sent Bernadette off again. We discussed school some more and I told her a little about Mrs Riddle. Bernadette wanted to pick me up from school every day, if that meant she could 'accidentally' bump into Mr Harris. She hadn't met any nice men in Auckland, they were all 'a bunch of deadbeats'. She had no shortage of admirers. Lots of men had asked her out, but Bernadette claimed she had high standards.

I skipped up our front steps, eager to show off my new shoes to Mum and Ed. Inside, Bernadette and I were surprised to find both Mum and Dad sitting around the kitchen table. They were having one of their secret conferences for they fell silent when we entered.

'What's happening?' Bernadette asked straight away. From the serious looks on their faces it was clear that something was up. Dad didn't answer. Mum held out her arm for me to come and stand with her.

'We've sold the house and the business,' she said bluntly.

'When . . . how soon do we leave?' Bernadette asked.

'Soon.' Mum hugged me close to her. 'Soon.'

It was as if a black cloud of darkness had suddenly descended on the kitchen, bringing an awful heaviness with it. Bernadette took a seat at the table. I wanted to say 'It's all over' but I said nothing.

Mum tried to look on the bright side. 'At least I won't have to show any more rude people through the house. Remember that couple from Remihana, Kevin?'

'They didn't buy the house, did they?'

'No, it was a family with four children. They have one of the grandparents living with them so they'll need the space.'

'Did they buy the yard as well?' I asked.

Dad's voice seemed to come out of nowhere. 'Adam Cleaver owns the yard now.'

'That fat pig from Auckland?' said Bernadette. 'How did he manage to get his hands on it?'

'There was an auction sale. Cleaver bought the yard.'

'As a bargain deal, I bet. What are we going to do? Can't we sue him or something?'

Mum looked to Dad to reply. Dad stared at the wall.

'We can't let him get away with it! I've met some law students at Varsity. Maybe one of them can help.'

But the way Dad looked, not a thousand law students could have helped us.

Bernadette got out of her chair and walked to where Dad was sitting. She leaned down over him and hugged him from behind with her arms folded under his chin and the side of her face pressed against his. Her eyes were closed but Dad's were open, still staring at the wall. Then Bernadette said, 'I love you.' I could have misheard that because her voice was so tiny that I thought perhaps I had imagined it. Or maybe it was another noise that just sounded like, 'I love you.' Whatever it was Dad must have heard it too because then he closed his eyes, raised his hands, grasped Bernadette's arm and rocked her gently back and forth. A single tear got squeezed out of one of his eyes. It slipped slowly down his cheek like a tiny snail and dipped under his chin. Then it fell to the table and disappeared in the swirly grey formica. Beside me, Mum reached over and put her hand on Dad's arm and held him. She just held him. She also had her eyes closed and I shut mine as well, letting the purple-black darkness swim in front of me, because it felt right.

I lay in bed that night and wondered what lay ahead for Ed and me in Remihana. What would our new house look like? Would he and I have to share a room? What would our school be like? Remihana had several schools, which one would we attend? I would have to make new friends and forget my old ones. Would my new classmates be like Sheree, Steve and Paul, or would it be a roomful of Richard Streets and Annette Luneys?

Then I fell asleep and had a dream about Sheree. I dreamt that she wasn't dead but had been sent to school in Remihana, except her new classroom looked just like our Standard Three room. We had moved and I was there with her. I was happy to see her and she was pleased that we could be together again. She tried to punch me on the arm but she kept missing and she grew more and more frustrated with every failed swing.

Mr Harris was standing at the front of the room. He had cut his hair real short and grown a beard so he looked like someone different. There was a merry-go-round outside with coloured lights and loud organ music. Mr Armstrong was all by himself on the machine, going round and round, and he waved at us each time he passed. Mr Harris and Sheree talked to each other about Sheree's special place. Mr Harris knew we often went there after school, he wanted to go with us sometime. Sheree explained that grown-ups weren't allowed there. Mr Harris looked disappointed but Sheree shook her head firmly and kept repeating that he couldn't come. Mr Harris walked over to my desk and opened it up. Inside was a pile of comics that I had never seen before, really old comics with dog-eared covers. Mr Harris said they were his comics but now I could have them. I wanted to read them right there and then but he said it was time to go home. I heard a bell ring somewhere in the distance and realised he was right.

I woke thinking I was in the classroom and the sight of our moonlit bedroom surprised me. Ed's loud breathing had woken me up. The strange dream stayed with me vividly. Sheree had seemed so real that it gave me a slight shiver to know that she wasn't here any more. I almost smiled thinking about the comics that Mr Harris had offered to me and how sad he had looked when Sheree told him he couldn't come with us. And suddenly I remembered about Sheree's secret place. I hadn't been to her secret place! It was the place that was more special to her than anywhere else in the world and she'd made me promise to go but I had completely forgotten about it! I panicked. I had to go there before we left Lumley. But what if I didn't remember about going in the morning? What if I didn't remember until we had left Lumley, when it would be too late? I had to go there now. Still in that panicky state I dressed, putting my clothes on over my pyjamas. The odd dream remained with me, hanging over my shoulder like a huge vulture.

I wasn't sure how I did it but I found myself walking down our driveway in the middle of the night. Then I was outside our gates, wandering down the street. I felt like a sleepwalker only half-aware of what I was doing. There was an almost full moon in the sky and the soft light glowed bluish on the partly melted snow making everything seem unreal. You could easily believe you were in an imaginary place, though whether it was from a fairy tale or a nightmare remained to be seen.

So much of the snow was melting that everything was wet and glisteny. My sneakers soaked through quickly and I soon lost the feeling in my feet. But I kept going. I was being propelled by something beyond me. Sheree's voice was in my head. 'C'mon Kev, don't be a baby. Let's go to my secret place, at night!'

At the edge of the bush I paused. With the cold and the wet I was truly awake by now and as usual I had lost my nerve. Peering into the shadowy expanse ahead of me all I saw were scary trees with huge arms and eyes and mouths. But there were other voices coming from within the bush, friendly voices. They called out to me on the night breezes. 'Come inside, we'll look after you,' they said. 'You don't need to be afraid.' Then I heard another sound, the roar of a car on the road behind me. I turned and was blinded by two glaring headlights, like the eyes of a huge beast. The car stopped just along from me and I saw that it was in fact not a car, but a van. It was Mr Hill's van and Mr Hill himself was sitting in the front seat, watching me with a steely glint in his eyes.

I looked all around, hoping there was someone else near that I could run to, but we were alone. Mr Hill motioned for me to come to him. He obviously thought I could be led over like a simpleton. I tensed up my muscles then, without any warning, I sprinted behind the van, back the direction I had just come. Across the road I slipped on the wet concrete and spun into a spindly tree at the edge of someone's property. I belted it back violently and ran on. The van U-turned and began to chase me. I ran so hard my lungs felt like they had exploded and my throat stung with saliva that tasted just like vomit.

The van zoomed in front of me then braked dramatically right in my way, so that I had no choice but to stop. The front passenger door flew open so that it was just about touching my arm. Mr Hill leaned over the seat at me and stared. I was like a frightened rabbit, too scared to run, too petrified to even move. 'Get in,' I heard. Had it been him talking? Where were the voices coming from now? Was it Ed mumbling in his sleep again? Was it Sheree? I kept thinking I was still dreaming.

'Get in,' Mr Hill hissed. 'Get in, you little fool. You'll freeze to death out there!'

Clearly, I thought to myself, he didn't want me frozen. Mrs Hill obviously preferred her meat fresh. I considered running again but I had no doubt that he would mow me down. I climbed up to the high front seat, reasoning that at least this way I had a fighting chance.

'Shut the door,' Mr Hill ordered and as I did he turned the van around again and began to drive.

He kept the van off the main street. We snaked up and down side roads where there was hardly any lighting and absolutely no people. On odd occasions the moonlight flashed into the cab and lit up Mr Hill's craggy profile. He wasn't wearing his cap, and I used the opportunity to inspect him closely. His face was like a model of the moon's surface, his mean expression set like concrete into the bumps and hollows.

'Where are we going?' I asked him.

'I'm looking for someone.'

I guessed we were on the hunt for other stray children who, like me, were stupid enough to wander the neighbourhood at night. We passed Lumley Primary then drove by St Peter's church. And then we headed out of Lumley, towards Dad's timber yard, except that it wasn't his any more because Mr Cleaver owned it. Perhaps Mr Hill was going to buy it from the big round man and use it to process little children by the van-load. I was going to be the first in a long line of victims destined for such a fate. Eddie would be next. But he had a cold. They wouldn't go for him while he had a cold, would they?

We passed the timber yard and kept driving. We were out into the real country now, where there was not one street light and just rolling fields and the occasional shed or house. A railway line ran parallel to the road here and I made a mad plan to leap out of the van and sprint to the tracks if I saw a train coming.

'Where are we going?' I asked again.

'I'm looking for someone.'

'You won't find any more children out here.'

'What makes you think I'm after children?'

'You're wasting your time. Why don't you just take me back to your cellar and finish me off now?'

Mr Hill looked sideways at me, then his eyes returned to the road. I stole occasional peeks at him and also stared out at the road in front of us. We had driven a long way out of town. The countryside was empty both in front and behind us. I looked down at the floor of the passenger seat and noticed that it was tidy. For some reason I had expected the inside of the Hill van to be dirty and smelly.

'Do you get the children to clean this van before you kill them?' Mr Hill ignored my question.

'I won't clean your van,' I told him bravely. 'Not me.'

Up ahead, the headlights caught a figure walking along the road. I gasped in surprise at the familiar shape in the flowing nightdress. The van braked and Mr Hill got out his side. I heard the hard sound of his footsteps on the metal on the side of the road then he opened up the rear doors and someone climbed into the van. Then Mr Hill hopped into the driver's seat. He turned the van around and we headed back towards Lumley.

'Where the hell were you going tonight?' he asked me when we were moving again.

'Nowhere,' I answered. I had this uncontrollable urge to look in the rear of the van to check that I had really seen who I thought I had seen on the road, but I resisted.

'You were headed somewhere. Running away, were you?'

I kept my mouth shut. The less he knew, the better.

'You didn't do a very good job of it. Where's your spotted hanky tied to a stick?'

'I wasn't running away.'

'If you say so.'

'Are we going back to your place now?'

'You want me to take you somewhere else?'

'No, I'm ready to die.'

'Well, bully for you.'

'They'll know it was you. My brother Eddie will tell them.' I realised what a shallow boast that was. Ed wouldn't have known what to tell anyone. He would probably hardly notice I was gone, let alone figure out where I had disappeared to.

I heard a low sound directly behind me. It was like a growl and a snort mixed together, not a snarl but not a sneeze either. The very back of the van was pitch-dark but I could make out a human outline. At first glance it looked like a sack but my eyes slowly picked out details. Long stringy white hair. The folds of a nightdress. Hands, claw-like hands shaking ever so slightly. Bare feet. Staring eyes. Not staring at me though. They were staring into something that only they could see. Another dreamer who couldn't or wouldn't escape their dreams.

'She's not a zoo animal!' Mr Hill barked, so unexpectedly that I jumped. But despite him I couldn't stop looking. I was fascinated by the woman. A thin line of saliva dripped from her mouth and trickled down the lines in her chin.

'Why are you staring at her?'

'I'm not.'

'Turn around and face the front then. She doesn't like it when people stare.'

'Is she sick?'

'Watch your mouth!' he warned me with a sudden anger.

'She's dribbling . . . ' I tried to explain.

'She's not sick. She is not sick!' The rage in his voice frightened me.

'Sorry.'

'She's not crazy.'

'I didn't mean it like that.'

He wasn't listening to me. 'People think they know. But they don't understand. She's lost, that's all. She's forgotten who she once was.'

'I didn't say she was crazy,' I replied. 'She's dribbling . . . maybe she has a cold. My brother has a cold at the moment.'

'She doesn't have a cold,' Mr Hill said, quietly this time.

'She could now since she's been walking through the snow.'

'She doesn't feel the cold.'

'I think I saw her one night. She was walking down our driveway.'

'She does a lot of walking, always at night. Sometimes she goes a long way, like tonight. And sometimes she just wanders close to home. When did you see her?'

'Ages ago. She's been taking things when she walks . . . I think.'

Mr Hill wasn't surprised. 'She picks things up on her travels. Souvenirs.'

'That's stealing.'

'Is it? What if the person taking the things has no idea of what she's doing? What if she doesn't even remember what she's done, eh?'

'She took some pillowcases from my mum. I know because I saw them on your washing line . . . I think.'

'I think, I think. Are you sure about anything?' He gritted his teeth and concentrated on driving. I dared not look back again so I focused on the way the headlights shone on the road ahead of us.

We didn't speak until Mr Hill quickly checked in the back of the van. He pulled a hanky out of his pocket and leaned back with one hand, carefully wiping his wife's mouth, all the while keeping the van steady on the road.

'I remember those pillowcases. They've got some design on them, haven't they?'

'Yes, my nana sent them to us.'

'We've been using them. I'll wash them and give them back.'

'It won't matter to me. You will have killed me by then.'

Mr Hill tucked the hanky back in his pants. 'You have to be the strangest boy I've ever come across.'

We passed the timber yard again and shot down the main street then turned back towards home. The bush rose up to meet us. I glanced at it wistfully and strained to listen but the voices had gone.

'What's in the bush?' Mr Hill said gruffly.

'Nothing.'

'Why were you going there then?'

'There is a place there.' The words slipped out of me. 'It was a friend's place.'

'Like a hut?'

'A secret place. I wanted to go there.'

'Couldn't it have waited till morning?'

'She wanted me to go there tonight.'

'She? You're too young to have a girlfriend.'

'She wasn't my girlfriend.' I paused. 'She was my best friend. She died on the mountain.'

'The little Humphries kid? The one who banged on my door a few months back?' He scoffed when he saw my surprise. 'You're not the first kids to knock on our door.'

We were coming up to our street.

'You miss this Humphries girl?'

'Not all the time, but sometimes I remember her, like tonight. I had a dream that she was alive.'

'Don't worry, death isn't so bad. It's the living that really gets to you.'

I didn't know how to answer that. 'We've sold the house,' I told him. 'We're leaving Lumley.'

'I know. Word gets around, even to me.'

The way he said 'even to me' filled me with sadness. It made me wonder what it must be like to be Mr Hill. I'd never thought of that. I heard more noises in the back of the van again. This time Mrs Hill was mewing like a little kitten. I thought about what it was like to look after a person like that, a person who took walks at night and stole things. And what it was like to have children laugh at you behind your back and make up stories about you and hit tennis balls onto your property and knock on your front door when they wanted a laugh. It seemed like such a sorry, depressing life that I wondered how Mr Hill managed to live through it day after day. It dawned on me that Mr Hill was all alone in the world. He had no one to talk to, no one except Mrs Hill and what sort of conversation could he have had with her? All the times I'd seen Mr Hill getting into his van and the occasional brushes we had with him, I'd never seen him in a good mood. Not once. My family cried a lot and we fought a lot but at least we had some happy times as well. It appeared to me that there were probably few if any happy times in the Hill house.

Mr Hill pulled the van to a stop outside our front gate and leaned across me to open the door. I didn't know whether to say thank you or not, so I bowed slightly and slipped down from the seat. I caught one last glimpse of Mrs Hill in the back. She was lost in her own world. I don't think she even knew I was there. She had dribbled all down her chin again. Mr Hill pulled out his hanky once more to wipe her dry.

'I would have given the pillowcases back but I didn't know whose they were. She takes so much stuff from all over the place and I'm not knocking on every second door just to return it.'

'You can leave it at the back door, if you want,' I told him. 'I won't say anything to Mum. She'll think it was Ed, since he takes things too.'

Mr Hill reached over, readying to close the door, as he considered what I'd said. 'By the way,' he added. 'Next time you and your brother want to visit you should wait till I'm in the house. You scared her that day. It took me all night to calm her down.' There was the closest thing I'd ever seen to a smile on his face as he pulled the door shut. I stood there, watching the van creep down our street and park outside their place. I saw him help Mrs Hill out of the rear doors. He took her fully in his arms and carried her up their steps. He must have been a strong man.

I stared carefully at our house as I walked down the driveway and it laughed back at me, with a mocking tone. In the moonlight the porthole windows looked like beady eyes, peering shiftily from the side of the house. On the lawn Ronn Karr the snowman had keeled over and was now just a pile of dirty mush. Inside, I placed my

229

sopping sneakers by the still faintly glowing fire in the kitchen. The crimson light made spooky patterns on the lino and the walls. Upstairs I undressed to my pyjamas and slipped between the covers. The sheets were cold but I warmed up quickly. I thought about Sheree's secret place and resolved to go there in the weekend. I would not forget. I lay in bed and listened to the night. The house was perfectly still. Even Eddie's breathing had cleared. I was glad.

I'm crouched down in the back of our car on the way to Remihana, holding the goldfish bowl against the floor so the water doesn't slop over the edges. Mum is driving. Dad has gone on ahead with the movers. Eddie sits in the front seat, singing a nursery rhyme. Oranges and Lemons. Our house is a tiny dot in the car's rear window. Outside is a spring so cold and wet it might as well still be winter. This is also a memory.

∾